LIGHT BEARERS

THE AWAKENING

MINDY HITE

Visit Mindy online at www.mindyhite.com

Light Bearers: The Awakening
© 2020 Mindy Hite

ISBN: 978-1-09832-293-9
eBook ISBN: 978-1-09832-294-6

Published by BookBaby

The persons and events portrayed in this work of fiction are the creations of the author, and any resemblance to persons living or dead is purely coincidental.

Printed in the United States of America.

Dedicated to you who need hope…

CHAPTER 1

Jolted awake from a terrible dream, I sat bolt upright in my bed, gasping for breath. My eyes widened, trying to take in any movement that might be hiding in the darkness. Gradually, as I became more accustomed to the small amount of light that filtered in through the moonlit window, I looked around the room and realized I was far from wherever my dream had taken me. With each deep, calming breath, the fragments of the dream slipped away, but the unease remained.

I sighed, shaking off a shiver and took a slow glance around the bedroom I had called home for the last eight years. "Sexy modern," the decorator called it; decorated entirely with a teenage girl in mind, sophisticated with just the right amount of color. My uncle insisted he wanted to spoil my older sister, Amelia, and me with our rooms, which was really an understatement because he had redone our rooms multiple times in the eight years since he'd become our guardian. He said it was important to stay ahead of the curve and insisted, "nothing but the best for his girls." I wanted to be grateful, I really did, but the truth was, I missed my old room. This room was glamorous, but cold. And although my old bedroom had hand-me-down items and mismatched furniture, it always felt cozy and filled with love.

Tears filled my eyes as I was overcome with the memory of my parents. Mom was so beautiful and loving and gentle with her touch. And I could still see the smile that covered my dad's whole face, remembering how easily that smile came to him. Our home had been old and small, but I would trade everything I had now to be back there again with my mom and dad.

Thinking about my parents wasn't helping me shake off the darkness I felt from my dream. I reached for my water, but it wasn't on my nightstand where I usually put it at bedtime. The last thing I wanted to do was walk through the dark house, but maybe moving around a bit would help me clear out the last remnants of fear from the dreams and put me at ease. I pulled on my robe and headed down to the kitchen to get a glass of water. The dark wooden staircase with its detailed wrought-iron features was grand in the daylight, but at night, and in my present mood, it felt more overwhelming than grand.

I tried to be as quiet as possible, getting my drink, not turning on any lights, but relying on the light of the moon to move about the kitchen. Sipping some water from my overfilled glass, I turned to walk back towards the staircase when I realized there was a light on down the hall. It was the middle of the night, so I was surprised to see the light on in my Uncle Derek's office.

As I approached his office, I could hear his voice, muffled through the heavy oak door. I assumed he was on the phone because I could only hear one side of his conversation. His tone was not the usual, lighthearted tone he used when he spoke to me; it felt more,

I don't know, sinister. I was surprised at my thoughts; clearly, my imagination was still in overdrive from my dream.

Come on, Sarah. You need to snap out of it. I coached myself as I shook my head.

Uncle Derek continued, drawing my attention back to him, "I know, it's almost too easy sometimes. They are so easily taken in." He laughed as though he was in on some kind of private joke.

I couldn't make sense of what I was hearing. Uncle Derek worked as the head of marketing for a lifestyle company, and he was very good at what he did. His success was evident in the opulent house we lived in, the cars we drove, and the designer clothes we all wore. Sometimes our lifestyle felt a little flashy, but extravagance was just his way. I felt like he always went overboard with us because he was trying so hard to make up for the loss of our parents.

I was rattled when I heard Uncle Derek's voice again. "We keep tempting them, pushing the things they think they need to be happy until it's too late for them." His voice had become almost frenzied and coarse, a distant echo of what he usually sounded like. This voice didn't sound like Uncle Derek. His voice had been a source of comfort over the past eight years since the death of my parents. But this voice . . .

"Yes," he paused as though listening to the other person on the phone, "That's right, empty. They want to be filled; we leave them empty." He laughed again like he'd told the best joke he'd ever heard. I couldn't help but wonder what the person on the other end of the phone was saying.

His laugh ended abruptly. I wondered if he'd heard me, and I took a step back away from the door.

"Oh, um," he cleared his throat. "Sir, I didn't know you were on the line." His voice sounded uneasy.

A sudden chill crept up my back at the disquiet in my uncle's voice. I had never known him to fear anyone of any position.

Regaining his composure, he replied, "The girls are coming along well, the older one especially." Pause.

"The younger one is slower to grasp the things I am trying to teach her." Pause.

"Yes, I completely understand how important this is." Pause.

"They will continue to be my top priority, Sir." Pause.

"I… I won't fail you." He paused again, stammering to find the words. "I know what's at stake," Uncle Derek uttered in a voice so deep and severe that I took another step backward.

The fear in his voice traveled through the polished wood door, and all of a sudden, I felt terrified of my uncle finding me on the other side of it. I moved down the hallway to the opening of the massive stairs, rounding each step so quickly I sloshed water out of my glass, but I didn't stop to clean it up. I raced silently to my room and heard a downstairs door open as mine closed. Back in my room, I realized I was shaking uncontrollably. With my back to the door, I looked around the room at all my expensive furnishings, and I heard my uncle's voice in my head. "Empty." The word rang in my ears.

I heard a sound outside my door and stopped breathing.

The water. He must have seen the water.

I waited there in the silence, trembling.

On the other side of the door, I could feel the presence of something.

Suddenly, the door between me and whatever was on the other side of it no longer felt like enough protection. I ran to my bed and climbed beneath the covers with my robe still on. I sat with my back against the headboard gaining a full view of the room and the door. I stared at the doorknob, willing it not to move. Gradually, my breathing slowed, and my heartbeat quieted to the point where I realized the house was silent.

As my breathing continued to slow, my brain unleashed a torrent of questions. What had I just heard? What had that phone call been about? Who was my uncle talking to? I assumed Uncle Derek was talking to one of his co-workers about a specific customer and the people they were targeting. But it didn't sound like they were trying to get them to buy their products because they believed it would make people's lives better. It seemed just the opposite. It sounded like they were trying to destroy lives. But that couldn't be right.

Then it seemed like his boss interrupted the conversation. I had never met his boss, but my uncle didn't call very many men "Sir." And who were the girls he was talking about; my sister and me? Why on earth would his boss care about making us a priority? Didn't bosses typically encourage more work, not more family time? Whatever he was asking of Uncle Derek didn't seem like a good thing; it had seemed almost hostile, just like the dream I had been having. But, could it be those two things were related?

I looked at the clock on my phone and realized the hour. Wow. My imagination was getting away from me. Hostile?

You've been watching too many movies, Sarah.

I slid down into my bed, confident that my dream had left me feeling fearful, having painted a dark shadow over everything since the moment I awakened. My uncle was so generous to Amelia and me. We wanted for nothing. And if we even mentioned a want, Uncle Derek jumped in and bought it for us.

We were so fortunate that he took us in when our parents died. Although he'd never planned to marry, much less have kids of his own, he took us in readily. I didn't have any memories of Uncle Derek before the accident, but he explained that it was because he had been so busy establishing his career. He said one of his biggest regrets was not spending more time with his family before bringing us to live with him.

I definitely heard the conversation outside his office door wrong. Uncle Derek was a good man. And I only heard one side of the conversation. As I talked myself out of my fear and into a more stable state of mind, I slowly drifted off to sleep.

I awoke the next morning to the sound of my alarm. Groggy and disoriented, I glared at my phone as I tried to find the snooze button before collapsing back on the bed. Even after falling into a restless sleep, I'd had weird and abstract dreams. I couldn't remember the dreams fully and couldn't make any sense of them. For that matter, I couldn't remember if I had actually heard my uncle talking on the phone last night. Had I dreamed that as well? My alarm went off again, and this time I threw off the covers and rolled out of bed.

As I stood up, I realized I was still in my robe, and my stomach dropped. I glanced over at the full water glass on my nightstand, and a chill ran down my spine as I realized that maybe I *had* heard my uncle talking on the phone last night.

"No," I said to myself. "I'm not going there again." I refused to believe that Uncle Derek was anything but the good man he was and had proven himself to be.

I opened the door to my bedroom and made my way to the stairs, resolved that everything was okay. My stomach growled, as I smelled something good wafting from the kitchen. I walked down the broad staircase, pulling my robe tightly around me as I walked toward the source of the tantalizing smell. As I entered the kitchen, Uncle Derek was leaning against the broad island at the center of the room, sipping a hot cup of coffee, and scrolling through his phone. He looked up at me and said, "Good Morning" with a bright smile, then went right back to reading what I could only assume was an email. Uncle Derek's workday started early and lasted long into most evenings, but he tried to be around whenever possible, even if it was just hanging in the kitchen as we started our day.

Martha was busy on the other side of the large kitchen, making her famous waffles, but we made eye contact as I entered the room, and she smiled at me as well. Uncle Derek hired Martha when we first came to live with him. She was a lifesaver for him (and us), and now, even though we didn't really need her, I couldn't imagine the house without her.

"Good Morning." I greeted my sister, giving her a quick side hug as I made my way to the coffee.

"Morning," Amelia responded. She was looking down at her phone, probably checking her latest social media obsession, and didn't bother to look up at me.

"Ugh." Amelia moaned loudly.

"What's the matter?" I asked with a slight irritation in my voice, feeling every bit of my exhaustion from my sleepless night.

"Jen feels the need to update all of us on her boring life; like who cares that you went to the grocery store yesterday," she said with disdain. "I don't post about boring stuff like that."

If I hadn't been so sleepy, I would have remembered that any outbursts from Amelia while staring at her phone were nothing to get worked up about. I knew she wanted me to respond about how ridiculous Jennifer was, but I was instantly irritated with her, so instead, I said with a bit of condescension in my voice, "Of course, we do have someone that handles all that stuff for us. Maybe you would post about it if you had to do your own grocery shopping." Martha smiled without looking up from her work. Uncle Derek caught my eye and smiled as well.

"No way," Amelia stated. "Even if my life were that boring, my followers would never know. How would people envy me if the most exciting thing I had to share was a selfie from the milk aisle?" She tossed her hair and gave me a cheeky smile.

Over the years, I'd learned it was just easier to agree with Amelia when she was like this. "That's true enough, I guess."

I made eye contact with Uncle Derek once more, and he gave me a wink in return. Suddenly aware of the time, he shoved his phone in his pocket, took one last sip from his coffee, and said, "You girls have a great day. I have a fun surprise for you tonight, so I won't be too late."

I took a bite of my waffle and thought about Amelia, still feeling slightly irritated with her even though she wasn't behaving any differently than usual. Amelia and I used to be close. We're only 17 months apart in age and were best friends from early on. When our parents died, we clung to each other as we settled into a new life with a man who was a stranger to us. Slowly though, we started to separate, and as I sat there looking at her, I wasn't even sure why we'd drifted apart.

Amelia made another disgusted noise at her phone. Maybe I needed to try harder to understand Amelia, even try to be more like her so that we could find some common ground again. I needed to find some way to reconnect. She was popular, and I was not. At school, I was in the crowd she would most likely avoid speaking to. She only acknowledged my existence because I was her sister.

"So..." I led into the conversation slowly. Amelia must have finished scrolling because she looked up at me. "You have been telling me that I need to find my dress for the Spring Fling dance. I was, uh, wondering if you would help me? You have such an eye for that thing, and you know, sadly, I lack in that department."

"Oh my gosh! You're going to the dance? Of course, I will *help you! I'm so excited you decided to go. This dance is going to* put you on the map, get the guys to notice you, and make the girls want to be you." Amelia put her phone down and rounded the table, squealing as she gave me the biggest hug from behind my back. Then, just as quickly, she slid back into her chair and grabbed her phone, on the hunt for the perfect outfit for me.

I forced myself to smile at her enthusiasm. I didn't care about getting on any map. I was exhausted from the events of last night and my overthinking of everything. I just wanted to go back to bed. But school was calling, and before I was fully awake, we were both dressed and out the door, stopping only for Amelia to take a selfie as we headed to school in her red BMW convertible.

After school, Amelia insisted we go shopping. She was so excited, and I was trying hard to get excited about any of the things she wanted me to wear. I liked to look put together, and I loved bright colors, but I couldn't have cared less what was trendy or what item was going to "really make a statement." By the time we finished shopping, I was exhausted from faking my emotions and excitement.

"Oh my gosh, Sarah, I'm so excited you have a dress, and I know just the guy to get to ask you to the Spring Fling." I felt like an extra in a story that was clearly more about Amelia than anyone else.

Yay, I thought sarcastically. I couldn't wait to go to the dance with someone that would prefer to go with Amelia but would say yes to taking me to get in her good graces.

By the time we got home, I was completely over the whole thing. Amelia insisted on stopping and grabbing dinner out even though I knew Martha had probably already made us something. During dinner, we didn't talk much as Amelia was blowing up everyone in her contacts to get me a date before Spring Break.

"The dance is only two weeks after Spring Break, and almost all the hot guys are taken," she informed me. "But, I think I've found you someone that won't be social suicide."

Wow. Amelia made him sound so great. A few minutes later, my phone beeped, notifying me I had a text. "Whatup Chad here, want 2 go 2 dance?" *Charming.*

All I knew about Chad was that he was in my grade and my math class, but we really hadn't interacted much. I showed the text to Amelia and asked what she thought.

"Sarah, he's the younger brother of one of my friends who graduated last year. You wouldn't know him. But Chad is pretty hot, and on the basketball team, so you should totally say yes."

I dragged myself up to my room to think about my reply. Even with Amelia's ringing endorsement of hot Chad, I was not the type to rush into anything. My phone buzzed again, and I assumed it was Chad, wondering what was taking me so long just to say yes. As I reached over to look at my phone, I saw the text was from Uncle Derek.

It read simply, "Sarah, can you come to my office please?"

My heart skipped a beat as I recalled the conversation I heard outside his office door last night.

What could he possibly want me for in his office?

I shoved my pile of books across the bed, then swung my legs over the side. As I stood up, I noticed the glass of water still sitting on my nightstand, but I pushed the errant thought from my mind and headed downstairs.

Before I reached the bottom of the stairs, I heard Amelia let out a shriek, propelling me to move much faster. As I reached Uncle Derek's office, I heard her thanking him repeatedly in a high-pitched, squealing voice. I didn't even need to be in the room to know he had given her another gift. I knew that squeal anywhere. I made it through the door just in time to witness her jumping to hug him. Uncle Derek loved us, but he was not an affectionate man, so in his usual Uncle Derek way, he patted her on the back with a closed fist the way most men hug each other.

Once she released him, he turned to me. "Here you go, Sarah." He handed my package to me, looking confident of the response he would get from me as well. It was the newest iPhone. I tried to bring up a smile for him, but it was tough because all I could hear in my head was the word "empty." I already had the latest iPhone. I'd only owned it for a few months. What more could a new one do for me? But I also didn't want to hurt my uncle's feelings.

"Wow!" I said, "Thank you for this. You really didn't need to; my other one works great."

"Nothing but the best for my girls." Uncle Derek said, smiling at me. "I already hooked them up to the plan. They are ready to go. They just need you to accessorize them," he added, winking at Amelia.

Amelia squealed again, "More shopping!"

Ugh, more shopping.

"Really, Uncle Derek, this was so generous, but I don't need another phone."

His face changed as he studied me. He looked almost disappointed with me.

Amelia piped in, "Seriously, Sarah, just enjoy it; we'll be the envy of everyone in school tomorrow. These aren't even out in stores yet." She waved her phone in my face as if I needed to see it to understand how great it was.

He smiled at her and then turned back to me. I hated that I had disappointed him.

"You're right, of course; thank you," I said to my uncle, giving him the best smile I could manage.

He smiled back at me, but I could tell he wasn't satisfied with my reaction. It wasn't that he'd expected me to squeal. If I had squealed, he'd have known I was faking it. But it was evident that he'd expected something more from me than I had given.

"I'm sorry I wasn't more excited." I apologized to him, "I didn't sleep well last night, and you know how shopping really takes it out of me," I said, trying to joke with him.

"I really do like it, thank you!" I said again, this time popping up to give him a polite kiss on his cheek.

"I'm glad, Sarah. I only want the best things for you," Uncle Derek returned with a seriousness to his voice that told me he was still disappointed. Uncomfortable under his gaze, I felt unsure how to cross this barrier that had grown between us.

"Well, I better go back-up my other phone and get all fifteen of my contacts switched over to my new present," I said, making a joke, still trying to lighten the tension that hung in the air.

"Yeah, you better get on that Sarah; it will take you all of five minutes!" Amelia laughed, wholly engrossed in her newest toy.

"Ha, yep. Thanks again, Uncle Derek!" I said as cheerfully as I could manage. As I moved for the stairs, I felt his eyes following me. When I reached my bedroom, I closed the door, trying to shake off the fear that once again seemed to have followed me up the stairs.

✶ ✶ ✶

My new phone buzzed. Annoyed, I thought, "If Chad doesn't stop texting me, I'm going to lose it."

He'd texted me pretty much daily since I said yes to his invitation a week ago, no doubt texting me at Amelia's direction. I looked over and saw that it wasn't Chad, but Uncle Derek texting us to come downstairs.

What now?

I texted back, "Proofreading my paper from American History. Be there in a couple minutes." I felt nervous, but I wasn't sure why. Things seemed back to normal with Uncle Derek, but then again, I hadn't seen that much of him in the last week.

When I approached the top of the staircase, I could see he and Amelia were already standing at the bottom, waiting for me. Amelia looked put out with my lack of urgency, but Uncle Derek offered a warm smile of encouragement to come on down.

"Hey girls, I know I have been working a ton, even more than usual, and I don't feel like we have had much time together."

"I know what this means," Amelia interrupted. "Vacay, right?" she asked, already knowing the answer. Our uncle had come to us with this apology many times, and each time he'd whisked us off to somewhere fun and expensive. With Spring Break starting next week, it was an easy guess that a vacation was on the agenda.

"I know it's been a little while, girls, so why don't we get away for a few days and have some real family time?" He looked at me for approval.

"It sounds great!" I said, and I sort of meant it. I really did want to get over these uncomfortable feelings, and a vacation might be the perfect way to reconnect.

"Vacay!!" Amelia shouted again, and we all laughed at her excitement. To my surprise, Amelia and I actually agreed on something: a vacation was just what we needed.

CHAPTER 2

"Why aren't we going someplace where people actually vacation?" Amelia asked again, flipping her long brown hair over her shoulder. As she sat with her feet propped up on the dashboard, it was clear she was annoyed that we hadn't been whisked away to some tropical paradise, but Uncle Derek didn't seem to care about her protest. She had already asked the same question numerous times since the day Uncle Derek told us where we were going. She had whined and griped, but she hadn't been able to sway him. As we pulled off the main road, her reason for asking was all the more evident as I climbed out of the Escalade and looked at the rustic cabin where we would be spending our spring break.

"We are here to toughen you girls up a bit," Uncle Derek laughed as he climbed out of the driver's seat. "Come on, Amelia," he chided, "give it a chance. I promise you're going to find some things to love here."

I was just thankful he didn't seem angry with Amelia's obvious and continued displeasure at our vacation destination. Maybe I was being paranoid, but since the night I received my new phone,

Uncle Derek seemed off. His otherwise even and jovial temperament was moody and on edge, so I tried to step lightly around him. Not Amelia, though. She was completely unaware of anyone but herself, and she didn't mind letting Uncle Derek know precisely what she thought of his vacation plans to Camp Tuano.

Uncle Derek always came to the camp without us, but he was adamant we go with him this time. Camp Tuano was where he went to de-stress after finishing big projects at work, or when he needed time alone with his thoughts. He called it his "sanctuary" and "home away from home." It was just all so strange that despite all the times he'd come here alone, this time he wanted us here with him. A thought crept into my mind as I recalled Uncle Derek's voice on the phone that night, saying, "The younger one is slower to grasp..."

I looked around and saw a ropes course through some of the trees just beyond the lake we'd passed driving in. I had felt a big case of the creeps when Uncle Derek turned the SUV onto the property, but there was no apparent reason why I should feel that way. Camp Tuano was set in the most beautifully wooded acreage, centered by a lake, far beyond the noise and light of the city. If this was Uncle Derek's sanctuary, it was clear to see why. The winding road from the highway to the camp was a constant reminder that we were leaving behind civilization and the hustle and bustle it had to offer.

It seemed like Camp Tuano should be a peaceful place, but I didn't feel at peace, and rightfully so. Camp Tuano wasn't a fun family camp. It was a war games camp where participants learned to hunt, shoot, and defend themselves against some unnamed, ever-threatening enemy. It had become popular with a few of Uncle Derek's work friends a few years back and had gained a reputation as a place where the rich and powerful came to let off some steam. Growing up in the south, Camp Tuano wasn't altogether as weird as it sounded. It was just weird that now, after all this time, Uncle Derek thought we needed to be here.

I jumped about a foot high when a gunshot rang out somewhere behind us. As my heart pounded in my ears, and I looked frantically around, Uncle Derek just laughed at me and told me I would get used to it.

He helped us get our bags into the private cabin where Amelia and I would stay. Uncle Derek's cabin was the next cabin over he reassured us, showing me the "x" on the little map that hung by the door in our cabin. He tapped a spot on the map and told us to meet him at the mess hall in an hour for lunch, then headed back out the door.

Amelia sat gingerly on the bed she had picked for herself, closest to the bathroom and farthest from the front door. "Ugh, can *you believe this? Maui . . . Cabo . . . those are vacation spots. What* are we doing here?" She looked around in disgust. "We even have to eat in a place called the mess hall."

"Seriously," I replied in agreement as she headed for the bathroom. I didn't mind the old rustic look or feel of the cabin, but as another shot rang out, I, too, wished we were anywhere but here.

"Ahhh!" Amelia shrieked from the bathroom. I ran in to see her looking in disgust at the single pedestal sink and a tiny mirror.

"Amelia, you scared me to death!"

"This is like my worst nightmare."

"Seriously? Your worst nightmare, Amelia?" I was technically a spoiled rich kid, just like my sister, but her tendency to overdramatize and exaggerate drove me crazy sometimes. "At least Uncle Derek let you bring all four of your bags, so you should still look

17

fabulous," I said, striking a pose, making good-natured fun of her obvious distress.

She looked at me, clearly annoyed.

"I don't know how your stilettos are going to look at the mess hall or on the gun range, though," I said, smirking.

Amelia shrugged. "I guess a tiny part of me was hoping that Uncle Derek was joking, and he would whisk us away to some exotic 5-star resort."

"Well, we're here now," I said cheerfully, "so I guess we try to make the best of it." She looked like she was going to cry, so I softened my words and said, "Or maybe he'll see what a bad idea it was to bring two city girls out here and never bring us again."

"One can only hope," she smiled. "I better change before we go to lunch."

She threw one of her suitcases on my bed and began rifling through to find the perfect outfit. I was pretty sure she didn't have the standard camo hunting gear, but hopefully, she would come out with a pair of jeans and not a party dress.

I was already in my jeans and t-shirt, so I took a few minutes to look around while she made her wardrobe decision. Spotting a camp brochure on our little table, I picked it up to read. I stepped outside on our porch to compare the map to the campgrounds in front of me. The trees were pretty thick where we were, but to our west, down the road, was the mess hall and entertainment center. Behind that was the lake equipment rental shack. Across the gravel drive were more cabins and more to the east of those as well. On the other side of the mess hall was the gun range.

I was startled again as I heard the screen door slam at my uncle's cabin. His back was to me, but I could hear his deep voice carry across the short distance to our cabin. "Yes, I'm here; cell service is terrible up here, you know. Yes, everything looks good; the new signs were a good touch. They shouldn't suspect a thing."

An all too familiar chill ran down my spine.

"You need to be up here in time for the meeting. They'll be distracted, and we have plenty to discuss." I could only assume the "they" he was talking about was me and Amelia.

Once again, I felt the same fear of being caught that I had felt that night outside his office. I took a step backward and quietly opened the door to our cabin, careful not to make even the slightest noise as I stepped back inside.

After locking the door behind me, I took a moment to slow my breathing and checked the clock. "Thirty minutes, Amelia," I announced, knowing she had probably already lost track of time.

"Okay!" she shouted back.

Knowing Amelia would be a while, I moved her suitcase to the ground and flopped down on my twin bed. Who was Uncle Derek talking to, and what meeting was he referring to? He'd told us this camp was to take a break from work, reconnect, toughen us up for the real world, etc. I knew Camp Tuano was a war games camp, but when he said we were going to family camp, I think I pictured it more like the three of us taking canoe rides, hiking together, and maybe even roasting s'mores. From the feelings I had so far, I didn't believe we were going to be getting any warm family fuzzies while we were here.

An ache went through my chest. I missed my mom and dad so much sometimes, it still took my breath away. Normally, memories I had of them felt warm and loving, but here, their memory felt soul-crushing. I sat back up and stuffed the sadness down into the hollow place where it resided in my heart. I might as well take a look in the mirror to make sure my hair wasn't too crazy, that my limited makeup was still in place, and that I was booger-free. Something told me Uncle Derek would not appreciate being embarrassed in front of his friends here.

When we arrived at the mess hall ten minutes late, Uncle Derek was pacing outside. He was wearing a dark green polo shirt with the camp logo on it. Under that logo, it read, Camp Director. Funny, he had never mentioned he was in charge of the camp before.

"Camp Director, huh?" I asked, teasing him.

"What? Oh yeah, I moved up to Camp Director this year. So, I will be busy with meetings and any disciplinary action that may come up," he said in a distracted way, not really looking at me. "But don't worry your pretty heads. We'll hang together at meals, and you girls are going to be plenty busy yourselves."

"Girls?" Amelia huffed.

"Excuse me, Princess," he said sarcastically, "You ladies are going to be plenty busy."

"That's better," she preened as we headed inside for our first look at the mess hall.

It was an interesting place. It looked more like a hunting lodge than a camp dining area. Heads of different animals were all over the wall. There was a buffet at one end with the kitchen behind it and picnic tables filling the rest of the room. They weren't typical size, but extended tables that could seat at least 20 campers each, and there were quite a few in the room.

There were only a few girls our age in the room and a handful of women. They all looked much tougher than us. I followed right next to my uncle as he headed for the buffet line. Amelia strolled a little slower, turning heads as she went. Once she reached my side and began filling up her plate, I heard her soft exclamation, "Ugh, cafeteria food. The salad is even iceberg lettuce." Uncle Derek just chuckled. I knew he had heard her, as that was her intent, but he didn't even bother to acknowledge her obvious misery.

When we sat down at one of the long tables, he introduced us to some of his friends. They all seemed nice enough. Drake and Thane appeared to enjoy the introduction, while Tristan and Carson, who looked a lot alike, seemed to have trouble even forming a smile. They did a side smirk, but it seemed almost painful. They definitely didn't give me the warm feeling the word "friends" should have implied. I got the impression they were soldiers, or at least they had been at one time. Uncle Derek kept up the conversation with them while we ate. Thane asked me a couple of questions, but then focused back on my uncle.

As they talked to one another, I noted that each of my uncle's friends also had leadership positions at camp. Drake and Thane were the Assistant Directors, a fact I knew from the titles stitched on their shirts. Tristan and Carson wore the same polos, but their roles weren't noted under the logo. My uncle had mentioned during the introduction that Tristan and Carson kept everyone in line here at camp. I guess putting "Enforcer" on their shirts would have been a little much. Their looks alone made me want to toe the line and avoid any disciplinary action.

We were almost finished eating when two younger guys came over, addressing our uncle and the other men first.

"Sirs."

"Good to see you, Tommy, Ben. How has training been going?" Thane asked with a smile.

"Good sir, we are learning a lot." Tommy and Ben were about the same height with dark hair, though one was definitely more muscular than the other. They had an almost boyish charm to their personalities, but their faces had a harder quality, especially the larger of the two. I wondered what their story was.

"Good to hear; we always like to know that our trainees are doing well," said Thane.

"Yeah, we do, because it makes us look good!" My uncle laughed. He seemed to notice their frequent glances towards us. "Oh, let me introduce you to my two nieces, Amelia and Sarah."

We exchanged greetings, but as usual, the guys were mostly looking at Amelia. It may have been the way she purred her responses to them. I couldn't keep myself from rolling my eyes at her when she leaned forward on her crossed arms, giving them a better view of her cleavage. Sitting next to her in my t-shirt, I felt every inch of being the younger, more naïve sister.

The guys sat down on the bench across from us, and when I tuned into the conversation, Amelia was admitting this wasn't typically her scene. She much preferred the mall or having her nails done.

After giving Amelia a thorough looking over, Ben smiled and said, "Could have fooled me. You fit right in here."

"Yeah," Tommy chimed in, "We'll have you completing the ropes course and shooting like a champ in no time." They all had a good laugh at this.

"Well, since I'm stuck here," Amelia flirted with Ben, "I might as well make the best of it. Hopefully, one of you will be my tour guide and help me get somewhat acclimated."

"I can definitely handle being your guide," Ben said with a smirk. "And I will take that role very seriously. In fact, one thing you can't miss out on is the bonfire tomorrow night."

"Um, yeah, why don't you come too?" Tommy asked with a sudden interest in me. He had obviously realized Ben had claimed the prettier sister.

"I don't know," I said. "This is our first time here at Camp Tuano, and we don't really know what plans Uncle Derek has for us, yet." I turned towards him, but he was leaning away, talking with Thane.

"Don't worry about it, Susan, your uncle won't mind," Ben said to me.

"It's Sarah, actually," I whispered to myself as he moved to talk to Uncle Derek.

I thought for sure Uncle Derek would decline their invite since we just met them, but to my dismay he said, "Of course, you girls . . . excuse me . . . ladies," giving Amelia a wink, "can go with them to the bonfire. All of the young trainees will be there. It's kind of a tradition."

"But Uncle Derek, I thought we came here to spend time together," I protested, almost hoping he'd provide a social rescue.

"We'll have plenty of time for that, and I have a meeting during that time anyway, Sarah. It works out perfectly. You two will be distracted and having fun, so I can do what I need to do."

I wanted to protest again, but decided against it since the entire table was listening to us, and I had obviously been overruled.

"Well, that settles it, then. You ladies are coming with us to have one of the best nights of your life. But, in the meantime, why don't you two meet us at the lake to work on your canoe paddling skills?" Ben asked confidently.

"Sure!" Amelia cooed. "I just need to run back to the cabin to change first."

"Okay, we have a quick meeting for the counselors at 13 hundred, so we can meet you at the lake at 14 hundred hours." He laughed and corrected himself, "I mean two o'clock. See you at 2:00."

"See you then!" Amelia smiled and waved them off as they left the mess hall together.

"Bye," I said to no one but myself.

"Okay, this place definitely has its benefits," Amelia stated, her eyes trailing after the muscular duo as she smiled at the view in front of her.

"Really, Amelia? It's obvious what they want."

"Oh, come on Grandma, what exactly is going to happen in a canoe? And so what if they want me for my assets, at least they want me. Well, I mean Ben did; Tommy was looking at you."

"Yeah, only once he realized you were already taken." She didn't argue with me. "Seriously Amelia, there have to be guys here who are less sleazy than Ben and Tommy; ones who might actually treat you like a person and not a conquest. I mean, don't you want guys to respect you, even just a little?"

"Oh my god, Sarah, look at that guy!" Amelia whispered excitedly in my ear.

There were guys everywhere in the mess hall, so I had to get her to clarify. But once my eyes were headed in the right direction, I needed no more help. He was hot, to say the least. Other-worldly was more like it. Although he was sitting with a group of guys all wearing the same counselor t-shirt, he seemed out of place in their midst.

Just at that moment, he looked up and stared straight at me. I immediately dropped my gaze and felt my cheeks redden. After a few seconds, I chanced another glance up at him just to make sure he was real. His eyes were still on me, but this time he smiled. His smile was the most beautiful thing I had ever laid eyes on. He was gorgeous in every way. Every inch of his face was perfection with the bluest eyes I'd ever seen. His broad shoulders gave way to his muscular arms, and he seemed to be glowing from across the room.

"I'm going to go talk to him," Amelia stated, pulling me out of my daze.

"What?! You're just going to walk up to him?" I asked in shock and feeling somewhat panicked. She had clearly already forgotten about Ben.

"Yes, dummy, I can't let a guy that looks that good slip away," she said to me, checking her makeup in her compact mirror.

The guys sitting with him stood and began to clear out. Amelia snapped her mirror shut, stood up, and headed straight for him. She had perfected the walk. Many heads turned, and eyes followed as she strutted in her white, skin-tight jeans and pink halter top. She complained about having to wear the flat, strappy sandals for five minutes in our cabin, but they seemed to be working for her now.

While most eyes were on her, Mr. Perfect Smile hadn't even looked up yet. In fact, it looked like he was trying to avoid looking at her. But, it couldn't be helped once she tapped him on the shoulder. He turned to look up at her, though he didn't have to look far. He was tall, and in her flat sandals, she only stood about a foot taller than him sitting down. He flashed that beautiful smile at her but didn't give her the full-body perusal most guys gave with their eyes.

After he said something to her, she put her hand back on his shoulder. My face grew warm at her boldness. He seemed to be trying to gesture that he was finishing up, so she pointed over to us. He looked at me, then his eyes moved slowly over to my uncle.

Next thing I knew, Amelia was walking him back to our table. My heart pounded, and I could feel the heat on my face rising. Without the aid of Amelia's compact mirror, I knew my cheeks were red.

"Lucas wanted to meet you guys," she said as she held onto his arm. "This is my uncle, Derek, and my sister, Sarah."

"Hello Sarah," he said, his voice as smooth and rich as I'd imagined it would sound. He reached across the table to shake Uncle Derek's hand. "It's good to meet you, sir. I obviously know who you are, but we haven't been formally introduced yet."

My uncle had a strange look on his face like he was trying to figure something out. "Yes, good to meet you as well, Lucas. It's your first year with us, I take it?"

"Yes sir, it's my first year at Camp Tuano. I did most of my camp years at a different location."

"Well, it's good to meet you, and I'm looking forward to seeing you in action," my uncle returned.

"Yes sir, I hope my skills don't disappoint."

Uncle Derek turned to us, "Well, girls, we need to get to the first counselors' meeting. I'll find you later." He waved goodbye, and he walked away carrying his tray.

Amelia, not yet ready for Lucas to leave, tried again. "So Lucas, tell me about you. Are you from around here?"

"No, I'm not from around here," he said kindly. "I hate to meet you ladies and run, but I have to get to the meeting as well, and at Camp Tuano, you definitely don't want to be late for a meeting."

"Aww, I thought we could get to know each other better." Amelia practically whined as she pulled on his arm.

"Well, maybe there will be a time later today. I'm at the shooting range this afternoon; not sure if that is really something that interests either of you, though." He pulled his arm away to reach behind his head as if he had an itch. I secretly wanted it to be because he didn't want Amelia's hand on his arm.

"Two of the guys asked us to go canoeing, so I'm not sure how long we will be. But maybe we can swing by later." She was switching to her jealousy tactic.

"Okay, see you later. Good to meet you, Amelia and Sarah." He looked directly into my eyes.

"You too, Lucas." My voice barely came as a whisper, my cheeks still flaming at his unexpected attention. Amelia looked at me oddly, then turned her attention to the sight of Lucas walking away.

CHAPTER 3

Amelia wouldn't shut up about Lucas as we walked back to the cabin to change. I wasn't exactly sure what Amelia would change into. There wasn't anything in her suitcase that screamed "roughing it," but when she came out in her see-through cover up with her bikini on underneath, I wasn't sure why I had even questioned it. I put on my swimsuit and changed into shorts to be cooler, but I was still wearing my trusty t-shirt. None of the guys would be looking at me anyway.

As we walked towards the lake together, we were already running late. Amelia was still incessantly talking about Lucas. She talked about guys all the time, and it had never irritated me before. I guess it bothered me because I didn't want her to be talking about THIS guy. Lucas seemed special and different. He wasn't like Tommy and Ben, yet there Amelia was, looking at Lucas the same way Ben had looked at her.

As we arrived at the lake, we spotted the guys with life jackets and two canoes ready to go. They waved as we came around the tree line.

"Hey, ladies! Are you ready to take these canoes out for a spin?" Ben grinned mischievously.

"I don't know; it seems like a lot of work," Amelia pretended to pout.

"Don't worry, I'll do all the hard work," Ben started giving my sister another full perusal. She had on her cover-up, but it left little to the imagination. I looked over to see Tommy doing the same. He glanced up to see my eyes on him and cleared his throat. He seemed to remember that it was rude to stare at another girl when I was technically his date for the canoe time.

"How about you, Sarah, you ready to take the canoe out?"

"I guess so," I replied reluctantly. "I haven't been in a canoe in a long time, and I'm not sure I have ever paddled one before."

"That's okay; I'll teach you the basics," he said with a wink. The wink surprised me because I thought he was into my sister, but I seemed to have gained his full attention now—nothing like feeling like the leftovers.

Getting into the canoe was a bit interesting as it was partly pushed into the water, and still halfway on the sand. Tommy had me climb up to the front seat. I did so as carefully as I could as the canoe teetered back and forth. I settled into my seat and reached back for my paddle, which was comical since I already had my bulky orange life jacket. The others had opted out of wearing the life jackets and instead threw them on the canoe floor. Amelia claimed the orange did nothing for her complexion and used hers as a cushion to make her seat more comfortable.

She didn't have as awkward a time getting in because Ben left their canoe almost all the way on the sand. Plus, he let her hold his hand as he coaxed her into the boat, "Your throne, Princess," he said with the sweetest voice. He ditched his shirt and was pushing them out in the water to the sound of my sister's squeals and laughter.

Tommy asked me if I was ready to go, and I said a quick "Yep," in reply. There was only a slight rock to the canoe as Tommy pushed us off and climbed in. I glanced back, and he, too, had removed his shirt. Better to paddle without a shirt, right? The guys certainly thought so, and to be honest, I didn't mind that much either. In that one quick glance, I could appreciate his tan and his rigid, built frame. I looked just long enough to earn another wink from Tommy.

With Amelia barely covered in her bikini and barely-there cover-up, and both guys shirtless, I seemed to be the only one still fully clothed. I left on my t-shirt and liberally applied sunblock every place the sun still touched. My life jacket was securely fastened around me, not because I couldn't swim, but because you couldn't see more than a foot deep in the water. What if I whacked myself in the head with the paddle and fell out unconscious, never to be seen again? It was a possibility.

"Okay, Sarah, put your left hand on top of the paddle handle and slide your right hand down halfway to the bottom of the paddle," Tommy instructed.

"Like this?" I asked back.

"A little lower, okay, that's good. Now, reach out in front of you with the end of the paddle, stick it in the water, and pull back. Lift the paddle out of the water at the back of your reach and repeat the motion."

I gave it a try. "Ahh! That's cold!" Tommy yelled behind me.

I glanced back to see I had gotten him with some water right in the face.

"Oops! Sorry."

He was smiling. "Watch it, newbie, or some might come back your way! This time stick your paddle in a little deeper, three-quarters of the way up the paddle part."

I tried that and did better, feeling the canoe surge slightly forward.

"That's better!" Tommy encouraged. "Now, you stay on the right side until you get tired and then switch to the left. I'll steer us, and you just add some power."

We paddled along while I got the hang of it and found a rhythm. I could tell I was using muscles I had never used before and would probably be sore later, but I also felt strong, almost powerful, as I helped move the canoe forward. As we came upon Ben and Amelia, we could hear them laugh. I saw some water spray up towards Amelia from Ben's paddle as he said, "Oops," which caused more giggles and squeals from my sister.

"Let's pass these clowns," Tommy said competitively as he stared down Ben with a slight grin.

I was more than ready to rise to the challenge and dug into my paddling. We pulled up alongside them. Amelia was sunning in the front with her legs crossed, but she didn't have a paddle that I could see. Ben noticed us, and I saw the challenge rise in him as he smirked and gave the nod.

"Around the island and back to shore," Tommy shouted. "Losers take the walk of shame!"

Without warning, Tommy yelled, "Go, Sarah!" and dug his paddle deep into the water. We were speeding faster than we had gone yet. As Ben matched Tommy's effort, Amelia let out a shout as the new speed was not conducive to her relaxed sunning position. I glanced back at her and noted she probably didn't feel too secure sitting on her life jacket instead of wearing it. I smiled as I focused on my paddling. I definitely had a competitive edge that rose up whenever I did something athletic, and with the wind in my hair, heart pounding, and adrenaline pumping, I could certainly feel it now.

I tried to maintain my rhythm, but it was a bit more daunting now that we were in a race, so I really had to focus. We were rounding the backside of the tiny island as I noticed my arms getting more and more tired. Part of me feared dropping my paddle in the water as my grip started to weaken.

"It's okay, Sarah, just lay the paddle across your lap and take a break. I'll need you when we come back out and have to go against the wind." Tommy shouted.

I glanced back. We definitely had the lead as Ben and Amelia *hadn't even rounded the corner on the backside of the island yet.* But Tommy was sweating from his exertion. My arms were already shaking, not having done work like this before.

We came around the island, and I felt what he meant. The wind was coming at us, almost pushing us backward. I started to paddle again, feeling like I couldn't lose to Amelia when she wasn't even trying, but paddling was much harder now. I realized that it had felt like we were flying because we had the wind at our backs. It was a lot less fun to work against the wind, and the shore seemed a good distance away.

"Nice and steady, Sarah, take breaks as you need to," Tommy coached.

We were about halfway back to shore when I heard Tommy swear. I turned back to look at him and saw that Ben was catching up, and my sister looked like she was a bit panicked.

"Okay, Sarah, we have to pick it up. Ben is strong enough to catch us. We have to win this."

I wasn't sure that I could even paddle anymore much less pick it up, but Tommy's voice had changed from fun and challenging to much more serious and demanding.

We were paddling for all we were worth. As far as I could tell, Tommy was equally as skilled as Ben. He kept us in a straight line, and we were moving forward. I let down my guard a little and paused for a rest.

"No, Sarah, paddle!" Tommy yelled.

I glanced back again, and Ben had gained on us. How was that possible? There were two of us paddling, and Ben was quickly catching up, even without Amelia's help.

"Don't look back, Sarah, just keep paddling!"

I started paddling again, barely able to pull my paddle through the water. My arms were shaking, and I was dripping with sweat.

Maybe that's why the guys took their shirts off.

Here I was layered in a thick life jacket, t-shirt, and swimsuit. Where had all of my adrenaline gone? I was wiped out.

"Paddle, Sarah!" Tommy yelled and then cursed in anger.

His anger scared me enough to dig my paddle in a little harder. I wasn't having fun anymore. I was just trying to keep Tommy from yelling again or from Ben beating us. We were getting so close to shore when I heard my sister shouting Ben's name.

I turned and saw the front of their canoe had edged up to the back of our canoe, still gaining as my sister cheered, no longer panicked with Ben's speed. I gave it everything I had and was so beyond thankful when our canoe hit the sand and slid up on it a few feet as our last burst of power brought us in.

Tommy was yelling and screaming, this time in celebration. He jumped out of the canoe, sending it rocking as he splashed over to gloat at Ben, who looked exhausted and furious. Tommy gave him a good hard splash of water, soaking my sister at the same time, who let out of scream of protest. And then he turned back to me and started splashing back my way as I was trying to climb out on shaky legs.

"We did it, gorgeous!" he shouted.

He lifted me out of the canoe in a big bear hug and twirled me around laughing.

"You're my lucky charm!" he shouted, giving a few more spins. "I have never beat Ben in a race before, ever. That was epic!" he shouted as he sat me down.

Feelings of warmth spread through me at his approval. I loved that I had helped make him so happy. My cheeks were flaming red, so I was glad he had turned back around to gloat some more at Ben. "How does it feel to lose, Benny boy?"

"Whatever, man," Ben replied angrily, "You had a huge advantage."

"Oh yeah, how's that?"

"Your girl could actually paddle. I had a princess sitting in the front that didn't lift a finger." When he said princess this time, it wasn't flirty and playful, but thick with sarcasm and anger.

"Hey!" Amelia protested, having finally made her way out of the canoe on her own. "You told me I wouldn't have to paddle." She glared at him with her arms crossed.

"That's right; my girl could paddle! Sarah, you were amazing!" He looked at me with more intensity as he helped me finish unbuckling my lifejacket. He slid it down my arms, dropping it onto the sand, but leaving his hands on my arms as he repeated, "You're my lucky charm."

I was embarrassed by his closeness and intensity. "It was no big deal," I said shyly.

"Oh, it's a huge deal." He pulled me to him, and he kissed me right on the mouth. He pulled back and looked at me with almost a possessive look as he turned to face Ben and Amelia, his arm around my shoulder, pulling me close.

Amelia was leaning into Ben; it seemed they had made up.

"Oh, did you forgive her already?" Tommy mocked.

"You bet I did. Amelia promised me she would make it up to me later," Ben said, winking back at Tommy.

Amelia's cheeks turned red at this, and she wouldn't meet my gaze. I came down off my high a little, feeling bad for her. A really good-looking guy had just kissed me. One that I had impressed. I had never been in this position of power before, so why was I suddenly feeling bad for her when she was always the one who got all the attention? I took a deep breath under the weight of Tommy's arm that no longer felt warm, but heavy and suffocating. As the guys continued to give each other a hard time, my heart hurt for her.

Amelia's obvious discomfort made me remember our conversation from a few months earlier.

"Amelia, you had sex?" I had barely been able to get the phrase out.

"Yes, prudy-prude. It wasn't a big deal," Amelia had said and rolled her eyes at me. "All my friends have done it, and they said if I didn't get some experience in now..."

"What if Uncle Derek finds out?" I asked, cutting off her tired excuse.

"I think he would be cool with it," she said casually.

"What?" I asked, startled at what she had just said. "What in the world could possibly make you think that?"

"He overheard me and Gemma talking about boys and stuff at the pool a few weeks ago and joked about making sure we used protection."

"He really said that?" I gasped with my mouth hanging open in shock. I honestly couldn't even imagine why he would weigh into their conversation, much less be so nonchalant about the whole thing.

"Well, it was something like that. And you shouldn't be so surprised, you know. It's no secret that Uncle Derek is pretty into the whole 'bachelor life, not being tied down to one woman' thing."

"I'm still shocked that he wouldn't think it was a big deal for you, though. He's a grown man. And our guardian. And you're still in high school," I replied. "What would Mom and Dad have said?" I was still kind of stunned by the whole conversation.

"Oh god, Sarah, Mom and Dad were so retro. No one waits for marriage to have sex anymore." Amelia went back to her phone again.

"Well, are you in love with Brian?" I asked.

"Umm, no," she said, dragging out her words. "Like I said, it just seemed like the next step. We've kissed a bunch, and so when his parents were gone one night, we just did it."

"Are you going to do it again?" I was still struggling to get my mind around something I saw as a big deal, and Amelia seemed to see as nothing.

"I guess so, but probably not with Brian, though. It wasn't all passionate like they show in the movies, but maybe we just weren't compatible physically."

I was having trouble breathing and felt seriously sick to my stomach. How could Amelia be so flippant about this? My mom had told us when you made love, you tied yourself to that person forever. In my mind, that was how it was meant to be. Forever. And now Amelia had just flippantly tied herself to a guy who just happened to be convenient, not realizing she would inevitably leave something of herself with him. It didn't seem right. But maybe I was wrong? Maybe I was just as backward as my parents.

"Sarah, if you are just going to judge me over there, at least go to your room so I can text in peace."

"Sorry, I'm still just trying to understand why you wouldn't believe what Mom had told us."

She shrugged off my shock along with the memory of our mom, "It's just part of growing up, little sis, and believe me, your day's coming too. You better get over it now, or else you'll still be all alone by the time you graduate. But whatever, it's your funeral."

I came back to the present to hear Tommy shout at Ben, "Okay, loser, walk of shame for you!"

"Walk of shame?" I asked. "What's that?"

"Nothing you need to worry your pretty little head about. Your man's not going in," he said with a nasty laugh directed at Ben.

Ben was glaring back at Tommy with such hatred that I was sure they would come to blows at any second, but I was still clueless as to why. It was just a stupid race.

"Okay, well, we better get back to our cabin. Thanks, guys, for a fun time." I said as cheerily as I could manage even though all I tasted was disgust.

※　※　※

The boys walked us partway back to the cabin and then took a different path headed to do some training. As we parted, Tommy pulled me in again, but I ducked my head to avoid his kiss and then pulled away with a friendly wave in time to see Ben slap Amelia on the bottom as he walked away without a backward glance.

Once the guys were out of hearing range, I asked, "Ames, are you okay?" She lowered her head at my question, but then she seemed to pull it together and gave me a big smile. I could feel her internal struggle, no matter how much she tried to hide it.

"Of course, I'm okay, did you see how hot Ben was in that canoe? We almost caught you guys because he has serious muscles."

"Amelia, that's not what I mean. I saw how you looked when Ben said you'd make it up to him. What did he mean by that? What did you tell him?"

"Sarah, let's just say I used my feminine charms on him so that he wouldn't be mad at me anymore."

"By feminine charms, do you mean sex?" I asked, starting to get irritated at how flippant she was being.

"We probably won't go all the way the first time, but it's not like it matters."

"Of course, it matters, Amelia! You're going to let a guy you just met use you because you were scared he'd be a little angry?"

"Sarah! Just shut up! I keep telling you that sex isn't a big deal."

"You can keep saying it, Amelia, but I don't believe you. I don't believe that once a guy gets what he wants and walks away, that you aren't torn apart by that. You can lie to yourself all you want, but you can't lie to me."

"Whatever, you're not Mom. You can't tell me what I get to do with my body," she said, glaring at me.

"You're right. I'm not Mom, but I'm your sister, and I genuinely care about you. Why is it easier to listen to Ben instead? To him, you're just a warm body. You aren't special."

"I'm not special? Thanks a lot, Sis," she replied sarcastically as she quickly turned to walk away.

I jogged a bit to catch up, trying to think about how I could get through to her. "That was not what I meant, Amelia. You are very special. He wants to use you to make himself feel good, and honestly, you'll end up using him just as much." When she didn't respond I continued gently and softly, "How much of yourself will you give away to try to make yourself feel better? Believe it or not, some guy might actually love you for you and not just for what you are willing to give him. Take Lucas, for instance…" At that moment, I wanted to rip out my tongue. I didn't want her to think about Lucas.

Sarah, what are you doing?

Amelia, of course, perked up at that suggestion. "Oh right, he wanted us to come see him at the gun range." Her smile returned.

"Amelia, I don't think he actually expected us to come." I tried to use another tactic. Why, oh why had I said his name? My heart was pounding just thinking about him.

"Don't be naïve, Sarah, of course, he wanted us to come. He was just playing hard to get."

"Are you actually going to shoot a gun?" I tried yet another tactic of stopping her.

"I don't know," she mused, "but I am definitely willing to let him teach me." She smiled and playfully bopped my nose. I couldn't stop the eye roll that followed. Thirty seconds ago, she was talking about having sex with Ben, and now she'd become completely focused on Lucas.

"I have to go change!" she said excitedly and jogged up the steps into the cabin.

I didn't follow her in but instead sat down on the steps, feeling the fatigue in my body. My arms and back were already sore, and I was sure, by tomorrow, they were going to feel awful.

My mind was exhausted as well. I kept trying to help Amelia, but it was like the harder I tried, the farther away she felt. She didn't want to be saved. She was all I really had left, and I felt like I was losing her, too.

I tried to think of a way out of going to the gun range with Amelia because there was no part of me that wanted to go. But I knew my sister, and I knew she would want me to come along. She would use guilt or some other tactic to get me to come, just as she had done many times before.

"You ready?" she asked from behind. I turned to see her standing there dressed in what could loosely be described as workout clothes. I hadn't considered what she would wear to a gun range, but her yoga clothes made sense. That was about as athletic as Amelia got. Her tight, black pants were the kind that had cutouts filled in with mesh. This particular pair had cutouts all the way down, but the first stripe was barely below her bikini line and wrapped under her bottom in the back. Their purpose wasn't for workout comfort, but for guys to be teased by a little skin . . . or a lot of skin. Her tank top was practically see-through to her low cut "sports bra." My outfit got an eye roll from her as I was still in the same sweat-stained t-shirt and shorts I'd worn to the lake.

"Don't you want to freshen up, at least?" she questioned me.

"To just get sweaty again? Not really." I earned myself another eye roll. "Ames," I protested, "I really don't want to go anyway; my arms are practically jelly, and I'm still bothered by the sound of all those guns."

"Please, Sarah, please," she whined. "I don't want to go by myself to a gun range."

My prediction came true. "How about neither of us goes then?" I coaxed.

"But then Lucas would be so disappointed. We don't want to be rude!"

I could tell she would not easily give up the idea of me going with her, and I was too tired to argue, so I stood up and started walking to the gun range.

Amelia squealed, "Thanks, Sis! I knew you would come."

✳ ✳ ✳

We could hear the shots from our cabin, and that was unsettling enough. But the closer we approached, the louder the shots grew, raising my anxiety and my desire to turn around and go back. We passed a sign pointing to an archery area, which seemed like it would be way more my speed, quieter at least.

As we turned the corner off the well-worn path, the gun range came into full view. There were several shooters, each in what seemed to be a lane, for lack of a better word, lined up along the same firing line. Downrange there was a large grassy embankment, which I assumed served as a safety barrier to keep the bullets from straying beyond its borders. Some of the lanes had paper targets that ran along a clothesline of sorts, while other lanes, the ones where people were shooting much larger guns, had targets that looked like mannequins, more or less. The whole scene was disturbing.

Other campers and counselors already took most of the lanes. The thought rolled through my tired brain that it was interesting that Amelia and I weren't campers, nor were we assigned to a counselor. I assumed because our uncle was the director, we were allowed to go where we pleased. From what I had seen, all the other campers, or trainees as they were often called, were on a strict schedule.

Amelia was looking around for Lucas, but I had already spotted him, my eyes drawn to him like a magnet. He was helping someone with a massive gun.

"There he is!" Amelia whispered, her voice sounding like a six-year-old who had just spotted Santa.

"He looks busy," I said, trying to sound disinterested.

"Well, we can make our way over there and see if I can catch his eye," she smiled.

A man, who I would guess was in his thirties, stepped in front of us.

"Can I help you, ladies?" he asked without emotion.

"We just saw our friend down the way, and we wanted to say hi," Amelia answered his question with the full power of her feminine charm.

"The gun range is not a place to say hi to your friends," he answered sternly. "You are either here to learn or to practice. Which is it?"

"Learn, I guess," Amelia said dejectedly.

"Okay, I'll have Steve set you up. But you need eye protection and hearing protection ASAP."

"Yes, sir," we both said in unison.

It turned out Steve's alley, that's what Steve said the lanes were called, was at the opposite end from Lucas. Once we had our proper protective gear on, he asked us what we wanted to learn to shoot. I bowed out as gracefully as possible, saying my arms were sore from canoeing, and I just wanted to watch for today. Amelia glared at me through her plastic glasses, which only made me smile. Both the glasses and the big headphone ear protectors were definitely spoiling the effect of her carefully planned outfit. She was not happy, mainly because the first thing Steve did was to put a big jacket on her to protect her from shell casings. She apparently had too much skin exposed. I was definitely enjoying the moment more than Amelia was.

Steve didn't seem too happy to be helping her either. He gave her a gun she could barely hold in her hands. After receiving his litany of instructions, she fired her first shot and then promptly turned around, still holding the gun in front of her. I dove for cover, almost face-planting as I scrambled for safety.

"Whoa!" Steve shouted as he placed his hands over hers and brought the gun to point at the ground. "You can't turn a loaded gun on people!" He removed the gun from her hands, fuming mad and shaking his head at Amelia's complete lack of gun experience. The guys next to her were snickering; although, why they hadn't ducked and covered like me made it seem to me like they had a death wish.

"What was the first rule I taught you?" he demanded.

"To never point a loaded gun at anyone unless I was prepared to kill them," Amelia murmured. Steve didn't look like he would be *giving her the gun back any time soon.*

"Well, I learned how to shoot," she said in embarrassment. "Let's go, Sarah." This excursion was not turning out how she had hoped. We were too far away for her to get Lucas's attention, and she was too busy with her lesson to catch his eye. But that didn't keep me from catching an occasional glimpse of him across the row of figures bent over in the shooting alleys.

I followed Amelia, placing my protective gear in the bins as we walked away from the gun range and into the clearing. I saw Amelia shaking.

"Are you okay?"

"No, that was super scary. I hated pulling that trigger, and once it went off, I just wanted that gun out of my hands."

I put my jelly-like arm around her. "Well, at least you tried; I wasn't even brave enough to do that."

She leaned her head into my shoulder, "That was humiliating, Sarah. I won't be trying anything like that again."

We headed back to the cabin to change for dinner, and while I knew she was talking about shooting, I was also hoping she meant she wouldn't try to get Lucas's attention again either. One could only hope.

CHAPTER 4

The next day, I finished breakfast and was trying to decide where to head next. Anything remotely related to using my arms was out. I was so sore and desperately wishing for a bathtub and some Epsom salt. I wished I had something, anything, to give me relief. I had already taken some Advil that I had in my bag, but it wasn't touching the pain I felt in my shoulders and arms.

Amelia had bounced out of the mess hall earlier after saying "gross" a few times and saying she needed to freshen up, an obvious ploy to get away from me. Her eyes were on Lucas as she said it, and my stomach rolled, making me regret the eggs and grits I had just eaten. Uncle Derek said he had a meeting with the camp directors, and with a quick "have fun," he was gone. As per the norm, I was on my own.

Looking around, I considered my options. The gun area had no appeal. I wasn't jumping every time a shot was fired anymore, but I wasn't too much better than that. Paintball seemed tamer, but not by much. I had glimpsed some of the bruises on those guys after they came out of the paintball field; no thanks. The combat arena was also a big no for me. The lake seemed like my best option. I loved the water; it always brought me peace, so I started heading there.

As I walked through a patch of trees, I realized a ropes course covered the entire area. And it wasn't a nice-easy-walk-until-you-make-it-to-the-end type of ropes course, but the kind that was high in the trees, where if you encountered someone else on the course, your job was to knock them off or throw them off with your bare hands.

Walking along the outskirts of the course, I saw two older teens locked into a battle trying to push the other off of a slim platform. One of the guys had a gash over his eye but seemed unaware of the blood running down his face. I felt my stomach turn again and walked a little faster. I had no desire to be discovered anywhere near the course by someone intent upon inflicting that kind of damage.

Emerging from the trees into a clearing, I looked over to see the beginning of the course. There were groups of guys and a few very muscular girls in gear or getting into what looked like harnesses, which I'm sure were helpful when the goal was to knock someone off the course. They were putting colored bands on their arms like maybe there would be teams trying to knock the other side out of the trees. I was contemplating that idea when my heart skipped a beat because I saw Lucas assisting at the ropes course.

I slowly started heading his way, instead of towards the lake. I couldn't seem to stop myself. I watched him work, getting the campers geared up in their harnesses, and I couldn't look away. I just kept walking in his direction, completely captivated by him. I needed to get a grip. I couldn't keep responding this way every time I saw him.

I felt the color rising in my face as I thought about talking to him, what I would say, how I would start the conversation. I slowed my pace, looking around to see if anyone noticed me, as I felt sure the thoughts running through my mind were displayed across my face.

I stopped abruptly, stunned by the scene before me. Amelia walked up behind Lucas and hugged him, wrapping her arms around him like they were already a couple. I thought about turning for the lake, but I couldn't seem to move, or look away, or breathe for that matter. Lucas slowly reached up and unwrapped her arms from around his waist, turning to face her very matter-of-factly. His back was to me, but it seemed like he was saying something quietly to her as he held her hands in front of him. She said something back as she leaned into him. He gently set her back by her shoulders as he shook his head, still talking to her quietly. She got mad, said something that seemed angry from my vantage point, and stormed off. When he turned back around to resume his work, I saw his profile. He looked sad, which was all the more confusing to me.

Just then, some of the other counselors at the ropes course walked up to Lucas, looking like they were congratulating him and pointing to my sister. Lucas's head snapped up and looked back in the direction of Amelia. He shook his head as he turned back to face them with a look that made them step backward, laughing and holding their hands up in protest.

"Dude, take it easy." I had somehow moved close enough to hear them, even though I didn't remember moving at all. "We were just giving you props for snagging the beauty."

Lucas relaxed, but had an expression on his face I couldn't understand. "Yeah, guys, I know she is a beauty, but also major off-limits."

"She's definitely not appearing off-limits, walking around in short shorts and bikinis," one of the guys added.

Lucas continued, "I mean off-limits because she's the Director's niece. He won't be too happy you guys are making comments about her."

I turned and headed toward the lake, no longer wanting to listen to a group of guys talking about my sister. As I turned, I saw Lucas glance in my direction, but I didn't wait to see his reaction. He was probably super annoyed that now the dorky, less pretty sister was coming to talk to him. I hurried off to the lake as fast as I could, my face flaming in embarrassment.

I don't know what I was thinking, even trying to walk up to him. I guess I wasn't thinking. I never approached guys at school. I talked to guys in my classes if they were sitting next to me or if they spoke to me first in the halls, but I don't think I had ever sought out a guy to talk to him. What was happening to me, and why was I so drawn to this guy?

Lost in my thoughts, I reached the beach and made a quick look around. It was just past breakfast, but already I'd had enough of people for one day and needed some space. There were floating obstacles in the lake to my left. Once again, people were wrestling and trying to be the king of the hill. I had no interest in watching that, so I walked along the beach in the opposite direction, past the kayaks and canoes lined up on the beach, close to the trees. I finally reached a spot where the water wars weren't visible and sat down on the sand. As I watched the water move in and out in small waves, wetting the sand and leaving its mark each time, I felt a little peace settle in.

I watched the water, smiling at the way it seemed to know its boundaries and taking comfort that the world still seemed to be operating as it should. I swirled my pointer finger through the water and the wet sand, finally feeling at ease, when I got a sudden feeling of being watched. A slight chill went down my spine as I slowly made my way to my feet and turned my head to the right.

"Hey there!" I whipped my head to the left to see Tommy standing there with what I think was his attempt at a sexy smile. It should be so easy to like him. At my school, he would have been one of the most popular boys with all the girls chasing after him.

I realized my hands had instinctively formed into fists at the sound of Tommy's voice, a fact that did not go unnoticed by Tommy. "Whoa there, easy Tiger," he said.

I tried for a smile, "Hey, sorry; you scared me." I exhaled slowly, trying to shake off the creepy feeling.

"Yeah, you seemed a million miles away," he said with a playful tone in his voice.

"I guess I was. This is such a peaceful spot," I commented softly, looking back at the water.

"Oh yeah?" he asked, which drew my eyes back to him. He seemed surprised and maybe a little confused by that. "Is this seat taken, Tiger?" He gestured to an empty spot on the sand as he sat down without waiting for my reply.

"I guess not," I replied as I sat down beside him, leaving some space that he quickly scooted over to fill.

"I saw you wander this way while I was working with some of my trainees, out there on the water. Whatcha' doing out here by yourself?" he asked while poking me in the side with his finger.

"Sometimes, I just need to get away for a bit to sort things out in my mind," I said, realizing I sounded like a crazy person. I bent my knees up, crossing my arms on top of them, my chin resting on my arms. I turned my head to glance at him.

The way he looked at me made me think that maybe he thought so too, but he said, "I guess I can get that." He glanced at the water for a breath and then turned back to me. "Do you spend a lot of time alone?"

"Probably more than I should," I said with a little huff of a laugh. Still resting my head on my arms, I continued to look at him. His dark hair was spiked up and wet from the water games. He peeled off his wet shirt and leaned back on his hands, looking back over at me just in time to catch me looking at his abs.

"Like what you see?" he asked, confidently throwing in a wink.

I could feel my cheeks flame bright red as I quickly averted my gaze back out to the water. "Sorry," I said softly.

"Oh, I don't mind at all that you're checking out the merchandise." He reached over and started playing with my hair that was loose down my back. I had chills at his touch, but they didn't feel like the good kind.

"Come on, don't be shy," he coaxed.

"Sorry." I cleared my throat and started again. "Sorry, shy is what you get with me."

"Tiger, I saw you row, there was nothing shy about you. You're competitive and fierce. You go after what you want, just like I do." He moved his hand to my shoulder to caress it. I knew I was supposed to like his touch, but I just didn't.

"Ouch, ow," I shrugged his hand off. "I'm still really sore from canoeing yesterday," I said to soften my shrug off.

"Oh man, I'm sorry, Sarah, I bet you are sore. You were such a champ." He beamed at me. "How about I give you a nice rub-down."

I felt sick at the thought.

"I'm probably too sore even to touch, so not right now. So how was the 'walk of shame' for Ben last night?" I asked, trying to change the subject, even though I had no desire to hear about someone being humiliated.

"It was epic!" Tommy's hand fell away as he gestured. And I changed my posture so as not to give him as easy access to my neck again. He went on about how this was Ben's first time to walk it and how Ben was still feeling the pain of it this morning.

"I can't tell you anymore, though. Let's just say it's pretty intense," he smiled at me. He was still flying high.

"Have you ever had to do it?"

"Yeah," he almost paled as he thought about it. "It was miserable and humiliating, but it was what I deserved and beat more of my weakness out of me."

"If it's so humiliating, why did you want Ben to go through it?" I asked. "You could have just kept it to yourself who won."

A flash of anger crossed his face, his body became tense, and his jaw clenched, but I could see him visibly soften before he spoke. "Ben has put me in the 'walk of shame' twice." His eyes shifted back out to the water. "He got what he deserved." And with that, he smiled a cruel grin, probably picturing the whole thing again.

"Was that why you challenged him?" I asked, my own anger barely disguised as I realized what I had been an unwilling participant to.

"Of course," he said nonchalantly, smiling as his eyes continued to gaze across the water. There was no remorse in his voice.

"Well, I better get going," I stated as I got up, brushing the sand off my shorts.

"Why?" he asked like my behavior seemed strange and unexpected.

Even though he didn't seem like a nice guy, I still didn't have it in me to reject him full out.

"I, umm, have to go because, umm," I stuttered along, trying to grasp for something to say. "I have an archery lesson. So, I need to get to that." I couldn't look him in the eye because of my obvious lie. I hated lying, but at this moment, I hated being next to him more.

He seemed to buy it. "Oh, okay, I better get back to my trainees anyway." He stood up and tilted my chin up to look at him. The guy I thought was cute before, no longer had any appeal. There was nothing attractive about the cold-hearted way he had treated someone he called a friend. His eyes grew suddenly intense as he leaned in to kiss me. I turned my head at the last second, and he kissed my cheek.

He looked taken aback by my rebuff. "Maybe you should take a little nap after your archery lessons. You seem a little off." He brightened a little, "Plus, you'll need your rest for the bonfire. Things get a little crazy, and it's been known to go late into the night."

"Yeah, a nap sounds like a good idea. See you later, Tommy," I said with a forced smile, walking backward and then turning to head off to what I hoped was the direction of the archery range.

Tommy just stood there looking at me with narrowed eyes, like he was studying me, trying to figure me out.

I was flustered, so I wasn't actually sure I was headed down the right path to archery. I slowed my steps and my breathing as I tried to get my bearings. I wasn't exactly sure why my interaction with Tommy had upset me so much, but I knew for sure that Tommy wasn't the guy for me. His size had even started to intimidate me on the beach. I hadn't noticed how big he was until his anger was directed at me, or was it at Ben? I wasn't sure, but I witnessed the full force of its intensity.

The sounds of gunshots were getting closer, so I realized I was probably headed in the right direction. I saw a clearing coming up on the trail, so I kept heading that way. I stopped abruptly when I heard what sounded like whimpering. I searched around for the sound when through the trees to my right, I saw a boy pushed up against a tree. He was held there by a bigger guy who looked a lot like Ben.

"You are so weak; you are nothing, you little piece of," I braced myself as he spewed a string of curse words in the kid's face. Once I heard his voice, I knew it was Ben, and I ducked behind a tree. "You will never make it as a trainee. Your life will consist of nothing but cleaning up the blood and mess when we're through, but you'll never be one of us." The kid was struggling now against Ben's hand at his throat, clawing at it to get a breath. When he started to go limp and slumped to the ground, I let out a startled sound. Ben turned to find the source of the sound, releasing the tension around the boy's neck just enough to allow him a breath.

From behind the tree, I could see Ben leaning over him, and the boy started screaming in pain. I couldn't see what Ben was doing to him, but the boy begged, "Please, please, I'll try harder."

Ben stood up and growled out, "You better, you're worthless and a waste of space. Walk of shame for you tonight." He kicked the boy hard in the side, and then walked off in the other direction, thankfully.

I was shaking so badly, I had to sit on the ground before I fell over. I could still hear the kid whimpering. He looked like he was maybe 12 or 13, but Ben would make anyone look small. Why on earth was he doing that to this poor kid? Maybe he was taking out his embarrassment and anger on the kid, from his own walk of shame.

I knew I had to talk to Uncle Derek about this. No one should be treated like that, no matter how bad they had screwed up.

The whimpering stopped, and I heard a groan. Still shaking, I leaned out from my hiding place to see the kid limping off, holding his side. I wondered if he was headed to the nurse. Wait, was there a nurse here? I had looked for one earlier because of how sore I was, hoping maybe she had some kind of treatment for muscle pain. But there wasn't a medical facility on the map, at least as best as I could remember. I would have to ask my uncle where that was as well. Maybe I could check on the boy there later. I didn't think he would appreciate me making myself known and letting him know there had been an audience to his humiliation.

Once the boy was out of sight, I slowly got up, bracing myself on the tree. The emotional weight of witnessing something so violent, had really taken its toll. I just couldn't stop thinking about Ben. I couldn't believe the playful, competitive Ben, whom I had raced against in a canoe, was capable of such physical and verbal abuse. Charming Ben, whom my sister was going on a date with tonight. I had to tell my uncle now, but I had no idea where to find him.

This camp was nothing like I had ever imagined. I knew it was a war games camp, but I thought it would just be a bunch of upperclass guys playing a grown-up version of make-believe. I really had no idea there would be so much real violence. Uncle Derek had always said he came here to relax, but there was nothing relaxing about this place.

I continued down the trail to the clearing to get my bearings. The darkness of the trail and the events I had just witnessed gave way to the light of the clearing as it opened to the archery field just ahead. All of the targets were lined up down the open field like soldiers ready for arrows to fly at them. It actually seemed peaceful there, which was surprising after what I had just seen. And then I saw him, just as he released an arrow that drove straight across the field and hit a bullseye. Even from the back and fifty yards away, I could tell it was Lucas. He quickly pulled two more arrows firing them down and hitting bullseyes on the surrounding targets. He lowered his bow and turned to look at me as if he knew I was there.

I gave a little wave to him, not sure if I should stay or go, but he smiled and nodded at me as he started walking towards me. My face heated as I realized I had once again shown up to a place where he already was, without being invited. I really hoped he didn't think I was stalking him or anything.

"Hey, Sarah," he greeted me easily.

"H…hey," I replied, barely able to get the word out.

"What brings you to the archery field?" he asked, still smiling that beautiful half-smile. His eyes practically glowed with life and kindness.

"I was actually looking for my uncle." I wanted to tell Lucas what I had just witnessed. I wanted to tell him everything I was feeling. He just seemed like he would listen and somehow make it all better for me.

"You won't find him at any of the activity stations," he paused to study me, but then continued, "At this time of day he's probably at the mess hall."

I looked at his wrist, but there wasn't a watch.

"How do you know it's time for lunch? Can you tell time by the sky or something?"

Lucas smiled and put two fingers behind his right ear, then leaned forward as if he were trying to hear something. And so, I listened as well. I didn't really hear anything except the wind moving through the trees.

"I don't hear anything," I murmured.

"It's not what you hear; it's what you don't," he replied. I still didn't understand, and he smiled gently at me. "Do you hear the guns?"

"No, I don't. Wow, I hadn't even realized." Between the hours of eight and five, it seemed like the noise from the gun range never stopped. "I can't believe I didn't notice."

He smiled at my observation, "If you let me get my bow put away, we can walk over to the mess hall together."

"Okay, yeah, sure," I said, hopefully not too enthusiastically. I watched as he placed his bow in its case and locked it. He had a simple wooden bow; at least it looked simple compared to all the offerings in the equipment shed behind us. He placed his case into the equipment shed and looked at me.

"Ready?"

"Yeah, uh, yes," I said as we headed to the other end of the clearing from where I had entered.

"Are you enjoying yourself here, Sarah?" he asked. I had to look up at him, way up, to reply.

"Well, umm, I like being outside."

"It's okay to be honest," he said, smiling.

I let out a short laugh. "Honestly, not really, everything here is a bit too intense for me."

"Yeah, I can see how this place could come off as intense. A war camp isn't exactly where I picture you enjoying yourself," he said kindly.

"Yeah, I can't believe I didn't notice that the guns had stopped shooting. The constant shots make me feel a little sick to my stomach, and on more than one occasion, I've found myself praying for them to stop."

"Praying?" he asked, raising an eyebrow.

"Uh, yeah, what I meant was, umm was... you know, like wishing."

"Oh, okay." He seemed to accept that.

Walking with Lucas, I felt calm for the first time in two days, even though I had just witnessed something so violent. As I saw the mess hall come into view, I was disappointed that we'd be going our separate ways, once inside. I wanted to ask him if he would show me how to shoot in the archery field, but all I could picture was him rejecting me as he did Amelia. I was the Director's niece, too, so he most likely had the same rules for me as well.

"Sarah, would you like to learn how to shoot a bow?" Lucas asked.

"Yes, umm, yes, I would like that. I mean, I would like to learn how to shoot." I involuntarily winced at my ability to form a coherent sentence as I answered a simple question. I tried to correct myself so he wouldn't think that I meant with him.

He smirked at my apparent giddiness and said, "Well, it's my shift in the archery field after lunch. How about you meet me there, and I can show you a few things?"

"Okay, yeah, that would be great." I couldn't make myself look at him but found myself beaming at the ground all the same. "Thanks."

"Okay, Sarah, I'll see you then!" I looked up, and he smiled a full-on smile at me. I didn't think his smile could get any better, but this was like looking into the sun. I was completely mesmerized and slightly stunned. He turned to open the door of the mess hall and held it open for me to enter ahead of him.

"See ya," I whispered as we parted ways, me to the table where my uncle was seated and Lucas toward the buffet line with the other counselors.

CHAPTER 5

I'm not exactly sure how I got through lunch. Although I know I ate some food, I couldn't tell you what. My uncle was engaged in an animated conversation with Drake for most of lunch. When a lull in the discussion happened, I quietly asked him if I could talk to him about something important. He said we could catch up later, but he had to rush off to another important meeting.

Amelia wanted to go lay out by the lake after lunch, but the last thing I wanted to do was be her bikini sidekick again. She was mad when I said I couldn't and definitely didn't believe me when I said I was taking archery lessons. But, thankfully, she wasn't curious about who was instructing me. As we exited the mess hall, I made sure Amelia was on her way to change before I headed back to the archery field.

Just then, a shot rang out. Clearly, the gun range was up and running again, my signal that lunch was officially over and Lucas would be waiting. I had butterflies in my stomach at the thought of seeing Lucas. As I turned from the pathway into the clearing that surrounded the archery field, I was surprised at how empty it was compared to the activity I'd seen at the gun range earlier.

"You ready for this?"

At the sound of his voice, I turned to see Lucas walking out of the equipment shed, holding a smaller bow, some arrows, and other equipment I didn't recognize.

"Actually, I am. I'm a little nervous though, my arms still feel a bit like jelly after canoeing yesterday," I admitted.

"I heard about the legendary canoe race."

"Oh no, what did you hear?" I cringed.

"It's okay, Tommy was ragging on Ben about beating him, and Ben mentioned that Tommy had some help."

Hearing Ben's name made me visibly bristle. "Did you have to watch the walk of shame thing?" I wondered if maybe I should tell Lucas what I had seen earlier. This might be the opening I needed to tell someone about Ben and the boy.

"It's mandatory to be present for any discipline."

"Discipline? So, like the camp administrators are there too?"

"Not necessarily, but the two disciplinary administrators were there."

"What actually happens?" I asked grimacing.

"You don't want to know, Sarah, it's a pretty terrible ritual."

I was glad he hadn't told me, and it made me feel a little better knowing my uncle wasn't present. Still, it made me sick that the administrators were not only okay with something like that but actually participated in it. I guess I thought it was just the counselors being cruel to each other. I lost my nerve to tell him what I saw as I realized that violence seemed to be a part of life at Camp Tuano.

"Sarah," he said my name gently, drawing my eyes up to his. "This camp is meant to bring out the worst in a person. Don't let it do that to you."

"Okay," I replied. I wasn't exactly sure what he meant, but just hearing his voice and looking into his eyes made me feel better. We lingered there with our eyes locked. The kindness I saw there almost made me blurt out what I had seen. Maybe Lucas wasn't okay with the violence either, but I wasn't sure I trusted my judgment when he was looking into my eyes.

"Let's get you geared up!" he said, changing his tone and the mood in one sentence.

"Okay," I said, my nerves a little more on edge as he moved closer to me.

"You're right-handed correct?" he asked. I nodded. "This is your forearm guard. Let's slide it on to right here." He slid the guard onto my left forearm.

"Is it too tight?" he asked as he checked the fit.

"Nope, feels good." I could barely hear my own voice over the pounding of my heart in my ears caused by his gentle touch.

"Okay, this is your finger guard. It will go on your pointer finger and middle finger like this." He demonstrated, and then I replicated what he had done by sliding it onto my fingers with the thick part in between them.

"Good, now we are going to test out your bow to see how it fits." Once he had me hold it and assess how easily I could pull back the string, Lucas declared it to be a good fit. He then asked me if I would like him to demonstrate. I readily agreed, and he positioned me safely back and to his right, allowing me to see how he held the bow. He showed me how to place the arrow, sight down the shaft, pull back the bowstring while maintaining control of the arrow, and then the release of the bowstring to send the arrow flying. His voice was rich and warm, drawing me in as he described each step of the lesson. He did a few more demonstrations and then asked if I was ready to try.

"Normally, a beginner would start out with blunted arrows, but there isn't such a thing at Camp Tuano, so please just don't point your arrows at anyone, okay?" His voice suddenly sounded serious, more direct somehow.

"Yes," I replied firmly, my eyes wide as I thought about the fact that in my hands I held something that could genuinely injure someone, even if by mistake. I tried to match my voice to the seriousness of his instructions. Once Lucas had me pointed at the target and showed me how to nock my arrow, I remembered the power I held in my hands. If I wasn't aimed at the target, I was to point the arrow at the ground, whenever the arrow's nock was snapped onto the bowstring.

Once Lucas declared me ready, I battled with my arrow falling off as I tried to get the nock clipped on the bowstring. Lucas didn't laugh at any of my sad attempts, he just kept encouraging me, which helped me to believe I could do it.

I finally got a few arrows headed in the right direction, but they weren't getting anywhere close to the target downrange. Lucas grabbed a movable target out of the equipment shed and put it at a 15-yard distance. My arrows could make it there, but they didn't have enough power to stick in the target. After I had made a few attempts at the target and not gotten a single one to stick, my arms protested that I stop. I confessed that to Lucas, and he graciously moved the target closer for one more shot. I got my arrow in it, nowhere close to the bullseye—high and to the right, but I was still very proud of myself.

"Well done, Sarah!" Lucas cheered me on. I jumped up and down in my excitement and then noticed the difference between my target and the ones downrange he'd hit so effortlessly. I started laughing.

He laughed along with me and asked with a knowing voice, "Something funny?"

"You know, for a minute, I thought I had actually done it, until I realized my target was like a thousand times closer than yours."

"Well you're no Robin Hood. But even he had to start somewhere." With that, he flashed a smile, and once again, I felt caught in his gaze. I could barely look at him when he smiled, mainly because of my own self-consciousness, but also, there was something almost brilliant to him. The longer I stared, the more I could sense there was something fundamentally different about Lucas. Sure, he was obviously nice to look at, but there was more to it than that. When I looked at Lucas, I felt at peace. I felt like I mattered.

I had to shake myself out of the trance I had faded into. "Hmm," I cleared my throat, "I guess you are a very experienced archer then?" I asked, smiling at him, still feeling dazed.

Somewhere during my archery training, I relaxed around Lucas, but I still caught myself staring back at his smile. I was having all sorts of new kinds of feelings around him, nervous, but at the same time, comfortable. I knew that when I was with him, I could be myself.

"I am very comfortable with a bow," he replied humbly.

I realized then that no one had joined us on the archery field and asked him why.

"Most counselors here are already pretty good with the bow and they don't feel the need to practice. The trainees are required, but they were here this morning."

"Well, who were you assigned to be here to train then?" I asked making a show of looking around.

Lucas laughed. His laugh was deep but so light and joyful. I swear, I couldn't think straight around him.

"It's kind of the least favorite spot for the counselors, so I get assigned to it because I'm the new guy. Most of the counselors were also trainees here at one point, so they have seniority," he explained. "The trainees can come for more training in the afternoons, but archery comes pretty naturally to them as well."

"Gotcha." I said, though honestly I wondered why archery came naturally to them. *Maybe it's a guy thing...*

"You saved me from an afternoon of practicing by myself, Sarah. I'm glad you joined me."

"It doesn't look like you need much practice," I responded kindly.

He smiled humbly in return.

"Yeah, like most of the guys here, it seems like they can't get enough of war and competition and hurting others," unable to hide the hint of disgust from my voice as I spoke.

He paused with a very calm look on his face, but he had narrowed his eyes at me. Not that he was angry with me, but that he was gazing into me, trying to figure something out. He glanced up at the sky, which made me do the same. When I lowered my eyes, he was looking at me again.

"I'm not like those other guys." His voice was soft but direct.

"I know," I interrupted. "I can tell you are different," I blurted out. "I mean, I see a good difference in you, not that you're different in a bad way." I tried to recover quickly.

He smiled. "I'm glad you can tell. And while we're on the subject, you are different as well and not in a bad way."

I blushed brightly as I said, "Thank you."

"My pleasure," he responded sincerely. "Sarah, there is something you should know. I'm not…"

"Sarah! There you are," Amelia shouted across the field.

Lucas's gaze and his voice had been so intense; it took me a minute to focus on my sister. She was wearing her see-through cover up with her bikini on underneath. Her cheeks looked sun-kissed, and she was beaming.

Embarrassed, I looked back at Lucas and saw his gaze was on the ground.

Once she was close enough, I turned my attention to Amelia. "Hey. Were you looking for me?"

I could tell then that her smile was fake. She looked back and forth between Lucas and me, pushing her sunglasses on top of her head and revealing a strained look in her eyes. "Have you been here all afternoon?" Until that moment, I hadn't realized how much of the afternoon had passed. Amelia continued, obviously irritated, and didn't wait for a reply. "Ben and Tommy kept me company for a bit at the lake. They want to eat dinner with us and then take us to the bonfire."

At the mention of the bonfire, Lucas quickly raised his gaze from the ground and looked at her face. His face seemed strained by her last comment, but I wasn't sure if it was the guys or the bonfire or both.

Amelia looked at Lucas with a bit of a glare. "So, if you're done with Lucas here, let's get going."

I didn't want my time with Lucas to end, but the tension was thick, and I could tell my sister was upset. I just wasn't totally sure why. Was she jealous of what she sensed between Lucas and me? Did she think I lied when I said I had an archery lesson?

"Okay, be right there," I said, expecting her to walk away. She waited, arms crossed, still glaring at Lucas.

"Lucas, are you going to the bonfire?" I asked him. His face looked sad, the same face I saw when he had the earlier interaction with my sister.

"It's not really my scene, but I may stop by knowing that you two will be there."

"Okay, I'll see you then?" I was still trying to get him to look at me.

"Just please be careful tonight. The bonfire is known to get out of hand. You both are priceless and precious, don't let anyone convince you otherwise tonight." He looked at Amelia first, and then he looked intensely into my eyes.

Amelia looked stunned but recovered quickly. "Whatever," she quipped as she rolled her eyes. "Let's go, Sarah. I need time to get ready." She grabbed my hand and pulled me along behind her.

"Thank you, Lucas," I said before allowing myself to be pulled entirely away. I hoped he knew I was saying thank you for many things: time with him, teaching me archery, making me feel alright for being different, for actually seeing me. And then a thank you for his words, I was priceless and precious. I looked back once more. His gaze was still on us, and he lifted a hand to wave goodbye.

On our way back to our cabin, Amelia tried to stay a step ahead of me. When I finally got her to talk to me, it was clear she was upset about me being with Lucas. I didn't offer her an explanation or any excuses, so she began informing me about her time at the beach with Ben.

She had barely started what most likely would have been a lengthy monologue on how great Ben was, when I interrupted her, "Amelia, he is not a nice guy."

"You don't know what you're talking about," she responded, dismissing me.

"I'm serious Ames, I saw him beating up a kid in the woods."

She slowed her fast-paced walk, "I'm sure it was nothing, the kid probably deserved it."

"What?" I asked, in disbelief that my sister could dismiss something like that so quickly. "I can't believe you'd say that. Does any kid ever deserve to be beaten up?" I could tell she was hearing what I was saying and thinking about the implications.

"Maybe it was self-defense for Ben, maybe that kid attacked him," she said with much less conviction this time.

"This wasn't self-defense, it was an outright beating."

"The counselors here know what they are doing, I'm sure it wasn't as big of a deal as you are making it out to be." My anger grew stronger as she dismissed me once again.

"I can't believe what you are saying, I actually saw a kid getting beat up and you either don't believe me or don't care." I had to turn away I was so angry. "Lucas would have never done something like that."

"I guess you and Lucas are all buddy-buddy now, huh?" I turned back to see her anger matching my own.

"That has nothing to do with this," I responded, a little taken back that Lucas was what she was upset about right now. "I wanted you to know so that you wouldn't go to the bonfire with Ben."

"Thanks for the tip, little sis, but I can handle myself." And with that, she stomped up the stairs and slammed the cabin door.

I sat on the steps for a few minutes hoping to let Amelia calm down. When I tried the handle, it was nice to see that at least she hadn't locked the door. After she got out of the shower, I tried to re-engage the conversation, but she still wouldn't listen to reason about Ben. I took my shower and dressed quickly, hoping I would have time to find my uncle while Amelia finished getting ready for dinner. I knew she'd be a while, and I needed to talk to him about what I saw. No matter how violent the camp was, I didn't think he would tolerate what Ben had done to the young camper. I tried Uncle Derek's cabin first, then some of the main buildings and the surrounding area, but I didn't find him, so I headed back to our cabin to get Amelia.

Once we were in the mess hall, we got our food and sat at our usual table. Uncle Derek wasn't there, and I worried again that I might not get to talk to him. As we started to eat, he came in laughing with a group of camp leaders and headed for the food. After he filled his tray, he sat down next to me, taking the spot directly across from Amelia. He asked us about our day, and before I could open my mouth, Amelia jumped right in to inform him of everything that happened to her, including seeing a snake. He laughed at her face when she spoke of the snake.

"The snakes here are beautiful creatures, Amelia, although somewhat deadly, so it's probably good you avoided it." He winked and chuckled as her jaw had dropped when he said deadly.

While I was glad it wasn't me who saw the snake, I was more focused on working up the courage to tell my uncle what I had seen earlier in the day. He was turning to ask about my day when Ben and Tommy arrived at our table, greeting my uncle and the other directors before asking if they could join us. Ben was sporting some bad bruises and scratches on his face and arms. He probably mirrored the boy he was beating on earlier. No way was I going to bring it up with my uncle while Ben was around.

"I sure hope the other guy looks worse than you," Uncle Derek laughed, motioning for them to sit with us. I looked across the table at Amelia, but she quickly looked away. Ben sat down across from me and put his arm around Amelia. Tommy sat on the other side of me, pulling me in for a side hug.

"Did you get your nap in, Tiger?" he asked as though we shared some intimate secret.

"Uh, no, actually, I couldn't sleep," I replied, trying to smile at him. That probably would have been true had I actually tried to sleep.

My uncle turned to me and asked, "So Sarah, how was your day?"

"Good," I replied, thinking more of my time with Lucas than anything else.

"Did you see a snake, too?" my uncle asked, teasing me.

As a matter of fact, I had seen a snake, and he was sitting right across from me. I looked at Ben, and he was looking at me with a weird expression, almost daring me to speak. Did he know I saw him? How could he know?

"No reptiles spotted for me, thank goodness."

"Well, what kept you busy all day then?"

"I had to keep it pretty low key since my arms are still killing me."

"Yep, I sure put her through some paddling school yesterday. And Ben too," Tommy said with a smirk at Ben. I saw Ben's fists tighten to white on the table and looked up to see Ben glaring at Tommy, like if there hadn't been a table between them, he would have his hands around Tommy's neck. The thought sent a chill down my spine, a reminder that I had seen Ben with his hands on someone's neck just a few short hours ago.

"Well," my uncle pressed, seeming not to notice Ben and Tommy, or not really caring, "Since your arms were out of commission, what did you do all day?"

"I spent some time by the lake, enjoying the water. I walked some of the trails. Checked out some of the fields and equipment." I said, hoping that was enough to appease him.

"You had an archery lesson too, didn't you?" Tommy asked.

"Oh, yes, I did," I replied, pretending like I had actually forgotten my archery lesson when in reality, I knew I never would.

"Well," my uncle held onto the word dramatically. "How did the archery go?"

"Umm, well," I fumbled, not sure how to answer. "Not that well, I only got one arrow into the target."

"It was your first time, I'm sure you'll get better at it," my uncle replied confidently.

"My arms felt like jelly, so it was good that my instructor was patient with me."

My uncle seemed taken back by that. "Who was this *patient* instructor of yours?" he asked, his voice turned more severe than the conversation warranted.

"Umm," I stalled, not knowing what to say because my uncle seemed angry, and I wasn't sure if Lucas would get in trouble.

"His name is Lucas," Amelia supplied, while looking at me like I had lost my mind.

"Lucas?" my uncle asked. "Oh, the new guy." His face seemed to relax a bit more at that thought. He looked at the other directors. "We may need to make sure he's settling in okay here. Camp Tuano may be a bit more intense than he's used to."

Suddenly, I felt a great need to either defend Lucas or run and tell him that something was coming. I couldn't think of anything to diffuse the conversation, so I changed the subject instead.

"Uncle Derek, tell me about this bonfire thing. You said it's a rite of passage or something?"

"Yep, it's a Camp Tuano tradition. The adults have our own traditions, but you kids will be out at the fire pit." He went on to tell me more about when it had started and why, but all I could think about was Lucas. Hopefully, I would get the chance to warn him at the bonfire.

CHAPTER 6

My uncle wasn't joking about the fire being massive. I saw it through the trees and felt the heat before we had even broken the tree line. Tommy was walking with me, his arm around my neck, the weight of it foreign and not very welcome. He was telling me about his day, his contests, and who all he had defeated. Though I had no interest in the conversation, he didn't really seem to need my input. It wasn't until we arrived at the fire, that he noticed I hadn't spoken a word.

"Sarah, what is with you today? I told you to take a nap." He looked a bit disgusted with me.

"Sorry, I guess I'm tired. I should have taken your advice," I smiled at him, if only to get him to back off.

"I told you so, and now you're probably going to be a big downer at the best party we have all year." He emphasized the last few words like he was in awe of the party, but still managed to seem disgusted at me. He pointed for me to sit down on a bench.

"I'm going to get you something to drink; don't fall asleep before I get back," Tommy said unkindly as he walked off to the other side of the fire where they had drinks and food set up on tables. I was surprised at the number of girls at the bonfire, because up until this moment, I hadn't seen many around camp.

Across the fire, I could see Ben and Amelia already standing too close for my comfort. I watched as he tugged her in for a kiss, hating that my warnings had fallen on deaf ears. He was bad news, but when I tried to talk to her about it again as we walked to dinner, she was having none of it.

"Sarah, Ben has been nothing but sweet to me, unlike Lucas, who looks away every time I show up. He also embarrassed me at the ropes course earlier when all I was trying to do was give him a friendly hug. If it comes down to Ben or Lucas, it's an easy choice for me." With a flip of her hair she had moved into the mess hall without another word.

As I stared across the bonfire at the two of them, I saw Amelia put her hands on Ben's chest, trying to push him away, but he was crushing his lips to hers. Should I go over there? I felt like someone needed to do something, but all of the people around them were giving whoops and whistles. Ben pulled back, grinning in victory, and Amelia ducked her head and touched her lips lightly.

Why did she get herself into situations like this? She had pretty much promised Ben he could have whatever he wanted from her, although, I wasn't sure it would have mattered if she hadn't. He seemed like the type that would just take what he wanted anyway. I got up and headed in their direction, running into Tommy on my way.

"Here ya go, Tiger," he said sweetly and in much better spirits. Then I smelled my drink and the alcohol that came with it. He had clearly had one or two already and forgotten his earlier frustration with me.

"Tommy, I'm only sixteen."

"Bottoms up!" he encouraged, completely unconcerned about my age.

"I'm good for now. Thanks," I said, trying to stall.

He leaned in heavily on me, pressing a wet and alcohol-laden kiss on my cheek, close enough to my lips to make me wonder if that's where he'd been aiming in the first place.

"Come on, Tiger, we got to get you loosened up." I felt my gag reflex as I realized my predicament might not be that different than my sister's.

"Come on, baby, let's dance," he urged, putting his hand on my forearm. I just ignored his comment and tried to shrug him off. He held fast though and my stomach dropped. "Come on." He yanked me forward, hard. "Dance with me." It was a command, not a request.

I felt like I had no choice but to let him pull me close. He was stumbling a bit, which made me question just how much he'd had to drink.

Back home, I never came to parties like this. They made me very uncomfortable. People always had expectations of you to get drunk or go too far physically. Yet here I was, starting to feel pressured about both as Tommy's hands slid down my lower back. "Tommy. Stop it," I said, my voice low and tight. Here I'd thought the bonfire would be roasting s'mores and singing songs. I could not have been more wrong. I wondered if my uncle knew what happened here.

I put my hands on his chest to put a barrier in between us. I kept increasing the pressure I was using to push against him as his hands started to move.

"Tommy, I mean it. Stop it," I said as I pushed harder.

"What is your problem?" He looked at me as though I were the one in the wrong.

"I don't like how you are touching me, please stop it."

"Oh, so the tiger's a tease, huh?" He leered at me.

"I have never teased you."

"Just the way you look at me tells me that you want me, so now you've got me." He pulled me tight up against him again.

"Tommy. Stop!" I shouted, giving a hard shove. He stumbled back a step, then smiled at me, set on coming back in to reclaim his ground.

"Trouble in paradise, Tommy?" Ben said, suddenly next to us. He had his arm around Amelia's neck, the crook of his arm practically keeping her in a chokehold. It was very possessive and stirred something in me.

"Amelia, let's go." I reached for her, but she pulled away from me.

"I'm having fun, Sarah; you should try it sometime," she slurred, making the guys around her laugh. She looked like she'd had a few drinks as well.

"Amelia, this isn't fun. Being groped by a guy you just met isn't fun. Getting drunk to fit in isn't fun. Please, let's just go."

The small crowd quieted as they watched Amelia, Ben, and I. Amelia stared at me for a moment. As I looked into my sister's face, I knew she wanted to leave, but I also knew she didn't believe she could.

"Come on, Amelia, let's go." I said more firmly, reaching for her again. Ben held fast to her though and said, "She's not going anywhere, Sarah. Don't worry, we know how to show her a good time."

I fixed my gaze on her. More than anyone else, I could see past the façade of Amelia's confidence and into the insecurity that drove her to whoever's arms seemed most convenient. What she wanted most, and what I wanted most too, was to be loved; yet if she couldn't be loved, she'd settle for being used. She traded her body to quiet her soul.

"Ames, this isn't what you want, and this isn't who you are," I pleaded to her as I gestured around. She seemed to grow angry at that.

"Shut up, Sarah; this is what I want, and this is who I am. Look around, you prude. No one wants you here anyway, and I won't stand here and be judged by you." She glared at me.

"Looks like I'm gonna win this challenge, Tommy," Ben said, punching Tommy in the chest. He didn't do it lightly, and Tommy took a drunken step back again, narrowly missing the edge of the bonfire this time. "Seems your girl isn't a team player this time." I looked at Tommy, and he swung his gaze to glare at me.

"Amelia," I pleaded, grabbing her arm as they tried to walk away, but she shook me off with a glare as they continued on to the drink table. I knew she wasn't going to change her mind, but I couldn't just leave her. I needed to find Uncle Derek; once he saw what was going on he would make her leave.

"I'm leaving," I said to Tommy.

"What? No, you're not, the party just started." His words were more of a threat than a statement.

"Well, it's over for me. I have no interest in being part of your challenge." I started walking quickly away from the fire.

"You're not going anywhere," Tommy snarled, grabbing my arm and yanking me around into him just as I reached the tree line.

"Let me go!" I shouted as I struggled against him. He held me firmly against him, and I felt the panic rising in me. "Don't touch me, stop it now!" I screamed. We weren't that far from the fire, but nobody around us even seemed to care that I was struggling.

"You're coming with me, you little tease." He yanked my hair down, causing me to scream in pain.

I was in full panic mode now. How was I going to get away from him? "Help me!" I screamed, still thrashing and fighting him. He was so strong, though, and my efforts to escape only seemed to fuel his resolve to keep me from it. But then I heard a calm but firm voice say, "The lady said to let her go." I couldn't turn my head as Tommy had a hard grasp on my hair, but I knew that voice. Lucas had come.

"What are you going to do about it, *Lucy*?" Tommy said to Lucas with a sneer. He didn't let go of me, but he loosened his grip on my hair.

"Tommy, you don't want to know, but I'll show you if you don't let Sarah go." There was such power in his voice that it shook me, and I knew it had rattled Tommy too because he loosened his grip and shoved me toward Lucas. I turned and fell into Lucas's arms. He caught me on my stumble and held me against him protectively. I turned my head to see Tommy still there, glaring at Lucas.

I looked up at Lucas, but his eyes were fixed on Tommy, his jaw clenched and set. When I looked back at Tommy, he looked scared. He backed up slowly, never taking his eyes off of Lucas's face. Once he was a safe distance, he turned and ran, but not in the direction of the fire, which was odd since I thought he would just grab more of his friends to take on Lucas.

As I looked toward the fire, I could see things had gotten way out of control. Everyone was drinking, even all the underage campers, and couples were practically having sex right by the fire. Amelia was nowhere to be seen.

"Let's go," Lucas commanded.

"I can't leave Amelia with these people; please, Lucas, you have to save her too."

He looked in Amelia's direction, then back at me, clearly torn between getting me to safety and rescuing Amelia. "Of course I'll go to her. But Sarah, listen to me. You run through these trees and wait for me on the other side. Don't stop, and don't look back."

I didn't hesitate to obey, running through the first sections of trees, just as Lucas had commanded. Once I was through the dense brush, I stopped, hiding behind a large tree just on the edge of the clearing. I felt so uneasy, like I was being watched or followed. It was so dark here. The trees, so lovely during the day, had become menacing when dressed in shadows. I heard a stick snap to my right and jerked that way, my heart pounding and my fists up.

"It's okay, Sarah," Lucas said, gently pushing my raised fists back to my side.

"You scared me." My heart was pounding, but not so much in fear anymore.

"I didn't mean to scare you." His voice was low, just above a whisper, but strong and comforting at the same time.

"Where's Amelia?" I asked, realizing he was alone.

"She wouldn't come with me."

"What?!" I said in disbelief. "We have to go back for her."

"We can't," he stated, his voice unwavering.

"Why not?" I asked, both panicked and confused.

"She refused to come with me, and she stated that she did not want my help. I can't rescue someone who doesn't want to be rescued. She has to want to come with us." He looked so sad as he spoke, I unconsciously put my hand out and touched his arm.

"Thank you for trying," I said sincerely. "I tried as well, and she wouldn't come." My voice matched the sadness and fear I felt inside.

"Let's get you back safely to your cabin." He grabbed my hand and led the way through the dark. Just like all the other counselors, Lucas was wearing his black counselor t-shirt, but somehow, even in the black of night, he brought light into the darkness I felt surrounding us.

I stopped for just a moment and looked at Lucas, my eyes unwavering. "Thank you for saving me, Lucas." Just having him beside me helped me feel better, safer.

He paused and turned to look at me, and somehow I knew he would always protect me if he could. "Let's keep moving, okay?" he asked with a half-smile.

"Uh, yeah, I mean yes." I fumbled over my words, glad he had only used a half-smile, contemplating the fact that his full smile usually rendered me stunned.

As we continued to walk, I could feel my fear waning, and my thoughts wandered back to the bonfire. "Were you at the bonfire? I didn't think I saw you until you stepped in to save me."

"No, I had just arrived and saw Tommy hurting you," he said, an edge to his voice.

"Thank you again for saving me," I said softly.

"I'm sorry that I even had to, but I'm glad I did, and I'd do it again." He reached to his face and for the first time I noticed a trickle of blood moving down his chin.

"What happened?"

"Ben and his friends didn't like my interference."

"Lucas, I'm so sorry."

"I'm fine, Sarah."

We walked slowly. "I'm still worried about Amelia," I confessed. "I mean, it's not like it's the first time she refused to leave a party with me. But this crowd is next level."

"I know. I wish she had come with me. I wish I could…"

I interrupted, "It's not your fault, she doesn't really listen to me either."

"She should; it's clear whose judgment I'd trust."

"Really?" I was truly touched, no one really valued my opinion on anything. "Amelia always tells me I just don't understand the world and that when I skip out on parties…or bonfires…that I'm being a prude."

"Holding on to yourself when everyone else wants you to change is not prudish, it's courageous."

I couldn't speak. Me, courageous? I had never felt courageous in my life. Fearful, small, unseen, and disappointing, yes. But courageous? Lucas was courageous, and yet here he was telling me I was too. I glanced up at him. He was looking at me, really looking at me, like he could see into my deepest thoughts. His gaze was so intense that I looked down, slightly embarrassed.

"There are many words I would use to describe you, Sarah, but those aren't any of them." He looked at me so intently I wasn't sure if he was angry.

Then it hit me. Wait? How did he know the words running through my head? Had I said those words out loud? How did he know anything about me at all? My eyes opened wide in shock, and my mouth dropped open. "What?" was the only word I managed to squeak out.

"You've been told many things about who you are and what you should believe about yourself. Most of them aren't true. You're courageous, Sarah, far more than you know; the words you've clung to don't define you."

A warmth I had never experienced before enveloped me at those words. Was it true? I found that hard to believe. My whole life up to that point seemed defined by the words of others: Nerd. Prude. Orphan. Those had been my truths, but the warmth and safety that I felt in that moment were hard to deny. Could he be right?

"Who are you?" I whispered in awe.

"I'm Lucas."

"I mean," I recovered from my disbelief, "you aren't like anyone else here. It seems like they are all out for themselves."

"They are, and they've all been lied to."

"And you haven't?"

"No, I see things very clearly."

We stepped off the path and onto the front porch of my cabin. My arms came up and crossed my chest in a subconscious form of self-defense, anticipating Lucas would lean in for a goodnight kiss. Instead, he gently reached out, and with one finger, raised my chin up so that my eyes would follow to look at him.

"I'm sorry things have been hard. I'm sorry that things might get worse before they get better." He paused. "But Sarah Joy, you are seen and valued."

My eyes grew large at that, "How do you know my middle name?"

He smiled gently at me, "Try to get some sleep."

I watched him walk away for just a moment, astounded at how he seemed to know so much about me; but as the distance increased between us, I was suddenly very aware of the dark. I ran down the path to Uncle Derek's door. I pounded hard on it many, many times and even tried the doorknob more than once, but heard only silence in reply to my shouts as the shadows seemed to press in around me.

Finally, I gave up and hurried into my cabin, shutting the door and checking the lock twice, praying Amelia had her key with her. As I walked to close the curtains of all the windows, the feeling of being watched was back full-force, and a cold shiver ran down my spine at the thought.

CHAPTER 7

The bright red numbers of the old digital clock read 2:00 a.m., and Amelia still had not returned. I had wrestled many times with leaving the security of my cabin to find Uncle Derek as the lights of his cabin remained dark, but I was afraid to going traipsing through camp in the middle of the night looking for him, especially considering Tommy was out there too. As I tried once more to summon the courage to go out, I heard a thump at the door.

Chills traveled quickly down my back as I slowly moved across the floor towards the sound. I stood perfectly still at the door, listening to hear if whatever had made the sound was still out there. I was freaked out, but panic wasn't going to help me right now. Lucas said I was courageous, and in this moment, I chose to believe him.

"Who is it?" I shouted through the door. The only response I could hear was moaning. *Amelia,* I thought with alarm. I cracked the door just a bit, and then opened it wide when I saw her slumped on the steps.

"Amelia!" I shrieked. She just moaned in response. Her clothes were torn, and her face was bloodied. Her hair was a mess, and it looked like patches of her hair were missing. "Amelia, who did this to you?" Not that I really had any doubt as to who it was, it was just what came out. She didn't respond.

I tried to get her to stand, but she was just dead weight, completely out of it. "Amelia, try to help me, please," I cried. Not knowing what still lurked outside, I wanted her in the relative safety of our cabin. She moaned again and started to vomit. To keep her from choking, I rolled her on her side. And in the faint glow of the cabin's porch light, I noticed blood in her vomit.

"Uncle Derek!" I screamed towards his cabin, and then I ran towards it. I banged on the door, screaming his name again and again, but there was no response. "Uncle Derek, please!" I shrieked.

What was I going to do? There was no nurse in this awful camp. Why was my uncle never around? Who could help me?

"Lucas," I breathed.

I started running through the woods to where I thought the counselors' cabins were. I was getting scratched by trees and tripping over roots, but I barely noticed. I was just desperate to get Amelia some help. I tried not to think about what would happen if I ran in to some of her assailants. A cold sense of fear passed over me, but I shook it off. I had no time for fear. For now, I was the only one who could help my sister.

I heard noise coming from the indoor training facility, a building I had avoided up until this moment. I had no desire to see a cage fight, but there was a lot of noise inside, which meant a lot of people, and I needed help. Light spilled out of the open door as someone went through it and then closed it behind himself. I ran to the door, but thought better of walking through it. I peered through a dirty window, but I couldn't make out anyone in particular, only shadows that seemed large and grotesque, fueled by my imagination and fear that were now both in overdrive. I heard someone cry out in agony.

I couldn't see what was happening, but the sounds made me certain I wouldn't find help inside. *Maybe Uncle Derek is in there.* I wasn't thinking rationally, but I couldn't just stand there either. I had to go find help, and this might be my only hope.

"Please, someone, help me," I groaned under my breath, hoping I'd find help once inside. I reached for the doorknob.

A hand closed over the top of mine, and I gasped, swinging my head around, eyes wide with fear.

"Lucas. Oh, thank goodness." I fell into his arms, feeling instant relief from the fear and anger and grief that had been swirling inside of me.

"Sarah, you can't go in there."

"What?" I asked, confused.

"You can't go in that building."

"Why not? Do you know what is happening in there? It sounds like someone is being tortured."

"They are," he said softly and sadly.

"What? Then we have to stop it."

"I don't have permission to stop it."

"Then, I need to find my uncle because he'll stop it."

"He's in there, Sarah, and he won't stop it," he said flatly.

"What? Lucas, what are you saying?"

"Your uncle isn't who you think he is. He isn't even your uncle." Lucas looked me directly in the eyes, and I could see his sadness at delivering that news, but I could also see the truth. I didn't want to believe it.

My mind was reeling, and I felt faint. "Lucas, I have to talk to him."

"No, you can't. Sarah, the world you think you and Amelia live in is only a shadow of what is true," Lucas continued.

As soon as I heard Amelia's name, I grabbed his arm and said, "Amelia. Lucas, please, she's hurt. That's why I came over here in the first place." I could no longer think about Uncle Derek or anything else. I grabbed his hand with both of mine and pulled him forward as I stepped backward. "Please, now. We have to go!"

He didn't even hesitate to follow me. As we ran back towards the cabin and my sister, I stumbled across the uneven ground in the dark. Lucas grabbed my elbow, helping me stay upright. I could feel warmth spreading through me at his touch, but I was so out of my mind with worry and fear that I didn't understand how that warmth was also making me feel calm. This wasn't my crush talking; it was something entirely different.

When we reached the cabin, Lucas dropped to his knees and started checking her over. He checked for breathing with his ear to her mouth and felt for a pulse in her neck. He was looking at the rest of her, feeling her arms and legs, probably checking for breaks. When he checked her ribs, she moaned again. I'm not sure if he heard a sound or not, but Lucas's head whipped around, and he stared into the woods.

"Let's get her inside," he said as he carefully scooped her up in his arms. I opened the cabin door, and he carried her in. I looked behind me once more, and while I didn't see anything or anyone, a familiar chill crawled down my spine, like someone was watching us. I closed the door quickly and locked it. I turned just in time to see Lucas laying Amelia on her bed.

Lucas prepared things to get her cleaned up, running warm water and grabbing towels. In the light, Amelia looked even worse. As I thought about what she must have endured, I could barely function. Lucas gave me firm commands as to how to help her, and that propelled me to action. I pushed through my own pain to take care of her. It was like I became someone else in that moment, Lucas's assistant taking care of this girl that I didn't recognize. I was on autopilot, just listening to his voice. As we cleaned her wounds and together got her dressed in new clothing, I finally found my voice.

"Lucas, will she be okay?" I asked, almost begging him to tell me she would be.

"I don't know, Sarah." His eyes held great sadness. "Physically, she will most likely make a full recovery, but as for the rest of her, it's really hard for me to see right now."

I felt a rock form in my stomach and shame engulfed me as I looked at my sister, broken and bruised. "I should have made her come with me," I choked back a sob.

"We can't push past someone's will. You tried to convince her, Sarah, and I know you have tried many times before to get her to see that she's worthy of so much more than she believes. You cannot bear the burden of this, and you aren't meant to." Lucas was speaking quietly but firmly, and when I lifted my eyes to his, I was shaken at the fierceness I saw there.

While I was numb from the shock of seeing my sister like this, I knew Lucas wouldn't lie to me. I was also flashing back to what he said about my uncle earlier.

"Lucas, what did you mean earlier when you said my uncle wasn't my uncle."

"Sarah, I will explain all of that to you. I promise. But right now, I don't like Amelia's color. I need to lie next to her," he said calmly.

"What? How will that help?" I asked, feeling a mix of emotions flash over me, concern, confusion, jealousy, anger.

"I'm not exactly what I seem either. You'll see." He stepped forward, taking my hand in both of his.

"Do you trust me, Sarah?" he asked gently.

"Yes," I stated without any hesitation. "I don't know why, but I do." I could feel the warmth and the calm spreading through me from where he held my hand. My breathing and heart rate slowed as well.

"I know this is all really unsettling, but Sarah Joy, you need to lie down and sleep. You will need your rest for what is to come." As he spoke those words over me, I was overcome with exhaustion. I tried to fight through it.

"I won't be able to sleep with Amelia like this, I have been up this whole time worried about her." I protested.

"Please, just try to lay down." A thousand questions filled my mind, but the exhaustion was like a heavy blanket.

"Okay," I replied. Almost helpless to resist, I laid down on my bed, fully clothed, shoes and all. He let go of my hand to pull my blankets up over me. I could feel the calm in the air; it was almost tangible.

Lucas placed his hand on my forehead and said, "Peace." I could not have fought sleep, even if I had wanted to. Lucas turned off the lights, and in the last remnants of my consciousness, I realized that Lucas had called me Sarah Joy multiple times. He never did answer me earlier, but I couldn't hold on to that thought as I slipped the rest of the way into sleep.

CHAPTER 8

I woke up the next morning to the light streaming in the windows. I turned my head to the right to see Lucas's back facing me. He was still asleep next to Amelia. *Amelia.* My heart skipped a beat in concern for her, but I tried to calm myself because I knew Lucas would have awakened me if she had somehow gotten worse. Still, I got up to look at her. I had to see for myself that she was okay. Lucas had Amelia wrapped in his arms with her back pulled up against him. He still had his camp shirt on, and she was still in the pajamas we had put her in a few hours ago. I walked to the end of the bed and to the other side to see her face. Her bruises were already fading, and the scratches on her arms had scabbed over. Some of her tissue was even pink, fully healed new skin. How was that possible?

Lucas had said he would lie next to her to help her. Had he somehow healed her? Who was he? Why did I trust him so completely? I noticed Amelia looked so peaceful in his arms. She was no longer moaning in pain; her cheeks were pink with life instead of the sickly gray they had been in the cabin light last night. I felt a surge of anger rise up in me as I thought of how she had looked when I found her and of the guys who had hurt her. I would make sure they were caught and brought to justice. My uncle would surely make them pay.

Then I remembered what Lucas had said about my uncle. Would he even care that she was hurt? My heart started pounding when I remembered Lucas's words, *not your uncle*. What did that mean? The peace that I'd felt in the middle of the night was gone, and once more, I was consumed with fear.

I had way more questions than I had answers. I wanted to wake Lucas, but when I looked at his face, I was startled by his appearance. His features had darkened some, and he had bruises on his face and scratches on his arms. Had he taken Amelia's pain, physically? What was happening to him? How was this even possible? Would I have to take care of Amelia and Lucas as well? Who would help me?

"Help," I whispered to the room.

Lucas's eyes slowly opened. He moaned in pain, touching his ribs, then closed his eyes in a wince.

I walked around to his side of the bed and knelt down. "Lucas, what's wrong, how can I help you?"

"I'm okay, Sarah, it will just take some time."

I touched his cheek lightly, running my finger just below a bruise around his eye that looked painful. As I was looking at Lucas's face, loud pounding on the door startled me, and I jumped to my feet.

"Sarah, Amelia, are you in there?" It was Uncle Derek.

"Thank goodness," I breathed a sigh of relief. I moved toward the door without a second thought.

"Sarah, you can't let him know that you know about him," Lucas said painfully as he strained to get up. I paused, suddenly unsure of what to do as I heard the rattle of keys in the door.

"Lucas, what should I do?"

He didn't get to answer because Uncle Derek flung the door open wide. He was followed in by the rest of the camp administration, Tommy right on their heels.

"Uncle Derek," I said, feeling guilty and embarrassed for some reason when in reality he was the one that had some questions to answer.

"What is *he* doing here?" Uncle Derek shouted, pointing his finger at Lucas.

"Helping," I said pathetically, trying to step in between the two of them.

"Helping? I bet he's helping." Uncle Derek was furious.

I looked at Lucas. It looked as though he was having trouble standing.

"What are you doing here?" he yelled at Lucas. Lucas just looked at him with a steady gaze.

"I already told you, he was helping us!"

Uncle Derek turned his scowl to me. I continued, "Amelia was attacked last night and left for dead on the doorstep. I couldn't find you, but Lucas came to help us."

He glanced in her direction, then turned his eyes to me and said, "I'm sure you're exaggerating, Sarah, she looks fine." But he didn't even move to check on her.

"I want this disgusting thing to answer me. What are you doing here?" he asked Lucas, his words held more meaning than I understood.

"Uncle Derek!" I shouted.

"Shut up, Sarah. This has nothing to do with you," he said, scowling at Lucas.

"What do you mean this has nothing to do with me? This has everything to do with me!" I yelled. He had never spoken to me in that way. When he saw the confusion on my face, Uncle Derek softened, remembering who he was talking to.

"Sarah, that wasn't what I meant. I just meant I have to do my duty as both your uncle and the camp director. He is in a girl's cabin, and he most likely harmed one of you."

"He did not harm Amelia, he was nowhere near her when it happened. And we are much better off than we would have been without him. He saved Amelia's life!" I shrieked, desperately trying to get through to him.

"Sarah, that's enough," he said, getting more irritated.

"No, Uncle Derek, you have to listen to me. Ben did this. I know it was him. You didn't see him at the bonfire."

"Sarah, Ben is one of our best leaders here. You're mistaken."

"No, Uncle Derek. I'm telling you the truth. I know what he's capable of. I tried to tell you sooner, but I saw Ben beating up one of the campers in the woods."

"There's nothing wrong with a little healthy discipline," my uncle said, his voice stern and direct.

"It wasn't discipline; he was strangling the poor kid and probably would have killed him if I hadn't come upon them when I did!"

I was still practically shouting at him, but my words didn't seem to have any impact.

"I've had no reports of any such injuries, and Ben is not the problem here. He," Uncle Derek pointed at Lucas, the color in his face climbing as his anger raged, "he is responsible, and he is not what he seems. He's not one of us." I watched as Uncle Derek traded a look with Tommy, who nodded his confirmation. "You need to trust me on this, and let your sad little crush go."

I gasped. It felt as if he had slapped me, not because he mentioned the crush, but because I had never heard him speak to me with such cruelty. The man standing before me was a stranger.

"What do you have to say for yourself?" Uncle Derek snarled at Lucas.

Lucas just stared at him, not flinching. I noticed then that his bruising was fading just a little, and the scratches on his arms seemed less distinct.

"Guilty it is then; come on boys, let's show Lucas how we handle discipline of the highest order here at Camp Tuano," he growled.

"NO!" I shouted, feeling the menace in my uncle's words. I grabbed onto his arm and tried to pull him back as he headed for Lucas. He shook me off easily; glaring at me with a hatred I wouldn't have imagined him capable. Tristan and Carson roughly grabbed Lucas's arms and pulled him to standing. They made Lucas seem small between the two of them, and I knew I wouldn't be able to stop them. I lunged around my uncle to get to Lucas and somehow got my arms around him.

Just as quickly, Uncle Derek ripped me away, grabbing me by the arms and pulling me back with more force than necessary.

"You will stay here and watch over your sister," he commanded still glaring at me. "Understood?" he asked, starting to move towards the door.

Taking my cues from Lucas, I didn't answer but just glared at my uncle in return. Searing anger ran through me toward this man who was supposed to be the person who loved me most in the world.

"Do you understand me?" he shouted again, his nostrils flaring.

He started towards me, so I gave one curt nod, maintaining my glare.

"Let's go, boys." Uncle Derek growled, turning away from me abruptly and moving to open the door, but I wasn't looking at him; I was looking at Lucas. Tristan and Carson still had a firm grip on Lucas's arms, so firm that I knew it was painful, but Lucas never said a word. His eyes were fixed on me as if he were trying to pass me strength with his gaze.

They pulled him along between the two of them, past me, and out the door. I noticed in that brief instance that his color was better, his skin was healing, and he was standing taller. I took a deep breath in and out as the door closed. Lucas's gaze must have worked because I was standing taller and despite the worst of circumstances, I felt . . . hope.

I paced the cabin, trying to decide what to do, feeling so desperate to help Lucas. I couldn't get Amelia to wake up, but she seemed better, and I knew she would be fine on her own. Maybe if I went after Lucas, I could help him escape.

I opened the cabin door to make sure it was clear. It wasn't.

The man standing guard outside was Steve, the guy forced to help us at the gun range. His look was passive and a bit bored.

"Get back inside, Sarah," he said flatly. He stood on the bottom steps with an automatic weapon in his arms and a pistol on his hip.

"Why?" I asked.

"Your uncle's orders," he replied, still keeping his voice monotone and bored.

"So, what, if I leave, you're gonna shoot me?"

"No, of course not. I'm here to protect you," he said without convincing me of a word of it.

I opened my mouth to protest when he said with a little more force, "Get back inside."

I stared him down with a glare for a few seconds. "Fine!" I shouted dramatically with Amelia-type flair, flipping my hair over my shoulder and slamming the door on my way back inside. I was angry, but quickly realized he did me a favor. I realized I was still wearing the same clothes from the night before. My hair was flat on one side from sleeping, and I had morning breath.

I tried to awaken Amelia again, but she wouldn't stir. She looked so healthy and whole that for a split second I wondered if I had dreamed the night before. I went into the bathroom, took a shower, brushed my hair and my teeth, and all the while, I worried about Lucas. What were they doing to him, and why? None of this was making sense. My mind bounced back and forth from all the things I had witnessed and heard in the last 24 hours.

Oh, Lucas, what are they doing to you?

As I pulled on clean jeans, a new t-shirt, and my hoodie, I began to strategize what I was going to do to help him. I paused as I tied my tennis shoes when the reality hit me that I didn't even know where they were keeping him. I had to find him before I could rescue him.

I need help.

My stomach growled, and I realized I hadn't eaten since last night at dinner. It was 11:30 in the morning. We had missed breakfast altogether. That's probably why my uncle came to our cabin in the first place. But that didn't make sense either. He clearly knew something was going on because he showed up angry and with all those people.

Well, I couldn't dwell on that now. Uncle Derek was clearly going to punish Lucas, no matter what. I had to find him. My stomach growled again. Food, I needed food. Steve would have to let me get some food.

Before I stepped back outside, I grabbed my phone off the charger and stuck it in my back pocket. Attached to my phone was a slim wallet that housed my ID and credit card. I grabbed the $100 in cash that I had brought. I wanted to take a backpack but thought that might seem suspicious. I took a look in Amelia's wallet. She had $160 in cash, so I decided to take that too. I wasn't even sure why I was doing this, but I felt the need to be prepared. As I was pulling the cash out of her wallet, I saw another ID behind it. I pulled it out. It was Amelia's picture, but some of the information was wrong, like her name and age. It was a fake ID.

I looked over to Amelia and felt deeply saddened by all she had lost and by my inability to stop it all from happening. I moved to her and touched her forehead gently. I spoke softly as I stroked her hair, "Amelia, I'm so sorry." Tears fell from my eyes as I gazed at my precious sister. "You are so special, and nothing that has happened to you can change that."

If the counselors could do what they did to Amelia and get away with it, what would they do to Lucas? I had to go try to stop them. I took the fake ID, wrapped the money around it, and tucked it into my other back pocket. I put Amelia's wallet back where I found it. I had to get Lucas away from my uncle, and then he would help me with Amelia. She would be okay; she had to be.

I tried once again to get her to wake up with a cold cloth, but she still didn't move. She was so peaceful, her cheeks a happy, sun-kissed pink once again. I kissed her forehead, pushing away the uncomfortable feeling that I might be saying goodbye. As I walked toward the doorway, I glanced back at her one more time and whispered, "I'll be back for you, Amelia. I love you."

✳   ✳   ✳

Steve had reluctantly agreed that food was a good thing and that my uncle wouldn't want me to be hungry. He locked the cabin door as we left for the mess hall, a fact that did not go unnoticed by me.

As we walked toward the mess hall, I tried to make small talk with Steve, pointing to the building where I had been last night when Lucas found me looking for my uncle.

"What's that building for?" I asked innocently enough.

"That's the main indoor training facility," he said, giving it a quick glance and replying like he was bored.

"What happens in there?"

"Fighting, meetings, discipline…"

"Oh, yeah, I've heard about that. Like the walk of shame? Ben and Tommy told us all about that, and about some of the more severe discipline that happens there."

"No, the more severe punishment happens at the infirmary," he said, his voice trailing off on the last word. He looked over at me, but my features were schooled to look completely innocent. I'm not sure he had meant to answer.

"Oh, that's weird," I said, "I thought there wasn't an infirmary on this camp. I had a super sore neck and shoulders yesterday and would have loved to have gotten some medicine." I giggled like I hadn't put two and two together, that they did harsh discipline at an "infirmary."

"What's this one for?" I pointed at another building, I knew it was the building where the cage fighting took place, but I wanted him to think I was just curious in general about the camp, not just one particular building.

"That's for hand-to-hand combat, not really up your alley," he replied dryly as we walked into the mess hall.

I giggled again, admitting he was probably right. We both walked through the line to get our food. I took more food than I could possibly eat. While I wasn't really hungry, I was thinking that I could eat slowly and make it last longer while I tried to come up with a plan for getting away from Steve. As we sat down, the rifle over his shoulder bumped me.

"What kind of a gun is that?" I asked, though I had zero interest in his answer. I thought maybe I could distract him while I tried to come up with a plan.

✳ ✳ ✳

By the time the mess hall had cleared out, I was still picking at my food with no plan. I was a lot more knowledgeable about guns, thanks to the questions I had pestered Steve with. And true to what I had suspected, he was happy to share his vast knowledge about the weapons he carried. The gun resting on his back was an AK47. The gun on his hip was a Glock 9. He was trained with pretty much any gun and made it clear he didn't hesitate to use them when the situation warranted. I wasn't sure if he was just bragging or warning me that he could and would use them on me.

The reality I still faced was that Steve could outrun me, shoot me, or knock me out within a second. What could I possibly do to get away from him?

I had no plan, and my stomach hurt a little from how much I had eaten. *That was it!* I thought with excitement. I would pretend to get sick to my stomach. I asked Steve another question as I picked at the last of my food and thought through my plan. Once I pretended to be sick to my stomach, where would I go? I thought about the exit, but that would bring the whole Steve-could-outrun-me-and-shoot-me thing in again.

I looked up as motion caught my eye, just in time to see the kitchen door swinging back closed as someone walked into the kitchen. The kitchen had knives and pans I could use, although again, Steve would overpower me in a second. I needed to stick with the stomach plan. They had to have a restroom. I could run back there claiming I was going to get sick. All of the other bathrooms I had encountered here had a high window for ventilation since air conditioning was lacking in most of the buildings.

Steve had been finished eating for a while and now drummed his fingers on the table, looking extra bored. He was probably wondering why he got stuck with this assignment. Hopefully, he would keep being bored and maybe a little disgusted, not needing to check on me in the bathroom.

I sat my fork down with a clank; it was now or never.

"You done?" Steve asked. I could hear the word "finally" without him saying it.

"Ugh, yeah, ugh," I moaned.

"What's wrong with you?" Steve asked, looking at me, but still sounding bored.

"I think I ate too much, ugh, my stomach," I faked. I had to at least get closer to the kitchen, or he might push me out the door insisting I be sick in the woods where he could keep an eye on me.

I got up from my seat, moaning, as I picked up my tray and headed to the tray return. Steve was not a gentleman, so I knew he wouldn't offer to take care of it for me. I heard him pick up his tray and knew he was following me. I hunched over as I walked, clutching my stomach.

"Oh, I think I'm gonna be sick," I moaned as I slammed down my tray on the stainless-steel counter at the tray return. "Is there a restroom in here?" I asked, sounding very pitiful.

I didn't wait for his response. I pushed my way into the kitchen.

"Bathroom!" I shouted as I clutched my stomach and covered my mouth, a worker with a shocked look on his face pointed to a door in the back, and off I went. Slamming the door and locking it, I immediately saw the window and felt immense relief when I saw it was already propped open.

Someone knocked on the door, "You okay in there?" It was Steve. Of course, he had followed me.

"Ugh, no," I started making retching sounds. There was a plastic cup next to the sink, I filled it with water and then proceeded to make vomiting sounds while I poured it in the toilet. I continued to act out a few more times with more water into the toilet. After a minute or two, I flushed the toilet.

"Steve," I said moaning, "I'm going to need a minute, I'm not sure I'm done." I said as pitiful as I could finishing with another moan.

"Oh, great. Okay, take your time," he said, clearly not enjoying his babysitting detail now.

In the short time I had known him, I knew it wasn't like him to be generous. He was probably trying to be agreeable so I wouldn't ask him to come in and help me clean up or to hold back my hair.

I turned the water on in the sink at full blast. And made my way to the window. It was high, but I could stand on the toilet seat to reach it. I was able to get myself up and my upper body halfway through the window, but then wasn't exactly sure what to do from there. I looked out, thankful this window faced into the woods so I shouldn't be seen. I used the edge of the window to pull myself to sitting, still facing in toward the bathroom even though my upper body was on the outside. I wiggled back, trying to give myself room to get my feet under me. There was shingle siding on the outside, so I used that as a grip to pull myself out further. My arms were screaming, they were still really sore, but I had to do this. I finally got a leg out and was straddling the window ledge. I wiggled and pulled and got myself turned around. Pushing feet first, I jumped to the ground. It was a bit jarring as the drop was farther than I thought.

I straightened up and looked around. I had gotten away from Steve for now, but I had to keep moving. He would be looking for me soon, and he would probably have some help. I had studied my camp map before I left my cabin. I headed in the direction of the one building that had been unmarked on the map. I took off running, being watchful of anyone around me. I moved as fast as I could through the woods, heading straight towards the infirmary.

CHAPTER 9

The heat of the midday sun was brutal, forcing me to take off my hoodie and tie it around my waist. Between the heat of the day, running, hiding, and my fear, I felt faint and was soaking wet with sweat, but I was determined to keep going.

It took me much longer to get to the infirmary than I wanted. Turns out, sneaking around in broad daylight wasn't the easiest thing in the world. I had to keep ducking behind trees and moving in different directions every time I came upon someone on the trails, but I finally saw the building that I thought was the infirmary through the trees up ahead. The building was unmarked and unremarkable in any way other than a large chimney that bellowed out a dark smoke into the clear sky.

What are they burning? It seemed odd to me that a fire was burning on such a warm spring day. But at this point, nothing in my life made sense.

I was overcome with the desire to sit down and weep on the spot. Everything I knew about my life was a lie. There was a part of me that wanted to go back and un-hear what Lucas said, to pretend everything was fine. But the truth of his words was affirmed by Uncle Derek's behavior when he was more focused on Lucas's punishment than he was on Amelia's well-being. He hadn't even let me talk to him about it.

But here I was, faced with the truth, and I had to help Lucas. I knew I couldn't just walk in the front door, so I began to move from tree to tree, trying to stay hidden as I went around to the side of the building that had thicker woods. I saw some open windows and crawled towards them, waiting to see if I could hear anything before I tried to look inside, but the only sound I heard was my heartbeat pounding in my ears.

I took some slow, deep breaths and tried to regulate my breathing. Less than ten hours ago, I had been frantically trying to find my uncle to tell him about the terrible situation with Amelia, and now I was overcome with fear that he might find me. And worse yet, I had no idea what he would do to me if he did.

Just then, I heard footsteps. I covered my mouth, unsure if my breathing would give me away. I sat, frozen, holding my breath, and praying I wouldn't get caught.

"You're not going to break him," I heard a deep voice say.

"I don't have to hear him actually admit it," Uncle Derek replied. It was good that I had covered my mouth because it stifled the gasp I let out at hearing his voice so close to me. "I know he came here for Sarah." He continued saying.

"Why?" the other voice questioned.

"Don't be stupid," Uncle Derek growled out. "He came for the exact same reason I brought her here. She was searching for truth," he said disgustedly. "She just wouldn't let up, and I couldn't keep my eye on her all the time."

"Well, if he did come here for her, that was really gutsy." I was thinking the other voice sounded like Tristan, one of the camp disciplinary administrators.

"No, it was stupid, and it will bring his death," Uncle Derek said fiercely.

"She must be more important than we previously thought for someone like him to be sent into the camp."

"She is, but up until this point, I've prevented them from telling her the truth. She has no idea of her value, and I have worked hard to make sure things stayed that way." I realized I was still holding my breath. I let it out very slowly, in disbelief, as he continued. "I have to find out what he told her."

"He's not going to tell you, and if you want to keep up this uncle charade, then you need to get back and smooth things over with her. She was furious with you."

"I know, and I will, but I hate that part of the job. It's disgusting to even have to fake an apology."

"I hear that, but if she's this important, you'd better do it fast."

"Ugh," he growled, his voice trailing as they moved away.

"Do you want me to take care of that 'thing' for you?" the other man said louder.

"Resume torture and make sure the furnace is ready; I'll be back to end him."

Resume torture and make sure the furnace is ready. I could not comprehend what I felt in my heart was about to happen. I knew they were talking about Lucas. I'd process what my uncle had said about me later, but for now, Lucas was being tortured, and I was clearly the only one here who would help him.

I heard a door slam and heard someone making their way into the woods. I waited another minute before I rose up to peer in the window. Looking inside, I saw an empty hallway. I saw a doorway across the hall from the windows and then a set of double doors that went to the left. I assumed Tristan had gone that direction as the other way seemed to lead to the front of the building. I climbed through the window and headed for the single door. Hearing about Lucas and what he was enduring pushed my fear down and increased my courage and my strength.

I placed my ear up against the door but heard nothing, so I opened the door slowly. As my eyes grew accustomed to the dark, I reached for the light switch and found myself in a small room filled with boxes. I closed the door quickly to take a breath and figure out my next move. The room was more like a storage closet, with no windows and only one door. It was bigger than a broom closet, but certainly smaller than Amelia's closet back home.

I put my back against the wall and slid down to the floor as a small sob escaped my lips. *No. Not now, Sarah.* Lucas was being tortured in this building somewhere and would most likely be killed if I didn't do something. I pulled out my phone, searching desperately for cellphone service to call the police. But again, just like in my cabin, there was no service. In reality, I knew deep down that even if the police came, they would be no match against the small army that seemed to be encamped here.

This was it. I was Lucas's only hope. I started looking in the boxes that were on the floor. Some of the boxes had camo pants and jackets. Two had masks of some sort. The next one I opened had paintball guns, so I assumed the masks were for paintball, though I had not seen these being used at this camp while I was here. I kept searching the boxes trying to find something or anything that would give me any advantage. The paintball guns were something, but there weren't any paintball pellets.

I opened the next box and saw arrows, lots of them, and a few sheaths. I opened the next one and found bows. They were more of the kind that I had used in the archery area, beginner's bows. I knew from my one lesson that I wouldn't be able to bring anyone down with these either, but Lucas probably could if I could free him. I might be able to use the arrows in my hand to slow someone down a little. I packed three of the arrow sheaths full of arrows and pulled out two bows, making sure the strings seemed intact and taut like Lucas had shown me.

"Lucas," I breathed. I continued looking through more of the boxes, even faster now, feeling the urgency of Lucas's situation. I found some roasting sticks, the kind used with marshmallows, and grabbed a few of those. In the last box, I found backpacks. I grabbed two and stuffed in some of the camo clothing that I thought would mostly fit Lucas and me. I looked at the ceiling again, hoping for an air duct or something to go through like in spy movies. There were none, of course. My options were slim, my plan unsettled, but it was time to go.

I listened at the door and didn't hear anything, so I peeked out. I didn't see anyone in the hallway, so I grabbed the backpacks and dropped them onto the ground outside the open window. I went back for the sheaths and bows, doing the same thing while keeping a close watch for any sign or sound of movement. I dropped some of the marshmallow skewers out the window, then headed toward the double doors, one sheath of arrows on my back and one skewer in my hand. I hoped that Lucas was in some shape to leave with me and that he was unguarded and no longer being tortured, neither of which was likely to be true.

I stopped once more to listen through the doors. I didn't hear anything, so I pushed one door open slightly, peeking inside. The hallway continued down to another set of double doors, and there was another hallway to my right.

I heard some muffled sounds to my right, so I moved slowly to peer around the corner. I didn't see anything, so I continued down the small hallway. I saw that it had six rooms, three on each side. Each room had a door and observation window, like a classroom or hospital, and each room was dark except for the last one on the left. The first two rooms were closed and empty, barring some old cabinets I could see through the window. But the second door on the right was open, and ironically enough, the room looked like an old hospital room with a metal table and medical instruments. A chill went down my spine as I realized those tools were the instruments they used for torture rather than for healing. The door of the lit room swung open, and I quickly ducked into the second room, crouching down below the windows.

"Wait, did you tie him up?"

"Yes, but it doesn't matter, that serum will have him out for a while. He didn't respond to anything else, so I don't know why Tristan thought he would respond to truth serum. When it's one of those, it only knocks them out. He should have let us pull another tooth."

I felt my head spin.

"It's just not as much fun when they don't scream."

"I know. Torture is much better when you get to delight in their pain and suffering." Both men laughed, a deep, low sound that made the hair on the back of my neck stand up.

Their voices were moving farther away in the direction opposite of the way I came. The last thing I heard was, "I have been away from our home base for so long I forget what true screams of agony feel like."

They have a home base where they torture people? I shook off that thought as fast as it came, focusing instead on the fact that Lucas must be in that next room since that was where they had come out. They said he was tied up, so hopefully, that would mean he was alone.

I waited another minute before I came out of my hiding place. I peered through the window and out into the hallway. There was no one, but I could see a silhouette in the lit room diagonal to my hiding place. I made my way quickly across the hall and tried the door handle. Thankfully, it was unlocked. I slowly opened the door and had to swallow a scream when I saw Lucas and the room surrounding him. He had open wounds on his arms and shoulders and across his chest. They looked almost like deep claw marks. Blood was dripping from more than one wound as he sat shirtless, slumped forward in his chair, held up only by his arms tied tightly behind him.

"Lucas," I whispered in agony, tears filling my eyes. He didn't even stir. I crouched down in front of him and saw his face. One eye was swollen shut, and three claw marks went across his face, tearing through his lip. "Oh, Lucas," I cried, choking back a sob.

"Lucas," I said a bit louder, but still a whisper. I wasn't as worried about someone hearing me as I was about hurting Lucas in any way. He still didn't respond, and I was hesitant to touch him.

I stood up and looked around the room, trying to find anything that might bring him comfort or revive him. All I saw were instruments of pain and evidence of their use. I even saw a few bloody teeth on a nearby tray. The last food I ate was a while ago, but I felt my stomach churn violently at seeing those teeth. This was so wrong. A person like Lucas shouldn't be suffering like this.

I continued my scan of the room. There was a sink, so maybe I could get some warm water. I turned it on, but it was running cold. I checked any cabinets that were unlocked, but nothing was in there that would bring relief, only more pain. There wasn't a single bandage or gauze pad. I couldn't even find a cloth towel. The water was hot now, so I added cold to it and wet some paper towels with the warm water.

Turning back to Lucas, I saw patches of hair missing from the back of his head, as well as some nasty bruises. It was clear from the discoloration of the area around his ribs that severe damage had been done; some ribs were most likely broken. I went to Lucas and tried to gently lift his head. It was heavy with the weight of his unconscious state. I wanted to cut his restraints as one of his shoulders seemed to be at a weird angle, maybe dislocated. But I knew I couldn't cut them until I had revived him. He would just fall face-first out of the chair, and I wouldn't be able to carry him.

I used the paper towels, starting at his hairline, trying to stop the blood flow from the gash on his forehead. Lucas jolted awake, his eyes wild as he inhaled through his teeth in pain. His eyes took a second to focus on me, but instead of looking relieved, he looked panicked.

"Sarah, what are you doing here?" His words were slurred because of the trauma to his mouth.

"I'm here to help you. I'm here to help you escape!"

"Sarah, you have to go."

"I'm not going anywhere without you," I said to him, hardly believing his words.

"You have to go and hide. I'll find you." Each word seemed painful for him to get out as he gasped. I knew his ribs must be broken with the way that he was struggling to breathe.

I didn't move. I struggled, wanting to obey him, and wanting to stay with him. I heard laughter and turned towards the door.

"Lucas?!" Asking him so many questions with just his name.

"Please Sarah, go." His eyes pleaded with me. I stared at him in stark fear but couldn't deny him. I headed for the door, running straight across the hall to another dark torture room.

The footsteps and voices I heard coming were so close, I thought they must have seen me. But they were still laughing and talking, and they would have immediately come after me if they had. I was sitting on the floor under the windows as I heard them go into Lucas's room. I hadn't had the chance to close the door, but they didn't seem to notice. I had my hand over my mouth again, trying to cover the sounds of my gasping breaths.

"Still sleeping, are you? Wakey, wakey."

I heard the sharp inhale Lucas took through his teeth again. The monster must have pushed on one of his wounds. I felt so sick to my stomach that I thought I would puke right there. I had to take deep, calming breaths. Lucas needed me, and I couldn't help him if I got sick and gave away my presence.

I could hear multiple voices now talking to Lucas. They were saying horrible things to him, cursing at him, and by the gasps and grunts, I knew they were hurting him again. It was all I could do to stay rooted in my spot and not come out with my skewer to stab them. That's when I realized I had left it on the floor by Lucas. I still had my arrows, but those wouldn't cause much damage. Plus, I could still see Lucas's eyes as he begged me to go. He didn't want those guys torturing me as well.

I covered my ears, the sounds of his torture too horrible for me to bear.

Another minute or so went by. I braced myself when I heard more footsteps thundering down the hallway.

"Have you seen her?!" I sat up a little at hearing my uncle's voice.

"Who?" another guy responded.

"Sarah!" he shouted.

"No, no one has been in here. Why would she be here, anyway?"

"She escaped from Steve. She tricked him and got away from him."

"What?" A couple of them chuckled. "Sarah got away from Steve?" Tristan asked, almost in disbelief.

"Yes, and he will be severely punished," Uncle Derek growled. I felt a little bad that Steve would be punished because of me, but then I remembered what Lucas looked like, and that feeling immediately gave way to anger.

"If that's true, why would she come here?"

"For him," Uncle Derek growled with such hate in his voice, my entire body tensed up. "She was asking Steve about the different buildings and what was in them."

"And he just told her?"

"Yes."

"Still, why would she come here? If she were just trying to get away from you, then why would she come for him?"

"She's a bleeding heart. It makes her weak to our devices, but it's also how I know she won't be able to leave camp without trying to help him."

I was trying to control my shaking as tears streamed down my face. My uncle was one of the monsters, and he was intent on finding me, probably to torture and kill me as well. He had been right at the cabin that Ben's treatment of that poor boy was nothing compared to what Lucas was enduring now. I felt despair. Deep, gut-wrenching despair. It reminded me of how I felt when my parents died. I felt paralyzed by the weight of it.

"Well, we haven't seen her."

Uncle Derek let out a string of curse words and some words I couldn't understand. I heard more slapping sounds as he raged at Lucas. I was only a half a second from screaming for him to stop and showing myself when he spoke actual words again.

"Get him up," he snarled, his rage no longer seething below the surface. "Take him to the whipping post. Carson is waiting for him. Let's see if that gets him to talk; maybe he knows where Sarah is hiding."

I still had my mouth covered, trying to keep the sobs from coming out.

"Keep your eyes and ears open. I know she will be here soon. She is weak, but she is determined. She never stays down for long."

Although Uncle Derek had said it with malice, his words filled me with resolve. I don't give up, and I am determined. I couldn't let them kill Lucas. I would fight until the end.

I stayed in my spot and waited until all the noises were gone. I knew from the sound of their footsteps that they had taken Lucas back the way they had come, but I had no idea how many people would be around Lucas. There was no secret passageway or anything that could help me get to Lucas. I had no weapons I could realistically use. No real brute strength to go up against these people that were now looking for me. I was sure there would be no one on my side in this, but what I did possess was determination. And that would have to be enough since it was all I had.

I was thankful that wherever the whipping post was that I couldn't hear anything. I don't think I could have stomached that sound. I had seen it faked in a movie once, and I was nearly sick at that. I wouldn't say I had a weak stomach, normally, but all of this was just so unfair and so evil, that I found myself feeling sick constantly.

Think Sarah.

I had to do something to get ahead of my uncle. They were at the whipping post; I doubted they would bring Lucas back to this room since he hadn't given up any information in there yet. Uncle Derek had said something earlier when I was outside the window about the furnace. That was probably where they would head to next. Where would the furnace be?

Then it came flooding back to me, the bellowing chimney I saw outside the building. It had to be through that second set of double doors, the ones I had seen right before I had turned down the hallway where Lucas was held. Maybe I could get to the furnace before the rest of them. Maybe I could turn it off or something to thwart their plans.

There were no outside windows in this hallway, so I wasn't sure if it was dark out yet, but for some reason, I hoped it wasn't. I felt surrounded by a sense of darkness that was waiting to overcome me at each corner; maybe a little sunlight would help that. I turned down the empty hallway and headed for the double doors.

I didn't hear any voices at the doors, so I pushed one open to look through. Unlike the others, this hallway was dark. I slipped through the doors and tried to let my eyes adjust. There was another hallway to my right. There was a bright red glow ahead of me coming out from a door on my left. I was still listening for sounds, but I knew I was at the right place because I could feel the heat even outside the door. I pushed hard on the weighted door, and it swung in, revealing the biggest furnace I had ever seen. I stepped to the side of the door to let it close.

The heat from the fire was so hot, I immediately began to sweat. The door of the furnace was closed, but I could see the bright light of the flames through the cracks. The fire reminded me of the glass blower's ovens that we saw on a class field trip in elementary school. Yet, the opening of this furnace was larger than any I'd ever seen. From the outlines of the closed doors, I could tell it could easily fit a body through with room to spare. If they were going to put Lucas in this inferno, there was no way that he would survive. It must have been how they got rid of the bodies that they tortured. Burned them so that there was no evidence. What a gruesome thought.

As I moved in for a closer look at the back of the furnace, I heard voices coming to my right and had to look for a place to hide.

There was a small door to my left. The door opened easily, and I quickly got inside. It felt small like a closet, but it was hard to tell. My eyes were having trouble adjusting even after only seeing the fire through the cracks of the furnace.

"Weren't you supposed to stay in here and guard the furnace?" a man said.

"So, it doesn't matter. I wanted to see Carson work those cattails. He is a master with the whip."

"It matters because Uncle was livid, one false step, and you'll be like Steve, with your guts hanging out of you."

"He didn't even notice I was there. Everyone was so focused on wanting that 'thing' to scream. What a disappointment."

"Well, stay in here this time. They will be coming our way soon. I'm going to check."

By then my eyes had adjusted to the darkness, and this time I realized I was in a broom closet. It had cleaning supplies and a few mops and brooms. The smell in the closet was putrid. When I thought about the smell and what they had to clean up in this building, it made me super lightheaded— better not to think about it at all. One of the guys had referred to my uncle as Uncle, like that was his name. Since I didn't have any clue who he really was, I wasn't sure if that name made sense for him or not.

My brain could no longer follow that train of thought as all my senses were brought back to the heat of the furnace. I was so hot and could hear the roar of the furnace. The quick look I had of the furnace showed me that there wasn't a big red "off" button or an easy to reach valve, and even if I had a firehose, it probably wouldn't be enough water to put it out. What was I going to do? I checked my phone, still no service. It was 6:28 pm, so past dinner time in the mess hall. Did Amelia ever wake up? Had she even noticed that I was gone?

I could hear the door open, and more voices came in. It sounded like even more men than were in the hallway earlier. *Apparently, the whipping post and furnace brought an audience.* I was disgusted at the thought.

This is it. I pulled out four arrows, two gripped in each hand as close to the arrowheads as I could get.

"Let's get rid of this infiltrator, this *thing* that has come in to infect us!" I heard my uncle shouting to the cheers of the men around him, "Throw him in!"

"No!!!" I screamed as I came out of my closet and into the room. Two guys were waiting to grab me, like they knew I had been hiding in the closet. Immediately, I plunged my arrows into their arms, fighting to get to Lucas, who was bound and gagged on the floor. I knew the arrows had done some damage, but it didn't matter. One grabbed my throat as the other one squeezed my wrists hard until I had no choice but to let go.

"Oh, there you are, Sarah," Uncle Derek said almost pleasantly, but he didn't seem to be surprised that I had been in that closet. My captors switched their grips to one holding me on each arm.

My uncle continued talking. "We have missed you. Steve is being disciplined right now for losing you and making me worry about you." He half smiled and spoke with kindness in his voice, but I could see his mask falling away. This was not a man who loved me; this was a cruel man, out for himself and some unknown agenda. My eyes fell away from him and onto Lucas. What I saw made my legs give out.

"You're a monster," I said with a choked sob as I glared back at him and then turned my head away so I wouldn't have to look at this evil man. My gaze fell on a woman in the group. Where there should have been sympathy or concern on her face, I only saw enjoyment and cruelty.

Uncle stepped towards me and grabbed my chin firmly, forcing me to look at him.

"Don't avert your eyes. You have been hiding here because you wanted to see what would happen. You wanted to see what we do to the corrupted." He jerked my head so that my eyes were on Lucas. He was lying somewhat on his side, and I could see the blood dripping from his open wounds where his back had been stripped of flesh from the whipping he had just endured.

"How could you do this? Who are you?"

"I'm your uncle, it's my job to protect you from evil people like him."

"You're lying, he's not evil."

"I will do anything I must in order to protect you, Sarah," he said with a smile that seemed like pure evil now that I knew what he was capable of. "Open the furnace," he commanded.

"No!" I screamed, getting one of my arms free from one of my captors and lunging at my uncle's face, scratching his cheek with my nails. My captors must have been distracted by the immense heat from the blaze, but quickly laid hold of me again, with a much firmer grip than before. A fraction tighter, and I was sure my bones would break.

Uncle slowly reached up to touch his cheek, pulling his finger back to look at the blood that now shown on his finger from his face.

Then, he lifted his gaze back to me. His mouth slowly curled into a smile, "Maybe she is one of us, a nice violent streak in her."

He moved back towards me and got right in my face as he gave his next command.

"Throw him in."

And they did.

CHAPTER 10

Between the tears and the blaze of the fire, I could barely keep my eyes open. I choked back my sobs, not willing to give Uncle Derek the satisfaction of hearing how much pain I was in. My new reality was that he wasn't Uncle Derek; he was the man they called Uncle.

"Sarah, you have to understand. Lucas was the enemy. He was beyond our help, and so we had to take matters into our own hands." He touched his cheek again, where I had scratched him. I wasn't normally a violent person, but I didn't feel bad at all for what I had done to his cheek.

My arms were going numb in the tight clutches of my captors, but I didn't care. My gaze was fixed on the blaze of the furnace as a groan from my gut came up, tears poured from my eyes, and my legs gave out. My captors had to hold me up. Lucas was being burned alive, and there was nothing I could do to help him. I had failed him, and now I was alone and at the mercy of whoever these people were. I hurt from my hair to my toes with physical and emotional pain as intense as when the news came that my parents were dead. I had only known Lucas for two days, but I just knew it wasn't meant to end like this.

Just as I had this thought, I was almost certain that I saw something different in the fire. *Did something move?* I blinked more tears down my cheek and stared so intently into the fire that I thought I would go blind.

I didn't see anything, though, and I knew my eyes must be betraying me. That last sliver of hope I had that he would somehow escape was gone. No one could survive the blaze of that fire. I could feel it burning my skin even from 30 feet back. I was already going to have the equivalent of a really bad sunburn, and if I stayed here much longer, it would be unbearable.

The men around me were celebrating. They seemed to be enjoying the ferocious blaze of the fire, completely unaware of the intense heat and the scalding fire.

Wait, there it was again. I saw another movement. Something apart from the dancing flames was moving around in the furnace. The object I was seeing seemed to be getting bigger, or was it moving closer? It was hard to tell as my eyes were now burning severely, and I was beginning to feel faint from the heat. I glanced at Uncle and saw he noticed the object as well. His eyes became narrow slits as he stared straight into the fire.

"Look," he said to the room in general.

The men around him quieted at the command and focused their gaze into the fire. I looked back as well. The object was even bigger and almost looked like the outline of a man. It kept coming towards us and getting larger. I knew immediately that it was Lucas. My sliver of hope hadn't been wrong. He was walking towards us. *How was that possible?*

As I could see his form more distinctly, it was also as if I could feel the power of something coming with him. The men in the room started to groan as if in pain. I looked at Uncle, and while he wasn't making noise, the feeling of pain was definitely etched on his face.

I could see the full shape of a man, but he was silver and had no definite features. Even looking at the luminous outline, I knew without a doubt that it was Lucas, and the light from his silhouette made the fire surrounding him seem as a shadow. He was at the edge of the fire now, and all of the others were screaming in pain, including Uncle. The quicksilver seemed to wash over Lucas as he stepped down out of the fire. The screams of pain rose to agony as everyone else in the room fell to the ground.

They were writhing in pain from some unknown source, covering their ears from some sound I couldn't hear, and screaming in distress with their eyes squeezed shut like they couldn't bear to look at Lucas. I had no idea what was going on. I felt calm and filled with peace at Lucas's presence. I was captivated by the beauty that wrapped itself around Lucas, and I was reminded of the subtle glow I'd sensed when I first saw him.

The platinum light made up the shape of his form, but I still couldn't see his facial features. My words couldn't describe the brilliance I was beholding. Each rapid breath of awe that I took was like breathing in what felt like goodness and love and life. Not even the screams around me could interrupt the beauty I was seeing and feeling.

Lucas walked slowly towards me; it was then that I fully realized my captors were writhing on the floor as well, and I was free. Lucas continued to move towards me slowly as if to avoid scaring me or to give me time to make up my mind about what I was seeing and experiencing.

He stopped one step away from me as I gazed up at him. The quicksilver was no longer flowing over him but seemed to slow, solidifying as his features returned to view. As he was revealed underneath, he was even more glorious to look at than before, which I wouldn't have thought possible until now. His perfect face, set with a smile, was beaming like the sun. The once metallic covering continued to disperse to reveal first his chest and arms, then his legs and the rest of his body. His body was fully formed, fully clothed, and glowing.

Lucas held his arms open to me. He was like a magnet pulling me towards him. I stepped right into his embrace and his arms came around me. I took a deep breath in and felt a calm rush over me. All of what I was seeing should have been freaking me out, but in Lucas's embrace, I didn't feel even one ounce of fear.

My breath had calmed entirely, and I was now breathing in what I can only describe as goodness. With each exhale, I was exhaling all of the awful I had been seeing and thinking and feeling. It felt like home, except better than any home I had ever known.

"You were supposed to be hiding," he said calmly. His voice was even more beautiful than before.

"I know, I'm sorry, I couldn't leave you," I said, not really feeling much remorse since I felt so right in other ways.

"I knew you probably wouldn't, I could see the resolve in your eyes."

"You're not mad?" I asked again, not really caring because I felt so good.

"I'm not mad," he said in the same calm, almost melodic tone. It was as if he were trying to be gentle with me not just in his touch, but in his words as well.

"Next time, though, you have to heed my words and obey."

"Next time?" I murmured, truly trying to care about what he was saying.

"Yes, this isn't over Sarah. We must go; we must run. Even now, others are coming."

"Okay," I replied. I held tight to him with the side of my face pressed firmly into him. He smelled like comfort. Even with what was happening around us, this was the happiest and safest I had felt in a long, long time. I couldn't even hear the screams from those around us.

He held me for another minute or so. It could have been an hour; I don't really know. And then he spoke, "Sarah."

"Yes?"

"It's time to go."

"Okay," I replied, not really knowing what I was agreeing to. He turned me around and walked me out of the room with his arm around my shoulder, gently leading me onward, the screams of agony behind us.

As we exited the building, I remembered the backpacks I had packed and stowed. I told Lucas where they were, and he rounded the building to grab them on our way out. We ran through the dark forest, Lucas carrying the gear and me following him. He was still glowing, though the glow had lessened some from when he first came out of the fire. At first, I thought my eyes were just adjusting, but I could tell now that the light was truly fading.

Although his glow was fading, his strength was not. He was completely restored physically, and if anything, he seemed stronger than I had ever seen him. I could tell the packs and running were no problem for him. I, on the other hand, was gasping for breath. I had slowed to a jog, and Lucas turned his head back to look at me, slowing down as well. We jogged for a little over an hour, but to my heart, lungs, and legs, it felt like we'd been running much longer.

Lucas turned back again to look at me and slowed himself to a walk. I quickly switched to a walk as well, gasping for breath. He didn't even seem winded. He slowed to let me walk beside him.

"Are you okay, Sarah?"

"Yeah," . . . "I'll be," . . . "fine." I bent over, holding my side. We were stopped now, just standing together while we waited for my breathing to slow down.

"I should have gone a bit slower," Lucas said after a minute. "It was hard to tell how fast I was even going. I haven't had this much strength in a while, if ever." It seemed as though his strength was a surprise to him as well.

"No, it's okay... really... I just need to catch my breath." I pulled in a deep breath and exhaled slowly, trying to will my lungs to open fully. My legs were dead, and my back was aching, but instead of mentioning that I continued with, "We can walk while I catch my breath... so we can keep going." I stood back up, arching my back to stretch it for a second, and then I started walking.

Lucas started to move forward in step with me and then stopped. I turned to look back at him. He had his arms open to me. I stepped into his arms, still unable to resist the magnetic pull coming from him. When I took my next deep inhale and exhale, I realized my legs and back felt great; there was no pain, and I was no longer tired.

I stepped back to look up at him. He seemed taller now than before, as well.

"What are you?" I asked a little breathless, not from exertion, but from being awed that Lucas had just healed me.

"What do you think I am?" Lucas asked with a small smile.

"I have no idea. I don't think I have ever encountered anyone else like you," I said, shaking my head in disbelief. Not only had he healed me just now, but I realized he must have healed me from the skin burns and heat stroke I had experienced from the furnace.

"You have encountered more of my kind, you may not remember it though, as you were very young." His voice sounded nostalgic, almost like he remembered me at a younger age.

"Lucas, had we met before this camp?"

"Not officially, no, but I knew you well."

I looked at him, not really understanding what he was saying and still shaking my head a bit.

"We will have plenty of time to talk, but we better get moving again." His voice was measured, encouraging, but at the same time, direct.

"Okay, I'm ready," I said with a smile. I felt like I could run for hours. I wasn't hungry or thirsty either. He had literally healed any need my body had.

"I'll try to go a bit slower this time." He gave me a small, half-smile.

A little while into our running, I asked, "Lucas, where are we going?" It hadn't even occurred to me to ask before now. I trusted Lucas. He told me to follow him and run, so I had.

"We are headed to a cave so you can sleep safely tonight."

"And then where to after that?"

His voice was gentle as he replied, "I'm sorry to say this, Sarah, but you can't return home."

"I wouldn't want to," I responded back. *Except for Amelia.* I was concerned about what would happen to her. I didn't say anything about it, though, as we continued to run. Lucas, my guiding light, ever before me.

When we stopped the next time, I was again gasping for breath and hurting all over, my good feelings were no more, but we had made it to the cave.

Lucas held out his arms to me, and without any hesitation, I stepped into them, taking a deep breath and exhaling. It took three or four deep breaths this time to completely feel back to normal.

Even though I wanted to stay right there in his arms, where the feeling of rightness and home was so strong, again, I pulled back, looking up at him. "Seriously, who are you?"

He gave a soft laugh and smiled at me. "Do you remember the Mythreal beings that your mom told you about when you were little?"

"Umm," I hesitated, taken aback by his mention of my mom. "Maybe, I'm not sure," I said, trying to think about my childhood and wondering how Lucas knew about my mom at the same time.

He just looked at me, waiting patiently for me to say something. Lucas's glow had lessened even more, and I wondered if that was why I wasn't instantly healed when we embraced.

"Mythreal, Mythreal," I pondered. "I don't remember that name."

"Did she tell you stories about creatures that helped people? That brought them healing and safety?"

I could see my mom's face. I could see her smiling at me even now, although I hadn't seen her in eight years. I closed my eyes to focus on her. I could see us snuggling in bed and her telling me stories. Was there one about beings that could help people? I remembered her telling me stories about a princess that went on grand adventures. She would help people and bring them into her kingdom of kindness.

I repeated that to Lucas, and he smiled his full-blown smile as he stared past me into the forest. "Was that what you were talking about?" I asked him.

"Not exactly," he said with his smile slowly fading. "I'm going to get us some firewood, and then we can talk some more."

What was that about, I wondered. He still hadn't told me who or what he was. I also had to find out how he knew my mother. I missed her so desperately that at times it was hard to fully breathe when I thought about her. I missed my dad as well, but we weren't as close. He traveled quite a bit while my mom stayed home with us. He was wonderful when he was home, and so of course, I missed him. But I truly ached for my mom. To have her hug me right now would be a dream come true.

"Are you okay?" Lucas asked, sounding concerned. I hadn't even realized he had returned to the cave.

"Uh, yeah, I'm fine, why?" I asked as I shook off the memories, looking up at him with his arms full of wood.

"You're crying," he said simply.

"Oh." I felt my cheeks, and he was right.

As I wiped my cheeks, I realized that with Lucas closer, I was already feeling better, not as sad. I watched him as he quickly started a fire. I wasn't even sure what he used to do it. He put more wood on his little fire, and before long, there was a definite warmth in the cave from the fire's blaze. I was certain now that Lucas's glow was dimming. When he walked out of the fire back at camp, he was brighter than the flames of the furnace.

"Lucas, why aren't you glowing as much?" I asked, quietly as he came to sit next to me. He didn't answer me right away, he was staring into the fire intently, maybe even remembering what it had recently felt like for him to be inside a fire.

He turned his head to look at me. "I think I'm using it up," he said with a small smile.

"Using what up?" I asked, feeling so curious about what was happening around me that I thought if I didn't get answers soon, my brain was going to explode.

"I'm not trying to keep things from you, Sarah," he said, putting his hand on my shoulder. At his touch, I felt the urgency to know leaving my body. All tension eased. "I just know that you cannot possibly take in everything that there is to tell you. Just know that I am here to help you."

"Help me with what?"

"Well, to protect you, and to help rescue you."

"If you had asked me at any time, I would have left with you."

"Would you have?" he asked, but it felt like he already knew the answer, so I stopped my quick answer of yes to think about it.

"You're extremely loyal, Sarah, and that's a good thing. Things had to unfold as they did for you to know the truth about your uncle."

"What about Amelia? Is she safe? That's the one thing that I feel pulling me back there. I don't know what they will do to her now."

"She has no idea who any of them are yet. She still believes that Uncle is your uncle. They will continue to try to turn her to their understanding. But she is stronger to resist now."

"Why is she stronger now?"

"When I healed her, it wasn't just physical. With what happened to her, she had wounds that were also mental, emotional, and spiritual. My touch helped to heal those things as well, leaving a mark that cannot be erased."

"You healed her, just like you have been healing me?"

"Yes."

"What mark did you leave on her?" I couldn't remember seeing anything different on her before I left.

"You'll see Sarah, just not yet."

I wanted to be mad that he was being so cryptic, but I couldn't even get the emotion to rise up in me. With his hand still on my shoulder, I was very peaceful. I felt like I could fall asleep.

"It's okay for you to sleep, Sarah. Let's get some things out of the pack for you to lie on." Lucas made me a pallet out of the jackets and made one of the bags my pillow. I laid down, struggling to keep my eyes open, but I had to have one question answered before I gave in to the heavy pull of sleep.

"Lucas, how did you know my mom?" He was sitting beside me, but he didn't look at me. He took a deep breath as he looked at the fire, and then his eyes shifted down to his lap as he answered.

"I was with her when she died."

"What?!" I asked in shock, sitting up to look him more fully in the face. All I had ever been told was they were killed in a car crash, and there were no witnesses.

"I held her hand as she died."

"Why didn't you get help? Why didn't you heal her yourself?"

"I tried but, but nothing happened. It wasn't my purpose, so I couldn't."

"What purpose, Lucas? Why couldn't you try to help someone, the most wonderful someone I've ever known? How could you let her die a horrible death?" Feeling angry at Lucas seemed wrong, but that was what had come upon me, hearing he couldn't save her.

"She didn't die a horrible death, even though that was the intention. She was at peace. She looked so beautiful as she talked about you and Amelia."

"She talked about me, what did she say?" tears welling up in my eyes.

"She adored you, and she wanted great things for you. She wanted you to know that she loved you more than her own life."

The tears spilled over in earnest as I cried. I thought Lucas would touch me to help me not feel this pain, but he didn't. I continued to cry, thinking about my mom and how some of her last words were about how much she loved me. I could see her looking me in the face, straight into my eyes, and telling me that she loved me. I could always feel her love, but when she said it looking at me like that, I felt it deep inside, like it was actually becoming a part of me. That love, her love, was still there.

"What about my dad?" I asked as my crying slowed.

"He was already gone when I got there," Lucas said softly.

"Daddy," I whispered as I cried, sobs coming out once again. I could see a picture of him laughing at something I was doing for my parents' entertainment. He had the most wonderful laugh, and I did just about anything to get him to do it. I had my eyes closed as I pictured that and was a bit startled when Lucas said my name.

I opened my eyes to see him looking at me. He looked deep into my eyes and said, "I'm sorry." I knew instinctively that he meant he was sorry for my loss, sorry for my pain, and sorry that he couldn't save her for me.

My sobs had stopped, and I took a shuddering breath. "Thank you, Lucas."

I felt lighter, having let myself remember them and cry for my loss and my pain and the journey that I had been on since that time. I laid back down, still sniffling but feeling spent.

Lucas reached out and touched my head.

"It's time to sleep, Sarah." I was powerless to resist as I drifted off to a peaceful, dreamless sleep.

CHAPTER 11

I awoke to a hiss, the warmth of the fire now gone. Alarm surged through me as I sat up, looking around. I was about to speak Lucas's name when a hand clamped over my mouth. My fight or flight instinct tried to kick in for a second before Lucas's whisper reached my ear, and I realized the hand clamped over my mouth was glowing.

"You're okay, but you cannot speak. He's here."

I wanted to ask who, but I knew who it was, the only person that would be hunting us: Uncle. How had he found us? We ran so fast, and it's not like he knew which way we went into the vast forest.

Lucas lowered his hand from my mouth, trusting me to not talk. I turned and looked at him, panic on my face, but with my lips clamped tightly together.

"We're okay," he whispered. "We are protected."

He grabbed my hand and pulled me farther into the cave to the back wall, where he had already set up another pallet. We sat down but didn't speak, the silence between us filling with unasked questions. Lucas provided the only light in the cave, which made me realize the hiss that I heard earlier was the fire protesting the water he had poured on it. Lucas must have found water somehow because we hadn't had any the night before.

His glow didn't seem as dim without the light from the fire diluting it. I looked at his profile. His head was resting back on the rock behind us, and his eyes were closed, his face relaxed. I thought about getting his attention to gesture to him how he knew Uncle was here when I heard voices.

The voices were arguing, but still too distant for me to make out what they were saying. As the voices moved closer, I heard someone almost above us say, "The signal was right over here, but it's gone." *Signal? What signal?*

Someone let out a string of angry curse words. It sounded like Uncle, but there was a difference to his voice, so I wasn't sure. Whoever it was, he was definitely furious.

"This is my long-term assignment," he yelled, his voice almost screeching. "You know what will happen to me if I can't find her." His voice changed from desperate to borderline hysterical. Chills slid down my spine. He kept ranting, but the words were no longer ones I could understand. However, the venom and the hate they were spewed with made me glad I couldn't understand any of it.

Obviously, he was talking about me. *Long-term assignment?* I thought back to the conversation I'd heard that night outside his office door and was overcome with a sick feeling in my stomach. Who had given him his assignment? What could be worse than the punishment I had already witnessed? And who would give out this punishment? All this only added to my long list of questions for Lucas. I looked over at him, and even though my senses were on high alert, he sat in the same calm position he'd been in earlier, eyes still closed. I had the oddest feeling he was concentrating on something, like he was in the position he was in so that he could fully focus. I wasn't about to interrupt, and it didn't matter anyway. My attention snapped back to what was happening outside, as the voices were now closer to the mouth of the cave.

The other voice that had been talking to Uncle sounded familiar but slurred.

Is that Steve?

I could hear his voice right at the entrance, and I knew that at any moment, they would see the opening and find us. Instinctively, I held my breath. I looked at Lucas, but he had not moved. I wanted to get our weapons just in case, but when I started to move, Lucas's hand clamped down on my wrist. I looked at his face. He still had his eyes closed, but I got the message that he didn't want me to move.

"I can't believe that you are telling me that the signal is just gone!" Uncle was back to screaming. "This is on you," he growled out with a terrifying hiss. I almost felt like his words were directed at me, but I had to remind myself that he couldn't even see me.

"Keep looking for them!" Uncle screamed again, scaring me to the point that I jolted. "She doesn't have the power to disappear; they have to be nearby!" He kept yelling, again in words I was neither able, nor wanted to understand.

I heard the sound of feet thunder overhead and movement in front of the cave. It seemed they had brought an army of men with them. Lucas was still in the same position, but he had released my wrist at some point. I was afraid to move or speak or breathe. I wasn't sure what they could hear or sense or see. It was becoming clear they couldn't see the entrance to the cave, although it was still open, or at least it looked like it to me.

What kind of magic is this? My mind raced in a thousand different directions.

"What do we know about his powers?" Uncle spat angrily with curse words added in, but he was no longer shouting.

"Sir, he is something we haven't encountered before. To be able to withstand fire and then debilitate an entire camp… None of our men have seen something like this from the enemy."

They were clearly referring to Lucas.

"If you would let us send a messenger to headquarters, we might be able to get more info…"

"No!" Uncle's voiced boomed. "They can't know she is missing. She is too important. My punishment will be unbearable if they find out." My skin crawled with the understanding that he was talking about me. I couldn't allow myself to imagine what would happen to me if they caught me. What was headquarters, and what on earth did they want with me there? It sure seemed like a whole lot of effort for someone that most people seemed to overlook.

Uncle ranted again in that horrible, spine-tingling dialect. Abruptly, he switched back to a language I understood, his words crystal clear. "I have suffered those two brats for eight years, catering to their every want and wish just waiting for the time to change them. Brat number one has come along nicely, but this one, the more important one, she has not been responsive to my tools."

Silence.

"I have to find her, and when I do, she will fall in line by whatever means necessary." The hurried sounds of footsteps leaving in a panicked search should have brought me comfort, but Uncle's words lingered.

By whatever means necessary.

Terror seized me. I raised my hand to my mouth to silence the sob that threatened to spill out. Lucas was still in his pose, but his hand grabbed mine, giving me a feeling of warmth and peace to battle the terror that raged in my head.

Once the voices had faded, we stayed seated side-by-side for a while. Lucas had released my hand, but the cold had seeped back in and was chilling me. I hunched down with my arms crossed. I wasn't touching Lucas for fear of interrupting him, but I was less than an inch away from him. Finally, his eyes reopened. He sat forward and took several slow, deep breaths. I was afraid to breathe myself, worried I would distract him from what he was doing. Slowly, he turned his head to look at me.

His eyes seemed dazed and unfocused like he was looking through me. He took another deep breath, and his eyes focused more. He blinked hard a couple of times, and then it seemed as though I was once again in his sights. I still didn't utter a word. He would have to be the one to break the silence.

"Sarah," he said, almost to reassure himself I was still there. The sound of his voice overwhelmed me with relief. I started sobbing. He wrapped me in his arms and held me while I cried. I couldn't believe I still had tears left after crying about my parents earlier in the night, but I guess my fear and relief had the power to bring them on again.

When my tears were spent, I slowly pulled away. Breathing deeply, I felt peace return. Lucas's glow was almost gone, but still evident as it was our only light source.

"What did you do? How did they not find us?" I asked him.

"We were protected by a power much greater than even I can claim. I served as the conduit of that power to this place."

"What are you talking about, Lucas? How did they even know where we were hiding?" I volleyed another round of questions, not sure what to ask or even if I wanted actual answers.

"The fire drew them. I shouldn't have made that mistake. I was trying to make sure you were warm and didn't think about the consequences. I led them right to us." He trailed off, seemingly puzzled by his own actions. He closed his eyes almost in pain as he shook his head.

"Lucas, it's okay, you just made a mistake."

"I don't normally make mistakes." His eyes opened, and he looked at me with confusion.

"Well, you also saved us, so you can let the other part go. We're okay. I'm okay," I said quietly, trying to encourage him. I hadn't seen Lucas confused before, and it was a little unsettling.

He didn't respond. I wasn't sure if I was helping or not, but questions were still racing through my mind, so I tried to pick one that was positive for him. "How were you not afraid? Was it because of this power that flowed through you?"

"I'm not affected by things the same way you are," Lucas said with sympathetic eyes. "The furnace was a bit of a recharge for me," he smiled. "What they intended for harm was actually used for good."

"How did you survive that? And what was the glowing?"

"The same power was with me in there, but the fire fueled the power. Fire wasn't created by them, but they use it now, and they can have control over it. Sometimes they do. Sometimes they can get the fire to do their bidding. But not this time. This time the fire remembered it's true master."

My mind felt like it might explode. "You know that just makes me have more questions, right? It just sparks my curiosity all the more," I said in frustration, shivering slightly.

"First, let's get you warm," he said and then added with a smile, "without the fire this time."

I put on more of the clothing layers I had shoved in the back-pack, then at Lucas's encouragement laid back down in an attempt to get more sleep. I didn't feel tired even though, according to Lucas, I'd only been asleep a few hours when Uncle arrived. I rolled onto my side about to ask Lucas my next question when he laid down behind me and put his arm around me, an extra layer of warmth and peace. I was still feeling frustrated by the lack of answers I was getting, but I was again helpless not to drift right off to sleep, safe in Lucas's arms.

I woke slowly to the chirping of songbirds and trickling water. The warmth of the sun on my body filled me with a deep sense of contentment, and I opened my eyes to the most beautiful sight I had ever seen. I lifted my head to get a better view and realized I was lying on grass, softer than any cotton and smoother than any silk I had ever felt. I continued to rub my hand over it as I sat up and looked around. I was on a grassy hillside with trees to my right and mountains to my left.

There was a stream nearby; I couldn't see it, but I could hear it. And judging from the direction of the sound, it was probably beyond the grove of trees. The trees overflowed with fruits of all colors, weighing down branches that were covered with the most vibrant green leaves. I breathed deeply of the freshest air I had ever smelled as I looked up at the piercing blue sky and wispy clouds floating effortlessly overhead.

I slowly got up, passing my hand over the grass one more time. As I stood, I took another deep breath and stretched out my body. It was a movement out of habit, though, because I didn't feel particularly stiff.

I looked down to see I was wearing a white dress. I smiled and twirled just to test it out. The skirt swirled effortlessly around me, coming to rest softly against me as my bare feet stopped moving. I giggled, and my laughter sounded like tinkling bells.

I heard the sound of trickling water and began to walk towards the trees in search of its source. As I entered the trees, I heard rustling all around, but I wasn't afraid. I instinctively knew it was the sound of life, of animals and other creatures, and I wouldn't come to any harm.

"Hello?" I called to see if there were any people nearby

As I made my way to the clearing, I saw the water. It was a river, not a stream as I had initially thought, and much larger than it sounded from far away. The water was moving, but it was peaceful and gentle as it wound its way downstream. I stood at the tree line, looking at the river when the color next to me grabbed my eye. It was a fruit, bright fuchsia in color and the shape of a pear. It glistened even though it wasn't wet on the outside. I grabbed the fruit off the tree, and it came easily into my hand, almost like it was anticipating that I would remove it. I didn't feel the least concerned that the food might be inedible, just like before, with the rustling of the animals, I knew I wouldn't come to any harm.

As I bit into the fruit, the juice was the sweetest thing I had ever tasted. The fruit was so juicy that the liquid ran down my arms and chin. I thought for sure that my white dress was ruined, but when I looked down, there were no stains, and my arm was dry. I wiped my chin with my other hand, but there was nothing there. Not even a sticky residue. I took a few more bites of the delicious fruit before I felt comfortably full. Then I gently sat the fruit down on the grass and watched as the grass started shifting to envelope the fruit, slowly covering it. Even the small mound where the fuchsia pear rested, disappeared. And then a small sprig of something came slowly out of the ground, growing before my eyes. I watched as the seed immediately sprouted into a sapling, and somehow I knew the growing plant would become a whole new tree.

In my awe, I had backed up almost to the water when the shimmering light of its surface caught my eye. I turned to look at it and gasped at the beauty before me. Not only was the water the clearest I had ever seen, but it sparkled as if it were made of diamonds. I knelt down beside it, touching the surface, releasing an array of sparkles. I couldn't help but smile as I swirled my finger in the water, sending the sparkles out in a pattern. I was fully overcome with joy as I played in the water. It was cool to the touch, so cupping my hands, I drew water up for me to drink. The water was the most refreshing thing that had ever entered my mouth. I had only taken one drink, but my thirst was gone. The last remaining drops of water in my hand fell back into the river, and I watched as each drip exploded into a cascade of light.

I sat at the edge of the river and stuck my bare feet into the water. Although it felt cool to my hands and mouth, on my feet, it felt warm and completely comfortable. I had the weirdest sensation of feeling even more alive with just my feet in the water. I stood and started to walk forward, noticing that the water was deeper than it looked from above. From this vantage point, I could see what appeared to be jewels on the bottom of the crystal-clear river. I walked eagerly towards them with the water almost at my chest.

The water felt so soothing. I took a breath and put myself fully under the water. My white dress floated around me; every movement elegant and unbroken. The jewels were much clearer. They were in the shape of small pebbles, but these were no ordinary rocks. The pebbles looked exactly like jewels: red rubies, blue sapphires, diamonds, green emeralds, and ones that were colors I couldn't even name.

I lowered myself down to the bottom of the stream to touch them. Picking up a handful, I let the beautiful rocks fall through my fingers. It was a rainbow pouring down from my hands with the blues, greens, reds, yellows, purples, and pinks. The light touched the pebbles and sent their colors in beams all around me in my underwater world. I realized I hadn't even taken a breath, so I inhaled deeply, able to breathe just fine underwater. I felt my neck just to make sure I didn't have gills, then laughed at myself when I didn't feel anything. In a world this perfect, of course, I wouldn't need gills.

I lingered on the bottom of the stream, playing with the pebbles and enjoying the difference of life underwater. After a few more minutes, I wanted to rise above the surface. It wasn't that I couldn't stay there forever, but I desired to be back on land.

I had the thought that I wanted to be on dry land and then I was; I hadn't even needed to walk out of the river. Looking down at myself, I realized my white dress was thoroughly dried. I felt so alive, rejuvenated, strong . . . and beautiful. The last time I remembered feeling this beautiful was as a little girl when my mom would tell me how beautiful I looked as we played princess together. The thoughts of my mom didn't bring on sadness and pain like they usually did. I felt only joy and love. I breathed in the goodness of that and continued walking back toward the trees.

Weaving my way through the trees, I heard it—a voice, the sound of which felt like something I had longed to listen to all of my life.

"Sarah Joy; My Joy. You are seen. You are Chosen. Walk in the Light." The voice, although not loud to my ears, moved through every part of my body.

"Who are you?" I asked. But there was no answer. I felt the truth of the words spoken over me, and I wished for a moment that I could write them down, but I was overcome with the need to lie down. With that thought, I was lying on the soft grass, rubbing my hand back and forth over it while sleep came over me like a warm blanket.

CHAPTER 12

My eyes opened, and I immediately knew I was back, back to normal, if that word even existed anymore. The day was upon us because I could see the rays of sunlight streaming into the cave. You would think waking up in a cave after what I had just seen would have been a little disconcerting or that I would have trouble making sense of all of the crazy that I had witnessed in the last two days. But the opposite was true; I felt rested and aware of where I was, and that Lucas was somewhere nearby.

Even as I thought of him, he walked back into the cave. I couldn't see his face because of the brightness of the light behind him and the darkness of the cave, but I knew it was him.

"Good morning," he said softly.

"Good morning," I said, feeling a little shy in the light of the day. I felt very much like a sixteen-year-old with a crush at that moment. I was overcome with feelings for him. He meant the world to me for what he had endured the past two days on my behalf. He was my protector, and I was so grateful that, for whatever reason, he had come for me.

I wanted to tell him about my dream, but I couldn't remember the details fully. "What's the plan now?" I asked instead, not quite able to meet his eyes.

He had come close to me now. "Sarah," he said calmly and waited for my eyes to meet his. Once I raised my eyes, he said, "That's better," and gave me a kind half-smile.

When I smiled back, he continued, "The plan is to get you to safety. We have to keep traveling, but they're still searching the woods for us. There's help coming, but we need to move farther away from the camp."

"Lucas, I know you're tied to my mom and all, but what does that have to do with me?"

"You are Sarah Joy, a chosen one."

"A chosen one of what?" I asked, having a twinge of memory of someone else saying that.

"The Eklesi."

"Lucas," I said, frustrated by the slow delivery of his cryptic messages. I didn't want to have to pull every piece of information from him. Surely, he could offer me more than one or two-word answers.

He chuckled, seeming to know just what I was thinking. "I know you are frustrated. You will learn everything in time, but for now, we need to keep moving." He stood up, quickly offering me his hand.

I made a face of reluctance at him but gave him my hand. He had already repacked our bags except for the pallet I had been laying on. While he packed up the clothes from my makeshift bed, I took off the outer-most layer of camo clothes as I knew I would get hot quickly in them. I went to put them in one of the packs, but Lucas quickly stopped me. One pack held water from a nearby stream. I had thought I had grabbed a backpack, but it was actually a water pack. Good thinking on my part, even though I had been unaware. He would carry that one since it was heavier.

I was a little nervous about leaving the relative safety of the cave; although, once Lucas stepped out of it, it didn't seem quite as safe, so I quickly stepped out behind him. My eyes began to water immediately because of the sun's brightness. I shielded them with my hands as I stepped forward a few more steps to be in the shade of a tree.

Lucas was looking at me. "Ready?" he asked.

I nodded, and Lucas started walking as I trailed closely behind. I had no idea where he was headed or what we would encounter, but I knew Lucas would protect me with everything he had in him; he had already proven that.

Lucas didn't have his glow of extra power, or magic, or whatever it was. The last of it had probably left him while he kept me warm last night. To think that he gave up that extra power and strength for me. He could have held onto it for longer and saved it for himself, but he chose to give it to me.

As we walked, Lucas explained some of what happened last night. Uncle's voice had sounded different last night because he was in his other form. I had to stop him there, because I had no clue what he meant by "other form." Apparently, Uncle was not human. The man I knew was only a form that he took in order to carry out his assignment with us. From what Lucas said about them, I was very thankful that I couldn't see outside of the cave last night.

We had an advantage over them, without the fire, they were now searching blindly for us. Apparently though, the danger was still very real, as Lucas continued to stop and close his eyes and listen.

After one break, as we walked on, I got brave enough to ask, "Lucas, what are you listening for?"

He replied, "I am listening for sounds of them, but I'm also listening for guidance."

"Guidance from who?" I asked.

"The Light." He said the name with such awe and reverence that I understood it wasn't just any light.

"Who is The Light?"

"The Light is The Light. Encompassing all good things: life, truth, honor, beauty, purity, love." He spoke slowly, giving each word weight.

He seemed to take on a different quality, just saying that phrase made it seem like he wasn't completely there with me anymore.

"I haven't seen a lot of any of those things around here," I stated sorrowfully.

He turned to look at me. I had succeeded; he wasn't as animated as he was before. I had snuffed out some of the good he was feeling, but I immediately regretted pulling him back. Having him fully back with me no longer seemed like it was worth it. But, as we were no longer separated, I couldn't be sure I wouldn't have done the exact same thing again if I had to do it all over.

"This world is filled with those who wish to bring the opposite of The Light. They only know darkness. They only want death, destruction, lies, devastation. They don't know good; they fear good because they can never have good." He paused, "Remember how I said that I'm not as affected by the things as you are?"

I nodded. He looked sad, and I wanted to erase that look from his face.

"The longer I'm here, the more I feel the things of this world changing me and affecting me more deeply. The hate and the hurt are taking their toll."

As I looked at him, I knew it to be true. He seemed to be pure, and our world was so tainted by evil and hate. How could he not be affected?

"I have to remember who gives me strength, power, and all of my abilities. Without The Light, I would be just like them. Wanting things only for myself and seeking everyone else's destruction."

"Lucas, I'm sorry. I shouldn't have said that. You are all those things you said of The Light. I lied when I said I didn't see any of those things around here." I paused, looking down at my feet. I realized that I didn't want to lower him to my level; I wanted to be lifted up to his, to all those good things.

I took a deep breath, knowing that I needed to be honest with him about how I was feeling. I spoke slowly, saying, "I just felt the separation between us, and I didn't like it at all. I'm sorry I brought you down. What I really want is to feel and hear and see all those good things."

My heart was beating wildly, just hoping he wouldn't say it wasn't possible for me. Hoping he wouldn't say I was doomed to be like all of those men back at the camp.

When my eyes came back up to his, he had a smile on his face, and he was glowing. Not like the glow from the fire, but the glow that was part of him, the glow I noticed when I first saw him. Even then, I knew he was different.

"Sarah, that is exactly what we want for you." He turned and gestured to go, "Let's keep going."

I was glad that I wasn't outright excluded from what he had, but I couldn't help but wonder what it would take to get to those good things. I continued hiking and following the only source that had some answers.

✳ ✳ ✳

We stopped periodically, taking listening breaks for Lucas and water breaks for me. Sometimes we walked, and sometimes we jogged. We ate some nuts and berries along the way, but my stomach still growled. We saw animals that Lucas could shoot, but without a fire, we couldn't cook them. He hadn't heard anything from anyone on the dark side. I couldn't help but think of them like that now. My only real knowledge of good versus evil was from the one Star Wars movie I'd seen. But as far as sci-fi went, I was pretty much living a good versus evil nightmare. Horrible creatures were out to get me and pull me away from all good things. They took on "other forms" and spoke screeching languages and burned people in fires. It was all too much to think about. Maybe it was okay that we didn't have food. I'm not sure my stomach could have handled anything anyway.

Lucas stopped so abruptly that I walked right into him. He didn't turn, but I could tell from his posture that he was listening.

After a moment more, he turned quickly and looked at me with his eyes wide.

"It's a scout, climb on my back and don't say a word." As he said this, he dumped the water and switched his pack to the front of him, already bending down for me to climb on his back.. As soon as my arms were around his neck, he took off running, dodging trees and bushes. If he hadn't had to dodge anything, I think he would have been sprinting, which was no easy task with me on his back.

I tried to make myself lighter by shifting my weight on his back, which of course, wasn't possible, but I wanted to help. I wanted to ask where we were going and if we were going to make it in time, but I did the best thing I could to help, and I didn't say a word. I wondered if they could track my voice or even hear it easier than they could Lucas's.

He ran for what must have been ten minutes without stopping. Once he stopped, I could hear his labored breathing coming in gasps. He hadn't been tired after those much longer runs when we were running away from camp, so I was surprised that he was struggling now. His breathing was slowing, though, which meant he had at least some strength left. I knew he was listening, and I continued to do my part by not saying a word.

Another breath and we were off running again. Well, Lucas was running, and I was holding on, doing my best not to strangle him as he carried the packs and me.

It seemed like the same amount of time had passed again when he whispered, "We are almost there." I had no idea where "there" was, but I continued not to speak. I even caught myself holding my breath, which really didn't help in any way.

We were now in a much denser area with a lot of rocks and bushes. Lucas lowered himself down and tapped my arm, letting me know it was time to get off his back. It took me a moment to unclench my arms, which had been locked in a very tight grip, strengthened by fear. Once I was off, he quickly stood and grabbed my hand, guiding me quickly forward and into the bushes.

He led me through bushes that were so thick they were snagging our clothes as we pushed through. It was mostly Lucas taking the brunt of the snags as I followed behind him, grasping the back of his shirt as he pushed his way through. The terrain became rocky under our feet, providing unstable running ground. Lucas pushed through the last few bushes, and I could see we were at a rock ledge. He looked up behind us to the rocks above, searching for something, and then he knelt down and looked over the edge of the cliff, looking to the right and to the left. He got up quickly and led me a few feet over to the edge and pointed down. I crouched down and peered over the edge, where I could see a slight ledge sticking out.

When I looked back at Lucas, he was lying on his stomach kicking and digging his toes into the dirt, almost as if he were anchoring himself in some way. My look must have registered confusion because he started gesturing to me with his arm and head. I understood that he was going to get me down to that ledge, but that seemed like an awful lot even for him. He held his right arm out to me. Even with the fear, I responded by reaching my right arm towards him, not sure what he wanted me to do. There didn't appear to be footholds to get down, but by the way he grasped my arm all the way up at my shoulder, and under my armpit, I was thinking that he wasn't planning on me using footholds, he was going to do all the work himself. He nodded and looked at me intently, like I needed to hurry. I grabbed his arm with my other arm and moved to the edge facing him and not the cliff. There was only a tiny ledge to catch me, and I shook with fear.

Lucas whispered, "Ready?" He asked it so quietly, I'm not even sure he said it aloud. Maybe he had just mouthed it. With panic on my face, I gave one quick nod. I tried to walk my feet down and under, but they quickly slipped off. He was still grabbing my arm, and I was hanging onto him for dear life. He was most likely going to have nail marks from my fingernails. My arms were fully stretched out, but my feet weren't touching anything. Gravity assisted in moving me closer to the ledge as I started to slide down Lucas's arm until our hands were grasped, and my arm was screaming. I could feel him letting go, and it took everything in me not to scream as I fell. I knew I had to lean forward if I didn't want to fall off the ledge backward.

I fell face-first into the rocks below, and with such force, I was probably bleeding. I saw something out of the corner of my eye and turned to see Lucas's legs as he was lowering himself down. He came over the edge with his hips and torso and continued coming until he was hanging from his fingertips. He dropped down with amazing calm and quiet. He gently turned me and pulled me back against the wall of the ledge to where we were hidden by the outcropping above us.

We were both winded, but Lucas still signaled the universal quiet sign to me. We both tried to take deep, quiet breaths to slow our breathing down. It was working until I heard footsteps. We had made it down here just in time, but here they were again. Did Lucas even have any power left to protect us? Would they find us? My breathing rate was increasing again, Lucas grasped my hand, and I tried to take deep, quiet breaths once more.

As the footsteps drew closer, he released my hand and pressed his palms back against the wall behind him. His eyes closed, and he took on that quiet look of concentration that I recognized from the cave. Here we were again, hoping that the power that flowed before would again protect us. I had stopped breathing altogether at this point.. My eyes were closed, and I, too, was willing the power that had protected us before in the cave to do it once more when someone started talking.

My eyes shot open as I heard someone say, "I followed the tracks, but they ended here at some rocks. I looked all around, but I don't see them."

I couldn't hear the response of whoever he was talking to. He must have been talking on a phone.

"I know that they couldn't have just disappeared sir, I'm just telling you that they aren't here."

Another pause.

"I don't think they could have gotten picked up here. There aren't any open areas for vehicles to get through."

Pause.

I looked over to see Lucas still with his eyes closed and a calm look on his face. I didn't dare move an inch, breathing as quietly as I possibly could.

I heard the man above pacing and reporting to the person on the phone, "I looked all down the rock faces and haven't seen anything. No ropes on any ledges or markings of any kind. The tracks stopped at the bushes."

Pause.

He uttered a curse word and then said, "How long do you want me to wait here?"

Another curse word, and then he mumbled, "Perfect. Hung up on me, and now I have to wait here for nothing."

That seemed like the worst thing I could hear him say. He had to wait here for who knew how long with us trapped on the side of a cliff. But then it occurred to me; he couldn't see us. While we were somewhat hidden, if he had really looked over the edge, he should have seen us. We must not be visible to him, just like in the cave. The Light must be protecting us.

A short time later, the pacing stopped, but I knew instinctively he was still up there. I could feel his presence. We stayed like that for a long time. The sun was beginning its descent, and unfortunately, it wasn't shining on us anymore. It was starting to get cold, and I was getting to the point where standing was difficult. I hadn't had food, our water had been poured out, and while the fear still lingered some, it was no longer fueling me. When I knew I couldn't stand any longer, I reached out to touch Lucas's hand. He opened his eyes to slits when he looked at me. What he saw in me must have alarmed him, because his eyes came all the way open as he fully turned his head to me. He stared at me before nodding his head like he had made a decision. He bent down and picked up some rocks and started lobbing them back over the ledge.

I heard a noise up above, and the man growled, "There they are!" His footsteps sounded more distant as he started running toward the sound of the rocks Lucas had thrown.

On the verge of collapse, Lucas pulled me to him. I breathed as deeply as I could, but the healing wasn't coming as quickly, if at all. I even tried to imagine I was pulling in some of his strength and energy. When the exchanges happened before, I didn't even have to participate, but this was different. I felt a little better when Lucas pulled me back just a bit. He switched to holding the sides of my face in his hands. He took a deep breath in and then exhaled right into my face. Some light floated out and towards me. I breathed it in as deeply as I could, feeling this time like I could go on. Lucas looked me over and then motioned me to the side of the ledge. He pointed, and I saw that there were some notches I might be able to put my feet on. I pulled and tugged myself up while Lucas helped from below.

I was still lying on the ground panting when he came up next to me and put his hand on my back. I tilted my head up to look at him. I knew we needed to go, but I was exhausted and very near tears. He gestured for me to stay. The enemy scout had started a fire while he waited, so I crawled closer to it as Lucas took off through the bushes. I fell asleep with my cheek on a cool stone, my body being warmed by the fire.

The smell of something cooking lured me from my sleep. The fire was out, but Lucas was right beside me.

"Okay, Sarah, you need to eat." I didn't need to be coaxed, but he did have to help me sit up. He handed me some bark that had some sort of animal meat cooked on it. I started shoving the pieces in my mouth, then slowed myself down so I could actually chew it. I didn't know what it was, but it tasted delicious. I think the bark it was sitting on would have tasted tolerable at this point, though. When I had eaten three or four pieces, Lucas took the meat away, to my dismay, but before I uttered my disapproval, he replaced it with the water bag that he had refilled. He helped me tip it up so that I could drink from the spout, and slowly lowered it before I was ready to be done.

"You've got to take it slow, Sarah," he said, handing me the food plate once again.

I immediately put another piece of meat in my mouth as I watched the canteen bag. Two more pieces of meat in my mouth, and this time I initiated the trade, greedily drinking more water down.

As my hunger and thirst were being satisfied, my ability to think more clearly kicked in, and I realized we were still in danger.

"Where is he?" I asked.

"I led him a bit off of our course. He was happy to find new tracks, but they will lead him nowhere." He smiled slightly.

His face fell, though, as he looked at me. "I'm sorry this is so rough on you."

"It's okay, Lucas. I'm guessing if I were still back there with them, it wouldn't be very pleasant either." I paused. "At least with you, I'm with someone who cares about me, and for the first time in a while, I feel hope." I continued to eat and drink.

"What was this?" I asked, holding up my bark with the meat on it. He had his own bark-plate with the same meat on it.

"Rabbit," he smirked. "I used one of the bows you packed and then cooked him quickly before dousing the fire."

"Thank you," I said quietly.

"Well, I couldn't very well let you starve, now could I?" His lighthearted attempt at humor made me smile.

We were quiet for a minute before he said, "Once you've eaten, we need to get going. He will come back here eventually, and I want you as far away from here as possible. We only have a few more hours to go before we reach a road, and then hopefully, our travels will get a little easier."

"Where are we going?" I asked in between bites.

Lucas paused and seemed to consider his response.

"Lucas?" I asked, growing a little concerned that maybe he didn't have a plan, and we would be running and eating rabbits forever.

"It's hard to describe to you where we are going," he said slowly.

"Okay, so what's one word you would use to describe it?"

Without hesitation this time, he said, "Safety."

CHAPTER 13

The motion stopped, and this time, I woke up very disoriented. My hands felt constricted like they were bound. I gasped and lifted my head.

"Are you okay?" I heard a voice whisper. It was Lucas, things were now clearer.

"My hands," I said with a raspy, dry voice.

"Oh, sorry." I felt him bend down and release my hands from his grip as I slid slowly from his back. He continued to whisper, "I had to hold onto them once you fell asleep because you were dead weight on my back."

The feeling in my hands slowly returned, along with pins and needles.

"I'm sorry I fell asleep," I rasped out.

"There's nothing to be sorry for. This is harder for you than I anticipated it would be," he whispered as he looked at me with sad eyes.

I tried to pull myself up to stand taller, self-consciously touching my hair, feeling a mess under his stare, and I knew I was blushing.

He was looking at me strangely when I lifted my eyes back to him.

"What?" I asked, feeling even more self-conscious of my appearance.

"I guess I'm trying to figure out what you're feeling right now. You looked embarrassed for some reason," his voice barely above a whisper.

"I'm just embarrassed that I fell asleep, and you had to do all of the work." I didn't want to add anything about my appearance at the moment.

"Sarah, if you remember from camp, I'm not easily swayed to do things I don't want to do. If I carry you, it's because I want to. You're not a burden to me."

"The reason I stopped was that we are nearing the road. I don't know who's out there and if Uncle has scouts watching it. I'm going to have you walk so that we don't draw any extra attention to ourselves, and we are going to stay back in the trees just a bit so that I can see what is going on."

"How do you know which direction to go?"

"I just know," he said with what would have seemed like annoyance were it coming from anyone but Lucas.

He took hold of my hand gently, "Let's go. And Sarah, we aren't going to talk while we walk so that I can concentrate."

I heard a car go by, and I held my breath as we moved through the trees, closer to the road.

Quit holding your breath, Sarah, it doesn't help anything.

We made it almost to the edge of the tree line, the wide grassy shoulder now the only thing separating us from the road itself. Lucas motioned me to stop as another car passed with its headlights on. I looked at Lucas once the beams of light had passed, and he shook his head at me. When he didn't seem alarmed, I knew it wasn't one of Uncle's scouts, so I didn't understand what we were waiting for. From my way of thinking, if Lucas knew these cars weren't scouts, why weren't we trying to flag them down for a ride?

Maybe we couldn't trust anybody, since there seemed to be some kind of plot to get Amelia and me to join whatever Uncle was involved with. My heart jumped as I thought of my sister. I trusted Lucas, so I knew that she was okay for now, but I missed her. I wanted her to know about all I had seen and heard, not that I could explain much of it. It also seemed really hard to picture her fleeing for her life, she was never one to be rushed. It would have been very hard to even convince her to come with us had she been able. I felt terrible pain at the thoughts of my sister, so I tried to focus back on what we were doing. Once we got to safety, I knew Lucas would help me figure out a way to save Amelia as well.

It wasn't long before my mind started to wander again. As we walked, I thought back to Lucas carrying me as dead weight. I hadn't even noticed I was starting to fall asleep. The last thing I remembered was him instructing me to climb on his back, followed by me hoping for another one of those dreams, like the one I had in the cave. I had even asked for another dream in my head, but I wasn't sure where my dreams came from, so I wasn't sure who I was asking.

I thought maybe I would ask Lucas about it once I was able to talk with him again. I was so thirsty at the moment, I wasn't even sure that talking would be possible.

I thought about how, on Lucas's back, I had fallen into a sound sleep, but I didn't remember dreaming anything. His walking motion had been soothing to me. He couldn't run carrying me anymore, and I marveled that he'd had the strength to carry me at all. Ever since the glow had completely faded, he seemed more human. He was still incredibly strong, but somehow . . . I don't know . . . my thoughts about who Lucas was swirled in my head.

I looked up at him as we walked and saw that his eyes were closed, yet we continued to walk forward. I also noticed that for the first time since he came out of the furnace, he actually looked tired. My heart hurt to see him so weary and I knew I couldn't let him carry me again, no matter how exhausted I was. It had been too much for him.

My thirst was becoming too much to ignore; it was all that I could think about now. I squeezed Lucas's hand. He opened his eyes slightly and looked at me. I motioned to my mouth with a grimace on my face. He gave a nod and pointed with his other hand through the trees and down the road. I could see some lights, so I nodded okay, I could make it to those lights. Fear slowly crept back in over the need for water. Who would be at those lights; who would we encounter next?

We stood back in the trees across from an old gas station that appeared to still be open. Lucas had let go of my hand and had his eyes closed in concentration. At some point, when we were someplace safe, I would have to ask him whether he was hearing something, sensing something, or sending out a signal of some sort to someone else. But at the moment, all I was really hoping was that he would hear we could cross the street to get something to drink.

When I just couldn't bear it anymore and was about to start pulling Lucas across the street, he opened his eyes. He was still looking straight at the gas station.

Without looking at me, he whispered, "I don't detect any scouts. We should be safe to go into the store and get some food and water."

Just outside of the door, Lucas paused, stopping my forward motion with his hand holding fast to mine. In the light, I could see he looked rough, and I realized I must look as bad if not worse. Lucas was looking in the store, then looked over at me and said, "I don't have my wallet."

My brain was so spent that it didn't compute for a second why we would need a wallet. It kicked in at that moment, and I realized we would need money to buy food and water. The man we could see through the barred windows would hardly be giving it away for free. I had a moment of panic and then remembered the money I had grabbed before I left. It was still in my pocket. I couldn't remember what had happened to my phone, but I still had the money. I reached into my front pocket and pulled out the wad of cash and then smiled up at Lucas. He gave me a small smile that showed his relief. I pulled off two twenties and put the rest back into my pocket.

Lucas moved towards the door, opening it for me. The old gas station smelled like gas, oil, and cigarettes, but I didn't care as I said a quick, "Hi" to the man behind the counter and moved towards the water in the see-through refrigerated case. I grabbed a bottle out and just started drinking. Lucas came up behind me and whispered, "Slow down, or you'll make yourself sick."

I did what he said and stopped drinking to take some deep breaths before taking another swig. It took restraint to go slow, but he was right, I would probably puke if I drank it too fast. Once I had finished off one bottle of water, I grabbed out two more and moved to set them on the counter with my empty bottle. I smiled at the man behind the counter, but he looked at me strangely, almost like seeing me was frightening him a little bit. I realized he was probably upset that I had drunk that whole bottle without paying for it. It was that or maybe the fact that we looked like we could have been characters from a survival show.

"I'm sorry, sir," I had to clear my throat because it came out as a croak, "I was just so thirsty." I cleared my throat again. "I will pay for the bottle I drank along with the other ones once I grab a few more items." I tried a smile again and showed him my money. He still looked taken aback for some reason, but he nodded his head like he understood.

Lucas was already in the food aisle with his empty water bottle, and he had multiple beef jerky sticks and a bag of trail mix in the other. He stared at the man behind the counter, but the man was turned away, hunched over talking on the phone. Lucas didn't seem concerned, so I didn't worry about it either as I grabbed some hand wipes along with the items Lucas held in his arms, then headed back for the counter.

After the man rang up a jerky stick, I opened it and started eating in between sips of water. His eyes never left me, and under his scrutiny, I felt suddenly very aware of my appearance.

Once the man had bagged up a few more items, including the wipes, I grabbed the bag, handed Lucas the money, and whispered, "I'm going to use the bathroom really quick." He nodded, looking at me quickly before looking back at the man behind the counter. I hurried off, knowing we probably needed to leave soon, but feeling secure nonetheless, as surely Lucas would not have allowed me out of his sight if our lives were in any kind of imminent danger.

CHAPTER 14

I stood at the sink and took a close look at myself in the mirror, sighing heavily at the sight before me. I washed the grime from my hands and face, then smoothed my hair back in a ponytail, still staring at the face before me. I looked like I had aged years. Suddenly, I heard a voice outside the door shout, "Put your hands in the air!"

I heard a muffled voice in return. "Where's the girl?" I heard another shout and then more voices, but I had already grabbed up my stuff and was pulling open the door. Had the guy behind the counter gone crazy? I had given Lucas the money, so surely the man didn't think we were stealing from him.

"I'm here," I said, trying to reassure the man I hadn't run off with something. I stopped dead in my tracks when I saw the police officer, his gun pulled and pointed at Lucas, who stood with his hands in the air.

The officer squinted his eyes at me as I slowly moved closer to Lucas, trying to put my hands in the air as well. But with one hand holding my precious grocery bag of goods, it was a little harder to do with the same air of calm Lucas portrayed.

"Decker," the officer said forcefully, but with less of a shout, "She the one on the flier you got?"

"Yes, sir," said the man behind the counter. I spared a glance at him, and he too had a gun pointed at Lucas. "I looked at it really good just to make sure."

"What flier?" I asked. My heart was slamming in my chest, but I latched on to the flier comment.

"There are fliers all over the place with your picture on it," the police officer said matter-of-factly. "They say you're missin'. Decker here called me when he recognized you."

I looked at Lucas, wondering if he had heard this conversation, but he was still looking at the officer who had a gun pointed at him.

"Decker assumed this must be the man that kidnapped you." The officer's eyes bounced back and forth between Lucas and me, his gun steady at Lucas's chest.

"Wait, what?" I asked, my hands slowly coming down.

"The fliers say that you were kidnapped by a man fitting this man's description. We didn't have any missing person's report on file, but I came just the same," explained the officer.

"This man did not kidnap me, sir. He's been helping me."

The officer looked at me like I might not know my own mind.

I took a quick glance at his nametag and said, "Please, Sergeant Tanner, I'm telling you the truth. My name is Sarah, and I *was* kidnapped, but not by Lucas." Lucas still wasn't looking at me, so I moved closer to him and touched one of his raised arms. "He's my friend, and he saved me from a very bad situation."

"Well, ma'am, that might be true, but we'll have to straighten all this out at the station."

He turned his attention back to Lucas and said, "Okay then. Lucas, is it? Turn around and put your hands behind your back." Sergeant Tanner holstered his pistol and, at the same time, quickly pulled the handcuffs from his belt.

"Please," I cried, "You don't need to do that."

Lucas looked at me as he turned and said, "It's fine, Sarah; I have nothing to hide." His eyes looked completely at peace as he put his hands slowly behind his back.

Sergeant Tanner handcuffed Lucas and then looked at me. In my exhausted state, I wasn't sure what to do next as he grasped Lucas by the arm and began leading him to the door.

"You need to come with me as well," he said to me as they started moving towards the door.

"Can I bring our food and water?" I asked a little pathetically, hoping not to be separated from my water so soon and still trying to get my brain to kick into gear.

"Of course, you can," he said, turning to look at me with a little kindness in his eyes. He moved to open the door and held it from the outside for us to walk through.

"Thanks, Decker. You did really good," he called to the man behind the cash register as I walked past him. I didn't hear if Decker replied anything before the door closed.

While we walked the few steps to the police cruiser, another police car was pulling in with his lights on. I felt Lucas stiffen next to me even though I wasn't holding onto him. His tension was palpable. I looked up at his face and saw that his jaw was clenched. Whoever was getting out of that car was not a friend to us.

His car wasn't the same as Sergeant Tanner's. I couldn't see the side description, but it was a different color. I glanced at Tanner and noticed he wore a look of confusion.

The other officer stepped out of his cruiser and said, "I heard the chatter on the radio, and since I was in this area, I decided to come see if I could be of any assistance. Is this the girl?" he asked, although I figured he probably knew who I was. He didn't wait for an answer before he asked, "I see you already arrested the perp."

I felt both Lucas and Sergeant Tanner move to shield me. I knew Lucas's movement was conscious, but I wasn't sure about Sergeant Tanner. I could still see the man in front of us. I didn't know him, but I had those familiar chills running down my back. He was with Uncle.

"I appreciate the help . . ." he looked at the Trooper's nametag, "Green, but I've got it under control." My estimation of Sergeant Tanner went way up as he continued, "We are headed to the station to sort this whole mess out."

The other man was staring at Lucas with conflicting emotions crossing his face. Sergeant Tanner glanced over at Lucas as well, but quickly turned his eyes back, "I know most of the Troopers in these parts. Are you new around here?"

The other man's eyes narrowed slightly, "Yeah, just transferred from Texas. Name's Trooper Doyle Green."

"I'm Sergeant Brian Tanner. Pleased to meet you." Still, Sergeant Tanner didn't move from in front of me, nor did he extend his hand to greet the other man.

Doyle smiled and said, "Well, now that we're friends, I'd be happy to drive her in for you, since you probably have your hands full with him," cutting his eyes to Lucas with a look of disgust.

The tension coming off of Lucas went up another notch at Doyle's comment. Most likely more for Doyle taking me than for the comment about him. The Trooper was now in front of us, and Lucas moved forward so that I was almost blocked from his view. My creepy meter was on high alert.

Tanner scoffed and said, "I know how to do my job, and the girl will be coming with me until we get this whole situation figured out."

Trooper Green's face darkened at the situation. His eyes shifted to mine, and his mouth curved into a snarl. His eyes were a little crazy looking, and I realized he was angry because he was probably supposed to bring me back.

I knew he wouldn't hesitate to hurt someone to get to me. "Whoa there, you okay, Doyle?" Tanner asked as he moved his hand to his gun and stood shoulder to shoulder with Lucas in front of me.

"Uh, yeah, I'm good," Doyle said as his face cleared, "Just got concerned for you there for a minute, and the girl too."

"I appreciate your concern, but don't you have a highway to babysit somewhere?" Obviously, Sergeant Tanner's radar told him that Trooper Green wasn't safe for any of us. His hand slowly moved to rest on his gun holster.

"Easy, friend. Just wanted to help," he said with his eyes on Tanner's hand. "I'll just head back to my car and follow you in." As he backed away, I could see him through a small crack between Tanner and Lucas. Doyle had his hands up as he backed away with a smile that was far from genuine.

"No need to follow us," Tanner commanded, "I got it, and it's time for you to get off my scene." His voice was cold and direct.

"Sarah," Tanner said quietly. "Please stay behind me."

I did as he said, and we walked around the front of the car without him taking his hand off of his gun. Lucas followed behind us, not taking his eyes off Doyle as he got into his car. Tanner opened the front passenger door, telling me to get in, at the same time opening the backdoor for Lucas with his left hand. He closed my door and then Lucas's, then moved back around the front of the car and stood by his door.

I turned quickly around to face Lucas and whispered, "Lucas, who was that?"

"One of them." He looked out the back window. I already knew who it was just from my feelings, but hearing it confirmed through Lucas made me feel sick that one of "them" had again been that close to me.

Sergeant Tanner was still facing Doyle's car. I could see both since I was turned around in my seat, looking at Lucas.

"Will he try something here?"

"I think he was going to until Tanner showed that he would protect us with his gun."

"Is a gun enough to stop one of them?" I asked, knowing they were capable of a lot.

"Yes, when they're in their human form, they can be killed just like you can. My concern was that he would shift."

"Why didn't he?"

"I would guess he had orders not to do that in front of you."

"Why would it matter if it was in front of me?"

"You still haven't seen them for what they are. My guess is that Uncle still hopes to bring you back and explain some things away. They are pretty frightening," he said, turning to look at me sadly, "it wouldn't be easy to forget once you had seen it."

"Was that why he started glaring at me?"

"Yes, I think so; you were the reason he couldn't get what he wanted without getting himself hurt. They're inherently selfish creatures and will avoid pain if possible."

"Lucas." Just saying his name, I knew he could sense my confusion, fatigue, fear, and everything else that was swirling inside of me.

He looked back at me with a small smile and sadness in his eyes, "I know, Sarah." I could see he desperately wanted to comfort me, but with his hands locked behind his back there wasn't much he could do. I took a deep breath, drawing on the strength I had seen in him and had seen in myself over the last however many days, and I was able to breathe just a bit easier.

"What happens now?" I asked.

"Our help was supposed to meet us around here. But I sense that there's Light at the police station. Tanner just needs to get us there, and then we'll have more help."

"Do you think Doyle will follow us?"

Lucas looked at me sweetly, but I knew the futility in my question; of course, he would follow us. Probably even try to run us off the road. Lucas confirmed it when he said, "Yes, and many more of them are nearby."

Finally, Doyle pulled out, and Sergeant Tanner opened his door. Lucas's gaze did not leave my face.

Tanner sat down hard in the car, "Okay, what's really going on here?" Neither Lucas nor I spoke, so he continued. "That was not a state trooper. I know all of the troopers from these parts, and I haven't heard anything about us getting a new one."

He had been turned to look at Lucas, but then he faced me, "Is he one of the ones that's been huntin' you?"

"Yes, sir," I said, as tears welled up in my eyes.

"Okay, well, he didn't give up easily, and my guess is that he is going to follow us, just like he said he would."

"And he will have friends here soon, as well," Lucas said from the backseat.

With that, Sgt. Tanner started the car quickly, backed out of the spot and peeled out of the parking lot. "I can tell good from evil. The young man sitting in the backseat is good, and the one huntin' you is evil. The rest we can figure out back at the station."

I quickly buckled my seatbelt as he pushed down on the accelerator and sped into the darkness of the forest. He picked up the radio and advised dispatch he was en route back to the station with one male and one female. A woman's voice answered, "That's clear."

He hung up the radio but pulled out his cellphone and placed a call. "Rhonda, have you heard of a new trooper, Doyle Green?"

We couldn't hear the response, but Sgt. Tanner continued, "Well, look him up for me and call me back, these folks I'm bringing in are claiming he isn't a trooper."

Again, her muffled voice was incoherent to anyone but Sgt. Tanner. "Alright, talk to ya soon," he said and hung up the phone.

Tanner was quiet for a minute, and then about came undone as he asked again, "What is going on here?" He quickly glanced at me, but immediately looked back at the road.

I looked back at Lucas, who was behind Tanner's seat, and he started to speak. "Sergeant Tanner, you are exactly right in what you are sensing; those men are evil, and they are hunting Sarah. I know you're already driving fast and have requested backup, but do you know any alternate routes that they wouldn't? That may help us get to the police station safely."

"Alternate routes, alternate routes," Tanner said softly, as if trying to find the answer by saying it out loud. "Yes, I have at least one we could try."

"Would they know about it?" Lucas asked quietly.

"No, this road is rarely used. It used to go to an old logging camp, but it passes through to town if you take the right road."

"It's worth a try," Lucas encouraged, "We have to make it there before they are back on our tail again, though."

"We should; it's just a minute away."

I looked back at Lucas to see he was looking out the back window. It all still looked dark, but that could change at any minute. Then, there was a flash of light that bounced off the trees on the curve behind us.

"With all due respect, Sergeant Tanner, floor it!" Lucas shouted.

And Tanner did just that. I faced completely forward, trying not to panic. Obviously, Tanner knew these roads way better than those guys, and he was a trained officer. He knew what he was doing. I glanced over to see that he looked frightened. I knew the feeling. I had been chased by these guys for days, but I still wasn't used to it.

"Here it is!" Tanner exclaimed, pulling a quick left. Lucas and I both swayed dramatically in the opposite direction, our bodies responding to the sudden turn.

"Once you're on the road, turn off your lights," Lucas instructed as Tanner complied. He also slowed as we were now on a dirt road, and it was kicking up dust. I knew he wouldn't dare stop, though. You don't stop when an unknown threat is chasing you.

"I count three cars that went past already," Lucas conveyed to us. "They must be focused on trying to see our taillights. Wait another minute before you turn them back on."

No one spoke for a minute.

"Two more just passed," Lucas reported.

"Seriously, you two, what is going on? Five cars trying to catch a police officer out here in the woods." He looked over at me with confusion and panic. "Who are you?"

I looked at Lucas, and he nodded at me to go ahead. "Sir, a man I thought was my uncle has had charge of me for the past eight years. I just found out two days ago that he is not who he said he was. He wants to bring me back to a place that I have no desire to go, and I fear for my safety. At this point, I'm still not sure what he wants from me." It was the truth. I had no idea why Uncle needed me back so desperately.

"Has he hurt you already?" he asked softly.

"Only with fear, not physically, thanks to Lucas," I said softly. I saw his gaze shift from the road to the rearview mirror to look at Lucas, causing me to look back at him as well. His head was still turned to look out the back.

Amelia was next on my mind. I wanted to tell Sergeant Tanner about her. Maybe he could help, but I held my tongue. Telling him about Amelia would open up a whole can of worms that I wasn't sure was safe to share.

"Okay then, let's get you to safety." He spoke with more strength and less fear in his voice. He turned his lights back on as we continued to bounce down the old dirt road. I saw some old logging equipment along the road that added to the eeriness of it all as he received a call.

"Yeah, Rhonda, what have you got?" I watched as Sergeant Tanner's jaw clenched. "That's what I thought. Okay, I'm gonna need a blockade of two black and whites at the road leading to the old logging camp off of Elm, along with safe entry at the station. Don't use the radios."

I could hear a noise that Rhonda was saying something in return.

"Yep, see ya soon."

Tanner peered up the road, and I knew better than to ask what he had learned about Doyle.

"What's your uncle's name?" Sergeant Tanner asked, catching my eyes on him.

"Derek Smith."

"That's the man that reported you missing?" he clarified.

"I assume so."

"Sergeant Tanner, how much farther until we get back to the main road?" Lucas asked.

"It's probably another ten minutes or so. Why?"

"I have the feeling that we'll have some company soon," Lucas said as if he wasn't completely with us. Maybe the power or "Light" or whatever was communicating with him again. "Is this road on GPS maps?"

"Sarah, check for me here on my computer." He guided me verbally through finding the maps. It was on the GPS map, but not as a through road.

"Hopefully, that means they'll dismiss it as an option," Lucas said, but I could tell by his voice that he wasn't set on that being likely.

I think Sergeant Tanner sensed it too as he pressed the accelerator down a little more, which caused us to feel every single bump and rut in the road.

We drove on for a minute or two before Tanner spoke again, "Lucas, how do you know Sarah, and how did you come to know that she was in trouble?"

I looked back at Lucas, just a quick glance, though, because with all of the bumping, I couldn't keep myself facing backwards. I had no idea how he would answer this.

Lucas had his gaze fixed on the rearview mirror and Tanner's face, "I knew Sarah's mom." He paused, "She asked me to keep an eye on Sarah before she died. For a while, I didn't know what had become of her. Once I found she had been taken in by a relative, I started looking into her uncle. Neither Sarah's mother nor father had a brother, and that tipped me off right away. Let's just say I'm glad I went with my instincts to follow them out into the woods."

How he managed to tell that story without telling a single lie, but also not giving away too much, was beyond me, but he did it. I don't know when, if ever, I would stop being surprised by Lucas.

"We've got company," Lucas said, his voice direct and without emotion.

"What?" Sergeant Tanner exclaimed. "Where?"

"I just saw a flash of lights behind us. It could only be them." Even speaking to Tanner, Lucas used that other tone of voice for "them" that sent chills down my spine.

"Well, I'm entering an area I don't know well enough to keep my lights off, but we got to keep going. Ain't no way I'm stopping now."

"Agreed," Lucas said, "We have a head start and a guide that knows what he's doing. We trust you, Sergeant Tanner." The way he said it was deep and reverberated in the car. I think Tanner probably felt that trust down to his bones as he pushed a little harder on the accelerator. We drove down the bumpy dirt road at a speed that I was sure wasn't good for his car, much less my insides as they were jarred about. All I could do was hope there wasn't going to be any wildlife darting in front of us or any other unforeseen issues.

A panicked minute or two passed where I was just trying to keep my breathing regulated so I didn't puke right there on Sergeant Tanner's dashboard.

I was still focusing on my breathing when I saw a glimmer of light up ahead.

"There!" I exclaimed as I pointed through the trees.

Sergeant Tanner called Rhonda again, so she could let the other officers know we were one minute out without giving away our position. He had just hung-up when a deer darted in front of us. Tanner swerved, narrowly missing the deer as he and I both screamed out in alarm. It was a miracle he didn't lose control of the car.

We were still recovering when we saw the paved road, the blue and red flashing lights of his backup serving as beacons in the darkness. Lucas had given updates that the headlights behind us had never gained any ground, and here we were pulling up to safety. Two cars were waiting on us, the number we were expecting. The drivers of the cars were outside of them. Sergeant Tanner blurred past them and kept driving.

Before we knew it, the lights of the town were in front of us. We had on our siren and lights and were flying through the stop-lights. We pulled into the station and right to a door on the side. Sergeant Tanner slammed the car into park, told me to stay inside, and got out to let Lucas out. He came around to my door and opened it while his eyes darted all over. I looked up to see two other officers looking around as well as they moved us quickly into the building.

Inside the bright light of the station, I let out a big, rattled sigh causing Tanner to look at me.

"You okay?" he asked.

"Yes, thanks to you, Sergeant Tanner," I responded, giving him a side hug.

"You're safe now," he said softly but with conviction. "And call me, Brian."

"Rhonda," he spoke over the top of my head. "Could you please find Sarah some clean clothes and help her get cleaned up?" I smiled at him again.

"Absolutely, sir. Come on, Sarah." I started to move towards her but hesitated as I looked at Lucas.

"Don't worry, Sarah," Brian said. "I'll make sure he gets cleaned up as well. He isn't in any danger. And you're safe here as well."

"Thank you," I said to Brian again. I reached out and grabbed Lucas's still cuffed hand. He gave me a squeeze and a nod, looking so tired. More tired than I had ever seen him. He let go of my hand as Rhonda led me down the hall and to the right, into the women's locker room.

CHAPTER 15

After Rhonda got me squared away, complete with all I needed to shower and brush my teeth, she gave me some privacy, saying she would still be in the locker room on the other side of the lockers if I needed anything. I really appreciated both the assurance that she was close by and the privacy, because when I stepped into the shower, I could no longer hold back the tears. They were mostly silent, but they streamed down my face as my body shook. What was this nightmare I was living in?

Lucas was so great, and I was grateful he rescued me, but part of me still wished I were back home in my bed, oblivious to the truths I had learned in the past few days. Then again, would I want to be in the dark about who I was living with? Would I want to be in a place with someone who was clearly trying to change me into something I'm not? I had to keep my mind focused on that, even though the fear was almost crippling. I wanted to be awakened to the way the world actually was.

I felt like such a child as the tears continued to come. All at once, I could sense my mom again. My eyes were already closed so

I could picture her leaning over me in my bed, singing over me and stroking my hair, touching my face, smiling at me. In my memory, I knew she was singing to me, but I couldn't remember the words. I felt calm settle into my body as the song lyrics slowly began in my mind…

My Beloved, don't cry as I hold you tight

Feel my warmth as you're hidden in The Light

I've counted all your tears

I've erased all your fears

Shadows are only revealed in the presence of The Light

In my arms, you can be sure that you're safe from the fight…

I felt so connected to my mom. As her song played in my head and my heart, I thought about how my mom's last thoughts had been of me. Even as she was in pain and dying, she made sure that Lucas would take care of me. Knowing that Lucas not only knew her, but was now taking care of me because of her, was so comforting. But it also made me realize there was still so much I didn't know. Lucas was the only one who could answer my questions, and he wasn't in the women's locker room.

I turned off the water and dried myself off quickly, then applied some of the lotion that Rhonda had given me. I pulled on the t-shirt and sweats she provided, grateful for something clean to put on, even if they were a little big on me. I had been warmed by the shower but was chilled by the events of the past few days. Honestly, I wasn't even sure what day it was or how many days it had been since the furnace, or the bonfire, or even arriving at camp.

I moved around the last bay of lockers as I was zipping up the hooded sweatshirt that Rhonda had lent me to find her sitting on the bench. She looked up at me as I came around. "Are you okay?" she asked with sympathy in her eyes.

I wasn't sure if she had heard me crying so I replied, "I'm better now, thanks." And I was telling her the truth.

Her eyes conveyed her sympathy as well as her pity. "I'm glad the shower helped. It seems like you have been through a lot over these last few days. Let's go find Brian and see if he wants to say anything to you before we find a spot for you to sleep."

"Okay, thank you."

She gave me a small smile before she turned to walk out of the locker room, holding the door for me.

We found Brian down the hall with a group of officers. Lucas wasn't with him. I felt my heart start to beat faster.

Where is he?

Rhonda had reassured me that no one tried to come through the blockade, but I still wanted Lucas near.

Brian stopped talking when one of his men nodded in my direction.

"You doing okay, Sarah?" he asked kindly, as he turned to me.

"I'm doing better, thank you," I replied quietly.

Rhonda spoke up, "She is about dead on her feet. Do you need to question her anymore, or can she get some sleep?"

He looked at me, wrinkling his forehead as he continued to really look at me, searching for some answers in my face. He took a deep breath, and after letting it out slowly, said, "We can talk more once you have had some rest."

"Where is Lucas?" I asked.

"He is in a cell. We have to follow protocol, but he won't come to any harm."

Lucas in a cell; it was wrong on so many levels, but instead of getting angry, I asked, "May I see him please?" Tears filled my eyes.

"I don't normally let that happen, but I will let you see him, so you know he is here and well. I'll come with you." I'm sure he had to make sure Lucas and I wouldn't talk about anything suspicious.

I nodded, feeling the heaviness of my head. The adrenaline had definitely worn off. "That's fine," I said softly.

We went down a hallway, and a guard let us into a room with two holding cells. Lucas was lying down on the bed but quickly turned to sit up when he heard us come in.

He looked so tired, but he was still beautiful, and he was here for me. He was looking at me intently, almost as though he were checking me over for harm. Then he relaxed his gaze and gave me a small smile, which did nothing but set my heart racing.

"I'm going to make sure Sarah gets some rest," Brian said from behind me, "but she wanted to see you first."

"Thank you, Brian," Lucas said, giving him a nod, the way guys do. I wanted Lucas to move towards me and touch my hand through the bars. Out of respect, I think for Brian, he didn't move to even stand from his bed.

Brian turned to me, "Lucas will be fine in here; he has a bed and a blanket. Let's get you settled now."

"Are you on high alert?" Lucas asked Brian.

"Yes, even my off-duty officers have been called in."

"Thank you, Brian."

"Once you two have had some rest, I'm going to need more answers."

"Yes sir," Lucas agreed.

Rhonda led me into an office where a cot was set up, along with a makeshift nightstand that held a small lamp and a bottle of water. It was better than a cave or a cell, I told myself, thinking again of Lucas in his cell. I was dead on my feet, and the weight of my exhaustion was evident the moment I laid down. I didn't remember falling asleep; my body just shut down.

I awoke the next morning, not because I was rested, but because something had woken me. When I sat up on the edge of the cot, my head spun a little, probably from dehydration or maybe the adrenaline crash I was most certainly experiencing. I grabbed the water bottle on the nightstand and drank the entire thing before standing up. I walked to the door and heard voices but couldn't make out what they were saying. I opened the door slowly. No one was in the hallway, so I started walking towards where I heard voices.

Walking down the hallway, I was better able to take in the building. Last night, when it was my sanctuary, it had gleamed like a palace. But this morning, I could see that the flooring was old, and the wall paint smudged and yellowed with age. The station was well taken care of, just older and well-worn in that small-town kind of way.

I was close to the door where the voices were speaking so I could clearly make out what they were saying now. A voice, which I recognized as Brian, spoke. "We've done all we can do, Rhonda.

This is out of our jurisdiction and out of my hands. I know in my gut that these two are telling the truth, but from what Lucas is saying, her uncle is bound to show up here with the right legal documents to take her with him."

"Well, you can't just let her go with him," a female voice said forcefully. I knew right away it was Rhonda. "You should have heard her crying in the shower. Her face and eyes showed that she has already walked through hell, and I'm not okay with just giving her to whoever caused that."

"I agree with you, Rhonda, believe me, but I can't change the law."

Rhonda must have made some sort of face or gesture because Brian continued with, "I'm on your side here, but she's a minor. Listen, this is a federal case now, and they'll check out her story before they let him take her."

"I guess that's the best I can hope for," Rhonda returned. "I'm going to check on her."

Rhonda walked out and almost ran into me standing there eavesdropping.

"Sarah, you're awake," she said, surprised to see me standing there.

"Uh, yes. Just trying to find the women's locker room again." By then, Brian had come to stand behind her.

"Oh, okay, yes, I'm sure you got turned around last night. Follow me." Rhonda led me back down the hallway toward the locker room.

After I had used the facilities, Rhonda walked me down to a break room area. "Would you like some breakfast?" I eagerly accepted her offer. Cereal and Pop-tarts were my options, and I took both. She also gave me a banana and a bottle of water.

"Is Lucas okay?" I asked, knowing from what I heard that Rhonda was on my side.

"Yes, he has already eaten and is now in the interrogation room."

"He really did save me."

"Everyone here believes you," she assured me, "but we are officers of the law and, as such, have to follow the law and our protocols. We might be a small-town station, but we still have to follow the proper procedures."

"I understand, it was just hard to see him behind bars."

"He's fine; his only concern is your safety." My breath hitched inside of me. His only concern was for me, even though I was the reason he was behind bars in the first place.

"Can I see him?" I asked as my eyes once again filled with tears. I needed to be close to Lucas.

"Probably not yet."

"Why not?"

"He's in the interrogation room with an FBI agent," she said matter-of-factly.

"Okay," I said, helpless to stop the tear that trickled down my cheek.

"Oh Sarah, I know it's hard honey but he really is okay."

"I believe you; this whole thing has just been more than I can take."

"I only know a fraction of it, but it sounds like it would be more than most people could take." She sat down beside me and put her arm around me, then continued. "Brian is a good man and a good officer; he'll get this whole thing straightened out."

After the FBI agent finished with Lucas, Brian let me in to see him in the interrogation room. I walked into the mirrored room and walked directly to Lucas. He was cuffed to the table, but his face was welcoming, and just being next to him felt like home. He couldn't hug me, but I hugged him. I didn't care that people were watching. While there wasn't the rush of goodness I had felt before, I still experienced the sensation of being able to fully breathe again. He smelled of soap and of something better than my words could describe.

I sat down next to him, so close that our legs were touching. He must have sensed my need because he leaned into me as if to give me extra reassurance that he was there.

"Did you get any sleep?" I asked, not sure of what we could talk about with people watching.

"Some, thank you for asking." He looked at me with kind eyes and gave me a smile. "How are you doing, Sarah? There has been a lot happening over the last few days."

"Is Uncle going to take me?" I blurted out quickly.

He looked a bit taken back that that was my first line of thought. "Sarah" he began, but I interjected, "I heard Brian talking, and he said you thought my uncle would have the right papers to claim me." I felt bad that Brian now knew I had eavesdropped, but I also needed an answer.

"Sarah," he said calmly, "Would I let Uncle take you?"

His question wasn't really a question, and there was a firmness to his voice that caused me to turn my head to look at him. I looked directly into his eyes. Even though he was sitting there calmly, his eyes were fierce. Staring into his eyes, I felt that familiar feeling of peace come over me.

"No, but the police seem to think they will have to let me go with him," I said weakly.

"Brian doesn't think that, and neither does the agent." He sat forward. "I will not let him take you." He said it fiercely, but for my ears only. I knew he wanted me to look at him, but for some reason I couldn't. I felt fear rising up inside of me once again. If the police couldn't protect me, how could only one man protect me? He reached out with his chained hands and tilted my chin, so I had to look over at him. I closed my eyes because his gaze was just too much.

"Sarah," he said patiently, "Sarah open your eyes, please."

"I can't," I whispered.

"Do you trust me?"

Of course, I trusted Lucas; of course, I did. So why was I so prone to fear? One man couldn't protect me, but one Lucas sure could.

"Yes, of course, I trust you, Lucas." I opened my eyes as I spoke, and he smiled just a barely-there kind of smile. I leaned into him again.

"Good," he returned. I took a full, deep breath, the fear subsiding once again. There were voices in the hallway. Lucas dropped his voice to a whisper, "Your trust matters because we won't be staying here until Uncle comes. I won't give him the chance to take you, not with legal papers, and not with force."

"But the police will stop you," I whispered back.

"I have a friend who is here to help." I wanted to lean back to look at him but knew I needed to be close to hear him.

"Who?" I asked.

"You'll see," he said with a deep sigh as he slumped down into his chair.

"Lucas, are you okay?" I asked, touching his arm. He was tired, but there was more to it than that, and I think he sensed I wanted the answer to contain more as well.

"I am getting weaker," he whispered without looking at me. Instead of the fear returning at his admission of weakness, I felt like it gave me more courage. I knew that each time he gave something of himself to me, it weakened him. And yet, he wasn't afraid. If he wasn't afraid, then I would try my best not to be afraid either.

"Well," I paused, trying to think of something to help, "why don't we just light a fire and throw you in?" I offered, joking with him to cover my anxiety.

He gave a soft huff of a laugh, "That's not how it works."

"It seemed to work great the last time," I said, smiling and trying to get him to smile.

He was looking at me, searching my face for something when a voice behind us said, "Sarah, this is Agent Owen Wright of the FBI. He wants to ask you a few questions."

"Okay," I nodded to Brian.

A man, who looked to be in his thirties, came around the corner, and just as I had done with Lucas the first time I saw him, I sensed right away that this man was different too.

"Lucas, you'll need to come with me while Sarah and Agent Wright talk," he said while unlocking Lucas's cuffs. He wasn't on alert, which led me to believe that Brian didn't fear Lucas but was continuing to follow protocol.

"That's fine, Sergeant Tanner."

"Lucas," I said his name, unsure of how much I should say.

"It's okay, Sarah. He is on our side," Lucas said with a smile. I read more into his statement, knowing he meant the agent was like Lucas. He was with the Eklesi.

✳   ✳   ✳

"Hi, Sarah," Agent Wright said, offering me his hand.

"Hi, Agent Wright." I shook his hand and felt the same warmth radiate from him that I usually felt with Lucas. I couldn't help but smile.

He returned my smile and said, "Please, call me Owen." He gestured for me to have a seat.

"Owen," I returned, sitting back in the chair that I had been in before. He didn't walk to the other side of the table but pulled back the chair that Lucas had been sitting in.

"We're fine in here," Owen said to another officer who nodded and walked out, closing the door behind him. Owen sat down.

"It's such a pleasure to meet you, Sarah, and I'm sorry things have been so rough on you." He was still talking at a normal tone, and I knew that others were listening.

He started by asking me all the same questions that Brian had done. He got up and started moving around the room at one point, making his way fully around the room before sitting back down slowly in the same relaxed position he had been in before. As he sat back down, he spoke in the same manner he'd been speaking all along; confident, relaxed, controlled.

"Okay, they can no longer hear us, so I can tell you what's going to happen next."

"What? How can they not hear us?"

"I have safe-guarded the room." He could tell I was about to speak, so he held up his hand. "They can still see us, so continue to act as before; you're just answering my questions. I promise we will explain all of this to you soon, once you are safe."

"Okay," I said, choosing to trust him, "What now?"

"I have the documents to prove that your abduction happened in another state. With that, I will be able to take you and Lucas with me back to your jurisdiction."

"Will they buy that?"

"I can be very persuasive."

"But can you lie?"

"I can't," he said calmly with a serious look on his face. I had only known Owen a short time, but it didn't seem like a serious nature came very easily for him. He must have been doing it for the benefit of our audience. "Everything in my documents is true." He continued, "You were taken by Uncle from somewhere other than this state, and you will be returning to that jurisdiction."

"Okay, what do I need to do?" I asked, hoping he'd reveal more of the plan.

"Nothing. Sarah, this situation is already confusing enough for you, and I don't want to give you more details than you need at the moment. I need you to just trust me and go with it."

"I think I can handle that. How long until we leave?"

"Sergeant Tanner really wants me to wait for his Lieutenant to arrive. Apparently, the Lieutenant needs to okay the transfer of custody, but he can't be bothered to come in to work until he's had his morning coffee. As an FBI Agent, my jurisdiction supersedes the locals, so I can take you whenever I want. There's no way we are waiting and risking your uncle showing up."

"Can they still hear us?" I asked, feeling a little nervous that they were hearing our whole plan.

"Well, not what we are saying right now, they are hearing us corroborate Lucas's story."

"They have been so nice to me here, but I'm so ready to be somewhere truly safe."

"We are eager for you to be there as well." Owen smiled warmly and placed his hand over mine on the table, letting his warmth flow and calm my fears. After about a minute, he removed his hand.

"Better?"

"Just a little," I said with a smile. "A little" was an understatement.

Rhonda came in not too long after to take me to the break-room and offered me a snack. She informed me that Brian had been on the phone the entire time trying to confirm Owen's story about Derek Smith. I wasn't sure what luck he was having or if Owen's identity was made up, just as Lucas's had been in the camp. I was nervous, then, when Brian pulled me into his office, Rhonda right on my heels.

"How are you holding up?" he asked me kindly.

"I'm doing better. I'm glad that Agent Wright believes Lucas and me."

Brian studied my face and asked, "So you feel safe to leave with him?"

"Yes, he is part of the FBI, and said he would get me into protective custody."

Rhonda jumped in, "Sarge, you don't think it's safe?"

Brian leaned back in his chair and let out a big breath through pursed lips, "To tell ya the truth, I don't know what to believe today." He paused. "Agent Wright has the badge, the credentials, and I do feel like he has your best interest at heart."

"But?" Rhonda prodded.

"But," He paused. "Everything about this situation seems off. A man claims you are missing and that he's your uncle, then come to find out he was the one holding you against your will. This Lucas that you have only known a short while seems to be willing to do anything to keep you safe. Now, Agent Wright shows up and says there are all these charges being brought against your supposed uncle." He took another deep breath and let it out slowly. "These just aren't things that our town usually deals with."

"If it makes you feel any better, this situation has been crazy for me too, and these things aren't something I normally deal with either." I gave him a small smile.

"Of course, Sarah, and I'm definitely not blaming you, I just want to make sure that I do the right thing."

"The right thing by the law or the right thing by me?" I asked, really wanting to know his answer.

"I'm hopin' to do both here," he said, looking at me. "Are you tellin' me that they aren't the same?" He seemed sincere in wanting to help me, and he had already proven that he would protect me even if he didn't understand the whole situation.

"No, I think they are the same, and I think I should go with Agent Wright. I just wasn't sure what you had found out on jurisdiction or whatever for me to be able to go with him."

"The law is on his side. The FBI does have jurisdiction. It's more how he came to be here. We haven't even filed a report yet."

"Sir," Rhonda piped in, "that was probably on me. While Sarah was sleeping, I ran Derek's name through any database we had access to. I didn't really find anything, but maybe my search triggered something in their system."

"I don't know about all of that, but I do know this…" he was interrupted by loud voices down the hall in the direction of the lobby.

Brian moved for the door just as it swung open. Owen was standing there looking like a fierce warrior. "Sergeant Tanner, I'm afraid our time is up. For Sarah's safety, I need to take her and Lucas right now." His voice conveyed his urgency.

"Is he here?" Brian and I asked at the same time.

"Yes, exactly," Owen said. "It's time for us to go. Derek and some of his friends have arrived to speak with the chief."

"Shouldn't we just arrest him?" Brian asked. You could hear the noise down the hallway growing.

"The arrest won't stick if we don't have a witness to testify." Owen said with such conviction in his voice that I shuddered. "It's time for us to go, Sergeant Tanner." Again, there seemed to be some sort of power in his voice.

"Where is your car?" Brian asked Owen.

"Already at the back door."

"Head for the back door, now," Brian said quickly, "I'll get Lucas. Rhonda move to the front, I'm sure the rest have already figured out what is going on."

Owen was reaching for one of my arms, but I turned and quickly hugged Rhonda and then Brian. "Thank you both. For everything."

Brian had a concerned look on his face as he let go of me, still holding onto just my hand. "If you can, let us know how things go for you, okay?"

"Okay, I will." I gave his hand a squeeze before releasing it.

"Sarah, now," Owen said, grabbing my hand. This time I went with him willingly as we moved quickly to the car. A minute later, Brian was there with Lucas who was still wearing handcuffs.

"We'll stall 'em as long as possible," Brian said, slamming the door and then running back inside.

CHAPTER 16

We drove through the alley behind the store next to us and turned down a side street. Owen maneuvered the car through the somewhat busy streets, making so many different turns that I wasn't really sure which way we were headed. I had been afraid to even breathe much less talk in case Uncle followed us.

I turned and looked out the back window.

"We're okay, Sarah," Lucas said softly.

"No one is following us," Owen confirmed. "For now, they can only see what I want them to see, but I won't be able to hold them off forever."

I nodded, trying to let that soak in. For now, we were out of danger. But what about the people that had helped us back at the station?

"Do you think everyone at the station will be okay?" I asked quietly. Lucas was sitting next to me in the back, and Owen was driving.

"Yes," Lucas spoke with such conviction in his voice; I had no reason to doubt it was true.

"I never thought I would be the one rescuing Lucas," Owen said with a smile as he looked back at us in the rearview mirror. "It seems you're always the one that gets sent to get the rest of us out of trouble." I could tell his words didn't bother Lucas as he flashed a grin in return.

"All of us need rescuing at one time or another." Lucas looked at me as he spoke. His words were certainly not lost on me.

"Any chance you guys are going to uncuff me anytime soon," Lucas asked with a mischievous smile. Owen passed the key back to me, and as soon as the cuffs were off, Lucas pulled me to him.

"Where exactly are we headed?" I asked.

"Someplace safe," Owen answered.

"I'm not really going into the witness protection program, am I?" I asked.

"No," Owen replied with a soft chuckle. "And I believe I said protective custody."

"So, what's awaiting me in 'protective custody'?" I asked Lucas.

"Training of sorts," he answered.

"Training? Training for what?"

"You might not yet believe this, but you are destined for great things."

"Lucas, I am trying so hard to be patient. And I know I don't understand everything, and yes, I realize that in time it will all make sense. But for now, can you please tell me *something*?"

"You know that I knew your mother, right?" Lucas began.

I nodded, anxious to finally hear how all of the events of the last few days tied together.

"I knew her because I was the one that taught her about The Light. Her 'rescue,' if you will, wasn't nearly as dramatic as yours." He paused, getting a far off look in his eyes. "She was all alone in the world. She had been left on the orphanage steps as a baby. She grew up there. Despite her hard years there, she was a very sweet and loving little girl. I met her when she was 12. I was there to transition her to a family, and to get a sense of her direction in life."

"Once I was sure of her direction, I placed her with a couple that couldn't have children. They understood The Light and raised her to do the same."

"My grandparents?" I asked quietly.

"Yes," he said with a pained expression.

"They died when I was young. I didn't really know them."

"They were killed, Sarah."

"By Uncle's people?" I asked.

"Yes."

I could feel the anger rising inside of me. "Why do they hate my family so much?"

"Because your family was and is very important." Lucas's words were measured and direct.

"But why? We aren't famous or world leaders, or anything." I could not wrap my head around the idea that all my family had been murdered.

"You're famous, Sarah, just not to anyone in your world. But to the Eklesi, your lineage is legend." He paused, letting the truth of my ancestry rest on me. "You come from a pure line of those who are called Light Bearers. They did great things for The Light and will continue to do so through you."

"But wouldn't the line have been broken with my mom since she was adopted? And what *is* a Light Bearer? And does that mean my father was a Light Bearer too? Did they know they were Light Bearers? Is this something that chooses you or you choose it?"

"No, you'll see, yes, yes, yes," Owen shot back in quick succession.

"Wait, what?" I asked, laughing, confused by Owen's rapid-fire answers to my questions.

Before he could answer me, another more alarming thought occurred to me: *What about Amelia?* It apparently wasn't just a thought, because Lucas answered me.

"Amelia is okay for now, Sarah," Lucas answered. "As for your other questions, the line came from your mother's biological family. Your grandparents were the end of another pure line, but they could not have children. The two lines were united, making one pure line again."

He continued, "A Light Bearer is a bearer of The Light."

"I kind of figured that."

Lucas continued, "Your dad was also a Light Bearer... " He hesitated for just a moment, then continued. "Amelia is still... undecided," He said, answering a question I hadn't even asked.

I looked at him in silence for a moment before turning my gaze out the window. *Amelia is still undecided.* I couldn't shake that thought from my head.

"Will I like the training?" I asked, trying for a lighter subject than what was brewing in my mind.

"I think you will enjoy it very much."

"Will I become like you guys? Able to withstand fire and all of that?"

Before he could answer, another thought occurred to me. "Lucas, can you tell me now, what happened in the furnace?"

"What you saw with the furnace was not a normal occurrence. That was a rare thing brought about by a complete inhabiting of The Light."

"Wait . . . The Light can inhabit things . . . er . . . people . . . beings?" The questions and confusion about this whole situation came rushing back to me. "Obviously, you're not a human, are you?"

He just looked at me like I already knew that answer.

Owen interrupted, "Lucas, it's time. We've reached the distance I'm able to shield us, but we are far enough away that they won't know where we've gone."

"Okay, let's go," Lucas replied.

I hadn't really been focusing on the storefronts and houses that we were driving by, but they were starting to blur. They had an iridescent quality to them, with bright prisms of light bursting through. I blinked my eyes rapidly, then rubbed them, trying to clear my vision.

"It's not your eyes, Sarah," Lucas said. I looked back at him, and everything in the car seemed normal, but behind him, the same thing was happening to the buildings and structures out his window.

"What is it then?" I felt my body start to tremor and tingle. "What is happening?"

"We're passing through the veil."

"The veil?" I asked, the panic in my voice evident.

"Yes, between your realm and ours."

"Lucas, how can you say that with such calm in your..." but my voice trailed off when I looked at him to see his eyes closed, a look of utter contentment on his face. The brightness of Lucas that had faded during our time in the woods was returning in all its glory. I turned to look at Owen. His eyes were closed, and his face was at peace too. Both looked as if they were breathing fresh air for the first time in years, like fish returned to the water.

"Is this the realm where you're from?" No one answered, and I didn't really need an answer. I could tell they were where they were meant to be. My tingling and tremors had ceased, and I felt the familiar sensation of warmth spreading through my body.

The buildings outside were no longer visible, just shiny prisms of light tremoring and shaking to the point that I could no longer look out the side window; it was just too disorienting. I looked out the front window, and it seemed as though we were headed for an even brighter light. The movement along the side of us made it appear we were moving at an incredible speed, but I didn't feel anything except the warmth circulating through my body. I realized I had a huge smile on my face, just like Owen and Lucas.

I leaned against the backseat as the feeling of utter peace flowed through my body and made my head feel heavy. I laid my head back, then rolled it to my right side to look at Lucas. He had his eyes opened now, and the brilliance that surrounded us matched the brilliance radiating from him.

"We're almost there," he said. His voice had taken on a different quality. Like a bell or something, except still deep and strong. It just seemed so perfect and clear.

We kept looking at each other, smiling. While Lucas's countenance was more radiant than I had ever seen it, I didn't have to look away. Whether my eyes were adjusting, or my body was changing, I wasn't sure. But I never wanted to change how I felt at that moment. I was utterly content, filled with inexpressible joy.

I sensed, more than felt, that we were slowing down. As soon as I had that thought, we passed through the bright light of the tunnel.

"We're here!" Owen's voice rang out.

Lucas and I both just laughed. Not at him, but instead, we laughed with the joy we all shared.

Owen stopped in front of a building made of white marble. Three flights of stairs led to an entrance graced by grand columns and a beautifully ornate overhang. The doors at the front of the building were solid gold and shone as if the sun were reflecting off of them though they were fully in the shade of the massive overhang.

Lucas and Owen climbed out and smiled at each other like two brothers who'd found their way home. Lucas opened the door and extended a hand to me. As I took his hand and stepped out of the car, I was once again aware of the warmth flowing through me.

I held Lucas's hand, then reached for Owen's hand as well, as together we headed up the stairs. It felt as though we were floating up the stairs, each step effortless and light.

Lucas gave two hard knocks on the right door. The doors were taller than us, more than double Lucas's height, with intricate carvings embedded in the gold. Before I had a chance to really look at them, both doors opened wide. We would have easily fit side-by-side through one of the doors, but with both doors open, the enormity of their size was all the more evident.

The room we walked into was just as beautiful as the outside of the building. The interior space seemed even larger inside than it had on the outside. The ceiling was filled with windows, some so clear I could hardly tell if I was inside or out, and some made of colored glass that sent shafts of rainbow light across the floor, like scattered sunlight through a tree. My gaze traveled from the windows, following one of the streams of light to the floor on which I stood. The sight of it took my breath away, astounded by the sheer beauty I beheld. The floor seemed to be made of jewels, pebble-sized in shape, but brilliant in color. I couldn't shake the feeling that I had seen those pebbles somewhere before. Unable to resist the urge, I reached down to feel the floor under my feet. I was surprised by how smooth it felt to my touch.

As I knelt down at the floor, I noticed that I no longer wore the police sweats, but instead, I was wearing a white gown.

Where am I?

My mind reeled with a sense of euphoria I had never felt before.

I had let go of Owen's hand to feel the floor, but Lucas was still holding my other hand and gave it a squeeze and a tiny pull as if to get my attention. Looking up, I saw someone else had joined us. The most beautiful woman I had ever seen was literally glowing before my eyes. She laughed at the bewilderment she must have seen on my face. Her laugh was the most magnificent sound I had ever heard. Slowly, I stood, my mind in a state of awe. The sound of her laugh and the brilliance of her face were simply mesmerizing.

She held out her hands to me, "Welcome to Ganheela, sweet Sarah Joy. I am Pneuma."

I still couldn't speak, but I gave her a slight nod of my head as I put my hands into hers.

"We have been so eager to welcome you."

I had no idea who "we" were or what this place was or why they would want to welcome me, but I shared her eagerness. "I am honored to be here," I said, surprised that my voice had a different, more beautiful quality to it as well. I laughed at the sound of my own voice, causing Owen, Lucas, and Pneuma to laugh along with me. Their laughter, unrestrained and overcome with merriment, filled me with such joy I almost wept. It was almost too much for me to take in. I looked down for just a moment, trying to collect myself.

The laughter trickled away as I looked at my feet, then Pneuma spoke. "Lucas, please take Sarah to rest. I think she needs more time to acclimate."

"Of course," he said, bowing slightly to Pneuma.

"Owen, would you accompany me, please?"

"Of course," he replied, bowing just as Lucas had. I wondered if I should bow as well. Instinctively, I knew I was in the presence of someone very special, someone royal. Lucas tucked my hand in the crook of his arm and led me away, but before I left, I bowed as they had. As I raised my head, I caught the delight in Pneuma's eyes. She gave me a wink and turned to put her hand through Owen's arm as they walked away.

I took a few steps and then felt my legs buckle underneath me, and just as fast, Lucas swept me into his arms.

"Come, Sarah, it's time for you to rest."

CHAPTER 17

As the light of the morning crossed my face, I smiled and stretched, moving my hands across the softest, silkiest sheets I had ever felt. I sat up and swung my feet around, pushing my toes through the plush rug at the side of the bed. I breathed in deeply, just simply enjoying my surroundings.

The walls of the room seemed to be made of only flowing white drapes. I watched as the breeze moved them gently as if to beckon me outside. I moved to stand and pulled back the fabric, stepping out onto an open patio that led right into the lushest garden I had ever seen. It was absolutely breathtaking.

The trees and bushes were laden with bright fruits. Each plant bloomed with brilliantly colored flowers, colors that I couldn't name and had maybe never seen before. The greens were more vibrant than any green in my world. The blue of the sky was more brilliant than a crystal-clear ocean. This was no landscaped garden. It was wilderness with no flaw, unstained by death. I couldn't take in the splendor of it all. I could hear birds' sweet songs and the rushing sound of water flowing in the distance. Beyond the trees, I could see the rays of the morning sun, soft and diffuse, giving way to a rainbow shining over a magnificent waterfall.

I breathed in deeply of the sweetest fragrance I had ever smelled. I wasn't sure if it was just one plant that I was smelling or a beautiful mixture of all of them. I closed my eyes as I took another deep breath. It was as if I could literally smell the splendor.

"Now you see why I couldn't tell you anything before," Lucas said softly behind me. I opened my eyes to look at him. "I could have never described it. This is something you have to experience," he said with a brilliant smile that I returned.

"Walk with me." He held out his hand to me, and we turned to walk down a tree-lined path that I hadn't noticed before.

"Lucas, is this where you're from?"

"No, I'm from a place that is far beyond your present reach. Ganheela is like a second home to me. Not completely the same, but with a lot of the same elements." I felt no frustration at his lack of details or information. I was completely content, except for the hunger I was beginning to feel.

"Can I eat one of these fruits?"

"Of course, try this one," he easily plucked a purplish-red, pear-shaped fruit from the tree right next to us. It was so shiny and beautiful that it almost looked fake. Once again, I felt an overwhelming sense that I had seen this before, much the same way I felt with the jeweled pebble floor in the entryway. But I knew that I had never been to Ganheela before.

"Are you sure I can eat this?" I asked. "It looks too perfect to eat," I said, smiling at Lucas.

He smiled in return and nodded at the fruit, so I took a bite, and immediately flavors as I had never tasted exploded in my mouth – sweet, tangy, indescribable. The fruit was so juicy that it ran down my chin as I took a couple more bites, thoroughly enjoying the flavor, the texture, the . . . it was almost like my five senses weren't enough to take in every aspect of this fruit.

Lucas was watching me enjoy the fruit. I wondered if the thoughts in my head were playing across my face as I ate. From the delight in his eyes, I knew they must have been.

"Aren't you hungry, Lucas?"

"No, but thanks for asking," he said, still smiling.

"I can tell you are feeling much better," I said, observing him from head to toe once more.

"I am, thank you."

We continued walking as I ate more of the fruit.

"What's this fruit called?" I asked.

"Fragi."

"Fragi," I repeated. "I love it."

After a few more bites, I felt full, but I hadn't even eaten half the fruit.

"Are you full?" Lucas asked.

"Yes, I am. But I don't want to waste this."

"You won't," he said, taking it from me. He grabbed a nearby flat rock and knelt down to dig a small, shallow hole, placing the rest of my fruit in it. He pushed the dirt up over the fragi, then gently pressed the soil down with his hands.

He stood back up, smiling at me.

"Hiding it doesn't mean we aren't wasting it," I said, smiling.

"I didn't hide it, I planted it." He grinned confidently and continued. "Your fragi will bring life to even more fragi."

Lucas was so great at putting positive spins on anything.

"Well, I guess now I need something to get this juice off my hands and face." But as I touched my hands together and then touched my face, the juice was no longer there.

"Are you sure about that?" Lucas asked, chuckling.

"I guess not," I said, feeling somewhat surprised. Just moments before, I was covered with the sweet, sticky juice of the fruit.

"We should get you to the water anyway."

"Why is that?"

"The water will help you acclimate to Ganheela, purifying you from what you're still carrying from your world."

"Are we still in my world?" I asked.

"Yes. Ganheela is a hidden realm within your world."

"Hidden realm?"

"Yes, when we passed through the veil, we moved into this realm that sits in your world, but outside of time as you know it. This is still the same sun and the same earth. But we are in an area that is pure and bountiful; outside the time of man."

"So, does that mean that the people in my world are sort of frozen right now?"

"Sort of. We left at a certain time in your world, and we will enter it at the same time. More specifically, we have stepped out of time instead of your world ceasing to move, if that makes sense."

"Sort of," I shrugged my shoulders and laughed at the impossibility of it all. Clearly, I had no idea what he was talking about. As we came to the edge of a slow-moving river, I felt overwhelmed by the brilliance of my surroundings. Rainbows of light were bouncing off the water at every ripple.

"Does this river flow from the waterfall I saw earlier?" I asked softly.

"Yes," he confirmed.

"Do we just put our feet in?" I asked, remembering Lucas had said we were going to the water to be cleansed, but not wanting to do anything wrong to mess up this wonderful place.

"How about we go all the way in?" he challenged. I looked at him with some confusion and saw he was holding out his hand to me.

"What about my dress?" I asked, still marveling that it was completely clean.

"It will be just fine."

"Okay."

I reached for his hand and let him lead me into the water. The river did not look very deep, but Lucas continued to lead me in until we were chest-deep in the water.

I started to resist him.

"I think I'm plenty deep here, Lucas," slight panic taking control of my voice. But as quickly as the panic rose in my voice, a familiar sensation came over me. The warmth I'd felt in the tunnel in Owen's car was back. The same warmth I felt from Lucas's embrace, now flowed again throughout my body, from my hair to the tips of my toes and fingers. I took a deep breath and reveled in the feeling. Suddenly, I wanted to go deeper. I wanted all of my body submerged. I took a deep breath, held it, and bent my knees until my head was underwater.

"How do you feel?" To my surprise, Lucas had joined me underwater and was talking to me, his voice almost as clear as if we were on land.

I hesitated a moment before I spoke because it felt so unnatural to open my mouth, much less talk underwater. "Wonderful." My eyes widened at the sound of my own voice, and once again, we both laughed.

I looked around at the brightly colored fish and crystal-clear water. "Lucas, I'm out of adjectives to describe this place. Just when I think I couldn't be more affected by this place, there is another shock to my system. It's so breathtaking under here."

"Let's sit while you take it all in," he responded with a smile.

So, we sat, under the water, as though that were the most perfectly normal thing any two people could do.

As we rested on the bottom of the riverbed, I felt pebbles under my hand. I looked down and once again saw they were no ordinary rocks. They were jewels. I gasped, remembering why I recognized the inside of the entryway earlier and why I felt like I had seen the fragi before.

"I just remembered that I had a dream about this place."

"I know, Sarah, I asked for you to have that dream."

I searched his eyes, waiting for him to continue.

"What we were fleeing from was so intense. Your world had just been rocked. The man you knew as your uncle turned out to be a complete stranger. A guy you barely knew was tortured, then walked out of a fire alive, asking you to trust him completely. I was concerned about how you were handling things, and I knew if you could have a brief break from that, you would fare much better."

"Did I actually come here to Ganheela during the dream?"

"Technically, no, your body was still in the cave, but your mind and spirit were able to be refreshed in a place like this."

I was about to ask a lot more questions, but Lucas reached out to grab my hand.

"You don't have to understand everything to appreciate it and to be changed by it. Rest, Sarah, that's why we're in the water. Be refreshed, mind, spirit, and body." At his words, my senses once again focused on the warm sensation flowing inside of me.

Feeling the peace of the moment, I closed my eyes and floated away with my thoughts.

Lucas touched my hand, and I opened my eyes, unsure of how much time had passed. There were still shafts of light dancing brilliantly over the surface of the water, but the sun had tucked itself somewhere behind the beautiful green trees.

"Pneuma is waiting for you," Lucas said as he gently pulled me to standing. I had never felt so good, so full, so happy. As we walked slowly out of the water, a question occurred to me.

"You said the water would purify me, and I definitely felt something there. It was the same flowing warmth I felt in the car when we passed through the tunnel. Was I being purified then as well?"

"We all were. Your world is overshadowed by the darkness, and the shadows have a way of clinging to you. The light we went through dispelled the darkness that had settled on us. Ganheela is a place where only The Light reigns; darkness has no place here."

As we walked back toward the house along the same path, we passed a knee-high plant where Lucas had planted the half-eaten fragi.

"Lucas, look! It's already growing! You were right. It wasn't wasted." Of course, he knew the fruit would grow the moment he planted it in the rich, fertile soil. The realization brought tears to my eyes.

He grabbed my hand and tucked it into his arm as we continued walking.

When we made it back to the patio, Lucas led me to the same flowing drapes I thought I had come out of earlier, but as he pulled back the drapes, the room was different, larger.

I hesitated because I didn't want to track water in, but when I looked down, I realized I was completely dry.

I looked at Lucas, and we both laughed at my constant state of surprise and delight.

"What will Pneuma want to talk about?"

"There's much she will explain to you: your past, things that are happening in the present, and she will discuss with you your future."

"She already knows my future?"

"She knows you *in* the future."

"She knows me in the future? Does that mean I stay here?"

"No, you aren't meant to stay here." His smile softened, then faded, but he was still radiant. I think the thought that I would have to leave pained him.

I moved on, not wanting to be the cause of his pain. "Does that mean that I will return here someday if she knows me in the future?"

He smiled again, finding humor in my persistent questions, "That, Sarah Joy, you will have to ask her yourself." He nodded his head at the opening he had created with the drapes. "She is waiting for you."

I knew I was supposed to enter alone.

I hugged Lucas just because and turned to step through the doorway.

CHAPTER 18

I didn't see Pneuma right away when I walked into the room, so I strolled around the room and took in my surroundings while I waited. I was still amazed that I had entered the house from the same patio and entryway I had exited earlier, but I was not in the same room. There were two windowed walls with sheer drapes, letting in the wonderful, sweet-smelling breeze. I noticed two sitting areas in the sunlight and a third one located more toward the back of the room, near a wall filled with thousands of books. The colors in the room were all light and bright, but at the same time, they felt warm and cozy like I could curl up on one of the couches and be forever at home.

The sound of water trickling made its way through the flowing drapes, an accompaniment to the music playing in the background. My body swayed to the music, although, until then I had been unaware of the sound at all. It wasn't an upbeat dance tune or anything, but something deeper, more melodious that made my body sway as if I were caught in a breeze and couldn't help but be moved by it.

While I let the music overtake me, I began to wonder where Pneuma was. Lucas said she was waiting for me, but she wasn't here. I stopped swaying, and tentatively asked, "Pneuma?" She materialized like a mixture of light and energy and fabric until all of her stood before me.

"Sarah Joy." When she spoke my name, her face lit up with delight, and she moved to hug me, a hug I gladly returned. It was not a short hug, but more of an embrace, a long, comforting embrace. Standing there in her arms, all I could think about was my mother. I didn't feel sadness, just a deep satisfaction as my heart and mind were filled with warmth and wonderful memories. As my head rested on her chest, I could hear her heart beating. I remembered how much I loved to hear my mother's heart when she hugged me or sang me to sleep in her arms. As a child, it was so calming, and in Pneuma's embrace, it also felt like healing.

"Did you know her?" I asked, somehow knowing Pneuma would know who I was asking about.

"Yes," She said but didn't elaborate. I felt an overwhelming sense of peace knowing my mother had at least experienced what I felt here before she left this earth. After another minute or two, I gently pulled back from Pneuma's embrace, feeling completely whole, possibly for the first time.

"Better?"

Though I knew she already knew my answer, I still responded, "Yes!"

"Then, come with me, child."

With her arm around my shoulders, Pneuma led me to one of the sitting areas and motioned for me to sit, taking the seat directly across from me for herself.

"I know you have many questions, but we have much work to do. We want you to gain as much rest and training as you can before you go back."

I nodded my understanding, though in truth, I wasn't sure I did.

"What is one question that you need me to answer for you?"

I tried to think of the questions I'd had for Lucas that he hadn't answered yet or even the new questions that had popped up since our arrival in Ganheela. But none of them materialized. I felt a slight ache in my heart as one question popped into my head, so I knew this was the question I should ask.

"Who am I?"

Pneuma was waiting patiently for me to ask, and when I did, a broad smile spread across her face. "You are Sarah Joy." I, of course, knew the full version of my name. I had heard it many times, especially since meeting Lucas. But each time Pneuma had spoken my name, a jolt went through me as if I were hearing it for the first time, and it held a much deeper meaning than ever before.

"You are Sarah Joy, a much-loved daughter of Mary Samantha and William Michael." I breathed in deeply, feeling empowered by the way she spoke this truth over me.

"You are Sarah Joy, a beloved granddaughter of Samantha Joy and Jonathan David." I let her words wash over me.

"You are Sarah Joy, a name that means princess of great gladness, and it represents you well, my beloved, because that is truly who you are."

"You are Sarah Joy, a fierce warrior who fights against injustice with the weapons of love." As her voice became stronger with each statement, I felt a new power, her power, coursing through my body.

"You are Sarah Joy, one who is set apart. You have been chosen for this time to be brought forth."

"You are Sarah Joy, and you are a Light Bearer."

The room seemed to reverberate with the last statement Pneuma made.

I was shaken to my very core and didn't even know what she meant by Light Bearer. If I were to think of anyone who was a Light Bearer, it would be Lucas.

Pneuma answered my thoughts without me even having to ask, "Lucas is a creature of The Light. His very existence is made up of light. But he is not a Light Bearer. You, my child, are a Light Bearer. You are human, and yet you have extraordinary giftings."

"I don't understand."

"You carry within your very being something that will awaken people. And by the time you leave here, you will carry even more of it."

"Pneuma," I whispered, my voice shaky and unsure of the truth of what she spoke over me. She made me sound like someone so important, but I still felt very much like me.

"Yes, dear one, I know you feel small. But that is not how we see you, and that is not what you must believe. What you believe is what you will become. If you believe that you are small, then you will find yourself small. If you believe that you are one who bears The Light, then a Light Bearer you shall be."

I didn't know how to respond. I could feel the truth in her words, but I was also just Sarah, one who feared a lot and, until this time in my life, had existed as someone small.

"Wrong belief and fear make you vulnerable to the Terrobah," Pneuma spoke this truth gently, but with great admonition.

"What did you say?" I had never before heard the word she used, but I knew exactly who she was referring to. I felt the vileness, the wretchedness of them, even more in this place of purity.

"Terrobah." She said it again as if the word meant nothing to her. At the same time, her very mention of their name made me shiver. "You have had the misfortune of meeting quite a few of them recently. I am so thankful that you have yet been spared one of their transfigurations."

"Pneuma, how did I come to be with one of them, thinking he was my uncle?"

"Uncle was a co-worker of William Michael."

"My dad?"

"Yes," she smiled sadly. "Even being a Light Bearer, your father was deceived by one of the Terrobah. More than anything else, the Terrobah are masters of deception. Lying is essential to who they are and is the birthplace of their power. And from that power, they produce the greatest lie of all: fear."

It hurt to think about my dad being manipulated.

"Why was Uncle trying to deceive him? Did he know what my father was?"

"Oh yes, he knew. The whole thing was set up. The accident happened in a different state from the one that your dad and Uncle worked in. Uncle showed up with the death certificates and the right papers to claim you girls within hours of the accident."

I looked at her puzzled and she continued.

"The Terrobah have been trying for centuries to break that particular line of pure light, your line, Sarah. The Terrobah are skilled at distracting many of our Awakened, including some in your line."

"Awakened? It's not just the Terrobah and Light Bearers?"

"No, there are many others. Terrobists are the humans that the Terrobah deceive into walking in darkness and acting on their behalf, giving them the ability to harness some darkness as well. Then, there are the Mythreal ones, beings like Lucas and Owen, who are creatures of The Light."

"Then who are the Awakened?"

"The Awakened are humans that know of The Light and have chosen to walk with us, but they are not Light Bearers. They do not have the power to harness The Light as you do. Then, of course, there are the rest of the humans, sadly oblivious to what surrounds them."

"It's true, I was so blind to what was around me."

"Most are, dear one."

"Does The Light hide from us on purpose?"

"No, we are in everything except the Terrobah. They are void of The Light. For all else, The Light beckons."

"How do we miss it then?"

"Humans have been misled and have fallen into selfishness and greed. They are easily satisfied with what the world and the Terrobah offer them. They become misguided in who they are and what they believe because they are told so much to the contrary."

"Even me," I said, feeling disheartened at missing something that now seemed so obvious.

"Sarah, you resisted better than most, and you were living in the same house and were constantly influenced by a Terrobah. And not just any Terrobah, but a high ranking one at that." She paused. "You thought he was your uncle, someone to be trusted, and yet you still knew something was wrong and resisted so many of his attempts."

"When did I resist?"

"Each time you said no to the newest trinket your uncle offered you. Each time you empathized with others who had less. Each time you adorned yourself with the beauty of your heart, instead of embellishing what was outside. Each time you spoke with kindness and gratitude towards others, expecting nothing in return."

I thought back to my new phone and Martha cooking in the kitchen.

"Sarah," Pneuma called my focus back to her, "You know how Uncle's job was to use images and videos to get people to want something?"

A shiver ran through me as I nodded my head.

"The Terrobah manipulate humans and other created beings to focus on anything but The Light." She looked so calm and peaceful that her words almost didn't make sense. They were manipulating people! By their deception, the Terrobah lured people to their own destruction, numbing them enough to hide the pain of their slow descent into death. And Uncle almost had me in his jaws. My mind ran to Amelia, who was still in his clutches and believing his lies.

Pneuma was saying something about humans losing their free will, at the hands of the Terrobah, all the while believing they were gaining freedom. But suddenly, I could no longer think of anything but my sister. In the splendor and magnificence of Ganheela, I had forgotten about the terror of the last few days.

The thoughts of Amelia slammed into me with a blunt force. What was Uncle doing to her now? Who would awaken her to the truth without me there?

Pneuma moved next to me and put her arm around me, returning my thoughts to the room and the beauty that surrounded me. Still, I felt sick and overwhelmed.

"Sleep." Pneuma breathed onto my face, and everything melted away to honey-flowing bliss.

There were no clocks in Ganheela, and though the sun moved in the sky, the light seemed to never change, so even the passing of time was not something that could be marked. I felt refreshed, so I knew I had slept, but my previous thoughts were still with me. I looked up and saw that Pneuma was sitting on the chair beside my lounging couch. She had been watching over me, protecting me from the things that I feared, just as my mom had done when I had nightmares as a child.

"Did my mom ever come here?" I asked.

"No, but we did take her somewhere like this in her dreams. It sustained her in her everyday life."

There was the deja-vu again. "I dreamed about a place like Ganheela too. Lucas said he asked for me to be taken there."

"Yes, Sarah, that is true. He cares greatly for you. But just as Lucas explained, you did not come here physically, nor did your mind or spirit. I sent you to the Land of The Light."

"Isn't that this place?"

"No, dear one, this is Ganheela, a land filled with The Light, but still adjacent to your world. The sun here is the same as the sun in your world. It is always light here because we sit outside of the time of your world. When you were in the cave, I sent you to the Land of The Light, an entirely different dimension."

"Is that where Lucas is from?"

"Yes."

"Will I get to go there again?"

"One day, yes."

"Why did I need to go there instead of here?"

"You needed to be fully satisfied, fully healed, fully without fear, and to feel fully safe. Those feelings cannot be gained completely here. You are still very much human here, just very saturated in The Light. You can still feel fear, confusion, and certain depths of hunger and thirst, although you can be fully refreshed in human form here."

"When Lucas healed Amelia in the cabin, did he take her to the Land of The Light?"

"No. Lucas poured The Light out of himself into her, which is why he was so drained."

I was silent for a few minutes,

Amelia.

"Amelia," Pneuma echoed out loud.

"Is she okay?" I asked, desperate once again to know what was happening to my sister.

"She has woken up and is well, but they moved her just before you came here."

I heard sadness for the first time in Pneuma's voice, and my eyes filled with tears. "To where? Where is she, Pneuma?"

"To a place for her training."

"To be one of them?"

"A Terrobist? Yes."

"I have to go back and stop her."

"You will when you are ready, but there is nothing you can do for her without training."

"How can I go on here with her in their grasp?"

"You make the choice to train in Ganheela knowing when you return to her, you will be stronger, wiser, and possess a greater ability to truly help her."

"Will I be able to save her?"

"Yes. You will be able to save her." She answered my question, but this time, when Pneuma wrapped her arms around me, she didn't answer my unspoken question.

But will I actually save her?

CHAPTER 19

My mind was so full of the things I had heard from Pneuma that I didn't think I would be able to speak again for a week. But as I floated on the river, Lucas and I easily kept up our conversation as we renewed our minds and spirits once again. Somehow the questions just kept pouring out of me. It must have been something about Ganheela that I could absorb and process more quickly.

"How do you keep," I paused, trying to say Terrobah, but just couldn't manage it, "them out of here? Out of Ganheela?" I asked.

"They would have been stopped by the guards before even entering the tunnel."

"I didn't see any guards."

"Because they didn't need to stop us. We had permission to pass."

"Are the guards like you?"

"Sort of, but they don't look human if that's what you mean."

There was still so much to learn, but in the peace of that moment, I didn't need to know.

"It's time for your training," Lucas said as we made our way to the shore.

"What's training like? Does it involve weapons?" I questioned, wrinkling my nose at the idea.

"Not weapons in the earthly sense, but the weapons wielded by Light Bearers. It's rooted in your mind and comes from The Light within."

We walked for a few steps before something occurred to me.

"Is that what you did to hide us from the, uh, them, in the woods."

"Yes, something like that." He pulled us to a stop. "Sarah?"

"Yes?"

"Say Terrobah."

"Why?" I asked, not really wanting to do what he asked.

"Right now, you fear them, and you fear to say the name. They cannot harm you here and saying Terrobah will not hurt you either. Your fear, if it remains, will give them power. Say Terrobah."

I knew what he was saying was true. I could feel the fear creeping along my spine. They had held power over my life for much longer than they should have. "Terrobah," I whispered.

"What?" Lucas asked, teasing me as if he hadn't heard.

"Terrobah," I said in a normal voice.

"What was that?" he asked, smiling.

"Terrobah!" I shouted.

"That's good," he said putting his arm around my shoulders. "Do you fear it less?"

I thought about it. "Yes! Yes, I do."

"The Terrobah feed on fear, Sarah. Don't give them any more ground with you."

"Okay," I said, not really sure how I would ever match up with any of the Terrobah I had already seen.

"I'm serious, Sarah. You are fierce, and after your training, you will be even more so. The Terrobah are the ones that need to be afraid."

I ducked my head, smiling and blushing at his praise. He raised my chin with his finger until my eyes met his.

"Do you believe me?" he asked with a small smile.

"Yes?" I replied, but more as a question.

"What?" he asked, seeming confused.

"Yes," I said it as a statement, although not much louder, understanding what he was getting at.

Still looking confused, he said, "I couldn't hear you."

I laughed, "Yes!" I shouted.

"See how your belief gives you power?"

"Yes!" I shouted again just for good measure.

"That's your first lesson in training. Pneuma will be glad you are coming in already prepared," Lucas said with a smile.

"I'm training with Pneuma? I thought it would be with you."

"No, she is much more valuable to you in training. I'll be on hand to help assist as needed." He smiled, lifting his head as if he was proud to carry the honor of assisting me. He was above and beyond me in so many ways, and yet serving me was an honor to him. I felt his devotion to me in every cell in my body as I beamed back at him. We laughed together as we continued down the path back to Pneuma and my home here in Ganheela.

✷ ✷ ✷

As we approached, I saw there were doors where the drapes had been previously. The doors opened for us, and we stepped directly into a new room. It was not a room I had seen before, though we entered the house through the same way.

I could feel that we were walking on a cushioned floor, much like I'd walked on at gymnastics as a young girl, but this room didn't look or feel like any gym I'd ever seen. The walls were all covered with softly muted colors of fabric that moved, stirred by a gentle breeze even though it seemed walls were present behind them.

Again, Pneuma wasn't in the room. I looked back at Lucas, who was smiling as he looked at me.

"She is waiting for you," he said simply.

Just as I'd learned from the last time we met, I spoke her name, and right in front of me, lights flashed, energy buzzed, and fabric swirled as Pneuma came into the room.

"Sarah Joy, my delight." She moved a few steps towards me, holding her arms out to me. I moved quickly into them and settled into her embrace. "How did you find the river, my love?"

"Refreshing in every way, Pneuma," I said softly, enjoying the peace that her embrace brought me.

She held my hands between us when she said, "Shall we begin?"

"Yes," I said. I knew this training was what I needed to save Amelia and awaken others to The Light. This was my purpose. This was my destiny. It was my turn to bear The Light. I looked intently at Pneuma, confident in my calling. "I'm ready."

"Good." She released my hands and gestured to two couches that had appeared.

"Are we sitting to train?" I asked in confusion.

"For the first part," she said with a smile.

I took a seat on the couch across from her and she said, "Let us begin."

A few hours later, I was lounging on the couch, Pneuma lightly stroking the top of my head. As a girl, I'd had court-ordered therapy many times after my parents died, so I understood the general idea of how it worked. I'm not sure Uncle would have taken me, but as I had lost both my parents and would be moving to a different state, the judge thought it prudent.

Pneuma's version of therapy was both more intense yet gentler than the therapy I'd had as a child. She untangled my past, talking about Uncle, revealing the bitterness and hate I harbored for him, feelings that could cripple me if left uncovered. Yet, as I uncovered more scars left by the darkness, the more I was healed by The Light. I asked her why she couldn't just take all of these things from me. She explained that my heart, mind, and spirit needed to be healed from the past so I wouldn't carry it into my future. "The human mind is an amazing organ. It doesn't have to hold on to the darkness as long as those thoughts and pain the darkness caused are given a voice. When the pain is spoken, the darkness that remains has to flee." That gave me pause. After this training, would I still be human if all the darkness in me was healed?

"Pneuma?" I asked, feeling suddenly shy.

"Yes, beloved?" she asked in return.

"Will this training make me like Lucas and Owen?" I asked, unable to meet her eyes. I very much wanted to be like them, but it didn't seem right to ask more of Pneuma than she was willing to give me.

When she didn't reply, though, I chanced a glance at her to see what she was thinking. She smiled knowingly at me, and I knew my question hadn't surprised her. She knew everything about me, even the thoughts in my head.

Once she had my gaze, she responded, "Lucas and Owen are immortal, while you, Sarah, are mortal. You have powers you can tap into, but you can still die. As a Light Bearer, you're an elevated mortal."

"Then how did Lucas get so worn down?"

"He had to take on mortal properties in order to exist among the Terrobah at the camp without detection. He was able, through The Light, to use his immortal powers when in need, but mostly he had to work without them."

"How could I see him so clearly when they couldn't?"

"They who, my love?" she asked with a cheeky smile.

I smiled in return, remembering I wasn't supposed to fear them, "How could I see Lucas so clearly when the Terrobah couldn't?"

"You, my love, are from a long line of those who pursue The Light. Within that line, there is remarkable purity and power giving you different properties than a normal human."

"I always knew I was different."

"Yes, but you used to think that was something to object to; do you think that anymore?"

"No, I am grateful to be a part of this lineage that enables me to help others. And I know I'm up to the task."

"What task do you speak of, Sarah?" she asked, but once again, I knew she already knew.

"I get the feeling that when I go back, I will be fighting the Terrobah and trying to awaken more people to The Light."

"Among other things," she said, confirming my suspicions. "Now, back to training. Please stand up." I stood, and with a swirl of her arm, the seats disappeared with electric light into nothing.

"We have been training your mind; now, it is time to train your body." With that, she made a small circular motion with her hand as some sparks of energy flew in my direction. I looked down at myself to see that my dress, still white and silky to the touch, had transformed into a martial arts uniform. I never thought of myself as a fighter, but dressed like this and with Pneuma as my trainer, I knew without a doubt that I could do anything.

"Lucas," Pneuma said out loud. And the next thing I knew Lucas was walking through the door.

"Waiting close by?" I asked, teasing him.

"No," he said, smirking. "But I can move with ease here, especially when Pneuma calls me." I returned his smile and readied myself to learn whatever was necessary.

Pneuma began to lead me through fighting techniques. It wasn't hand-to-hand combat like I had seen at camp. It was more about projecting energy and blocking the attacks of the darkness. I was shocked at how easily it came to me.

Pneuma said, "Sarah, when I give you a command, it is important that you not only hear my command, but believe you are capable of what I am saying." When I believed what Pneuma said and followed her command, I became a conduit for The Light, and what once seemed impossible had now become second nature.

I learned to use The Light to create a shield around myself and project weapons that were like extensions of myself. I could tell they weren't super strong yet, but the fact that I was projecting anything at all was amazing to me.

"Pneuma?" I asked, looking at my hands as weapons illuminated out of them.

"Yes, Sarah?" she said in return.

I looked up into her knowing eyes. "How is this possible? I couldn't do any of this yesterday, either here or on earth, and now it seems almost easy, like I could have always done it."

"To some extent, you have before. The Light passed through you on numerous occasions, you were just unaware."

"Did I hurt anyone?!" I asked in alarm, looking at my hands like they were now deadly weapons.

"No, my love, not at all. Your touch brought life to them, a sense of peace, maybe even love."

"Hmmm," I laughed slightly, feeling delighted at the thought that my touch had somehow already helped people. Then, I remembered, "Was that why Uncle was so uncomfortable with our physical affection?"

"Yes," Pneuma responded matter-of-factly. To Uncle, a fist bump or a pat on the back was affection at its peak. Even when I was really distraught, he rarely put his arms around me.

"Why wouldn't he have wanted to feel those things?" I asked, feeling confused.

"To the Terrobah, The Light is mortally painful."

I thought about the last time I had touched Uncle in the cabin with Amelia, and he had looked down at my hand on his arm like it was the worst thing ever. I thought he was just furious, but I had actually been hurting him.

She knew where my thoughts had gone, and so she continued explaining, "The Terrobah are so dark and evil that anything of The Light causes them actual physical pain. That is why, Sarah, your weapons are made of Light." She let me think about that for a moment.

"Let us try the sword again, shall we?" she asked, sunnily, drawing me back.

I took a deep breath while I looked at my right hand, and the sword started forming. I reached out in front of me, and the sword lengthened, brighter this time than the last time.

"And retract," Pneuma said. I stopped thinking of the sword, and it disappeared.

"Very good," she smiled, her delight in me shining through her eyes. "It looks like Lucas has our targets ready."

I turned around to see that there was a line of ten or more black figures that seemed like target mannequins. They didn't have faces, and they were all at least a foot taller than me. They were standing on their own as if they were actually men. Lucas closed something on the back of one of them and stepped aside.

Pneuma moved toward the targets, and I followed. She had Lucas demonstrate how to harness The Light into a pulse, a ball of brilliant yellow light and energy. As he forced the pulse towards a dummy, it didn't rip apart or explode as I thought it would. Instead, it was like a wave of energy that pushed it backward. Once he demonstrated, then I followed suit, holding my hands as though I were already holding the ball of light, and watching it form there between them. I was surprised at how well I was able to use it on my first try.

Then, Lucas demonstrated harnessing The Light into a sword. I fully expected him to swing it and likewise push the dummy backward, but this time it crumpled to the floor.

I looked back at Pneuma in confusion.

"How . . . uh . . . ?"

Pneuma explained. "The Terrobah will use blunt force. They will want to draw blood and kill. You are harnessing energy that will halt or slow their nervous system."

I'm sure I still looked confused, so she explained further.

"When the Light coursing through you and emanating from you passes through them in any way, whether it is a block or a weapon strike, it passes through them with an electrical current that disrupts their nervous system. Blocks will halt, weapon strikes will stun for longer, and can even stop their nervous system if delivered with enough power."

"You mean, kill them?" I asked, thinking about the last part.

"Not exactly," she said. "The Terrobah cannot die. When you stop their nervous system completely, they will dissolve…in a way. They are then taken back to their home and are tortured for failing."

The word torture made me feel sick. The only torture I had ever seen was at camp and having to watch Lucas go through that was awful. I didn't like to think of subjecting anyone to that.

"I know it sounds awful, but the Terrobah themselves cannot be returned to The Light. They made their decision long ago. You will be fighting for those who can still come to The Light, for those who have no idea of the darkness they are trapped in.

"But if The Light affects the nervous system, then The Light can hurt normal humans as well," I remarked, not really asking a question. I watched as Lucas put the target back up, almost like he was recharging it, even though we had moved down the line to the next one.

"Yes, that is why you must use your power only on those who need to be stopped." I was staring down at my hands of death as Pneuma spoke, but when she stopped speaking, I looked up and saw her looking at me with an intensity I hadn't seen before. It was overwhelming, and I took a step back. I wanted to avert my eyes, but I couldn't.

"Pneuma?" I whispered.

Her face softened back into a smile. "Sarah, you will be just fine, more than fine. You will be brilliant."

The intensity of her gaze changed so quickly I couldn't find my voice.

"Have no fear my child, I was gazing at you to see if there were any ill intentions in you. There are none. If it is at all possible, you will never hurt a human." She put her hand on my shoulder, and I breathed deeply, recovering complete peace.

"Let us continue," she said as she gestured to the next dummy.

As I reached out to strike the dummy, my sword had already formed. Pneuma and Lucas both smiled approvingly at me as my target slumped to the floor.

✳ ✳ ✳

Though time was not measured in Ganheela, I felt as though days had passed since my training had begun. I had just finished off a row of targets in quick and efficient fashion to hear, "Impressive, Sarah. Very impressive!" Lucas's pride in me was obvious by the way he was glowing.

I beamed at him, and the love I had for him affected everything within me. It was a love I had never experienced, a pure and unconditional love. I would do anything for him, and he had already proven he would do anything for me. I couldn't really find the words to describe what I felt with my entire being. He was like a father, brother, savior, and best friend all in one.

I realized how long I had been staring at him and felt redness creep into my cheeks as I dropped my gaze. When I raised my eyes, Lucas was gone. Pneuma was looking at me, and I wasn't sure what I was seeing on her face.

"His level of devotion to you is something we do not often see." I couldn't decide if she was saying this was a good or bad thing.

"I'm sorry," I said, feeling like it was somehow my fault.

"You have nothing to be sorry for. You and Lucas have a great love for each other. Even with your mother, you did not know a love like this. You were too young yet to understand unconditional love." She paused. She swirled her hand, giving us a love seat to sit on together.

We sat, and she pulled my head to her shoulder, wrapping me in her arms. "I am the one that should be sorry. Maybe if I had explained better," she said, almost questioning herself. I had never heard one moment of confusion or uncertainty out of Pneuma before this moment.

I knew she would continue when she was ready, and so I waited, enjoying her presence, peace, and love.

"Sarah, what do you feel for Lucas?" she asked me.

"Everything good," I whispered. "I love him so much."

She didn't say anything, I knew I wasn't in trouble, so I continued.

"It's nothing like the love I saw in movies where it was about taking and loving for your own gain. I want everything good for Lucas, and I would do anything for him."

Still, she said nothing.

"I know Lucas and I are different beings, and so it's not really about earthly things like going on a date or anything," I blushed again. "In fact, I love you with the same love, it's so strong, and it makes me feel completely whole. It's just a little bit different with Lucas."

"That is all as it should be, my love, you have done nothing wrong." At her words, relief washed over me.

"The world distorts what is good and pure, but there is nothing wrong with the love you feel for Lucas. The difference you feel for Lucas is because you were created to feel those feelings towards a man. You have a brotherly love for him, but you also feel romantic love for him."

It was true. I was in love with Lucas.

"Your hormones and your brain are labeling your feelings for him as romantic love. Without drawing too much attention to the pleasant nature of his human form, the security, affection, protection, and peace he's brought to you throughout your journey together have made for a powerful combination."

She continued, "I have never seen Lucas so drawn to anyone either. Your connection to each other will always remain." I felt her hesitate, "but you have different missions. He will take you back, but he cannot stay with you. You will have The Light and the overwhelming sense of love, but you will not have him physically present."

I could see now why she was being so gentle with me. That news was devastating. If I hadn't been in Ganheela and in Pneuma's arms, I'm not sure I could have handled hearing it. Part of me probably would have died right then. But I did have Ganheela, and I was in Pneuma's arms, so her proclamation didn't seem that life-altering. I would be okay; I already knew that, even as a tear rolled down my cheek. I would still have The Light and Lucas's love. I would always be tied to Lucas in some way.

"Does he know how I feel, all of it?"

"Yes, my love, and because he was in human form and took on those properties, he has felt the same type of love for you. That is why he is still so drawn to you, these feelings are a first for him."

"I'm surprised more of his rescues don't fall for him," I said, with a laugh, overwhelmed to hear he shared my feelings.

"Many have before, but you and Lucas went through an experience unlike any other he has had before. You love each other so deeply now because of what you walked through together."

I wasn't feeling sad anymore, but I did feel a small amount of loss. Pneuma gently lifted my chin, and I looked at her.

"Sarah Joy," she said, making sure she had my gaze. "Do you think this will hinder you, or will you choose to continue to walk down the path that is before you: To be a Light Bearer and save many from the evil of the Terrobah?"

By hinder, I knew she was asking if I would move away from The Light because I couldn't have Lucas. I took a deep breath, and I could feel the gravity of what I was committing to. I would not turn my back on the call I was given. This wasn't a choice. This was my destiny.

"I will be a Light Bearer," I said in full voice and with the conviction of my whole being. Had I been in my world, I'm not sure that proclamation would have come so easily.

CHAPTER 20

I felt a slight tinge of worry that things would be awkward between Lucas and me. But they were the same as they had always been, maybe even a little sweeter as I knew how he felt about me, and I wanted to savor the time I had left with him.

In my time here, I'd grown so much, even more so since my last conversation with Pneuma. I said as much to Lucas as we walked beside the river, and he agreed.

"You have grown, Sarah, and not just emotionally and mentally, but physically as well." He motioned to my reflection in the river. I was surprised at what I saw there. Although no time had actually passed in my world while I was in Ganheela, I easily looked 19. I said as much to Lucas.

"Sarah, you've grown up, and when you go back to your world, this change in you, all that you have learned, will change where you fit in. Your appearance had to change to align with all the knowledge you have gained and for you to accomplish your upcoming work."

Training, while it didn't seem any harder, seemed more intense. Pneuma instructed me to resist an attack from a man in all black who represented the Terrobah. But there was no mistaking Lucas's blue eyes beneath that mask. He had just unloaded about ten arrows at me and was now charging. I forgot myself for a moment, and he had his weapon out and at my throat before I could regain my composure.

"I'm sorry," I said, feeling defeated. I tended to get myself into trouble because little things could distract me. I knew this couldn't happen when I was with Uncle. He would use every scheme in the book when he came at me. But unlike Lucas, he wouldn't stop until I was on his side or dead.

"Sarah," Pneuma breathed softly.

I looked at her.

"You have nothing to feel defeated about." She smiled at me gently. "You are doing remarkably well." She came to me and touched my cheek. When I was in combat, I became taller and more formidable, an added benefit of The Light, so I was slightly taller than her instead of the other way around. She rose though, to look me directly in the eyes.

"You are thinking about Uncle, but do not let him have this power over you. The only reason we told you about him was to give you wisdom. This wisdom is intended to give you power, not him. With The Light in full power inside of you, what can he do?"

I felt the confidence rising in me as her voice grew stronger.

"Nothing, he is powerless against you and will flee from your presence. He is all talk and schemes, but you are light and power! You are love and strength! Make him flee from you or dissolve trying, Sarah!"

I felt empowered and ready to go again. I looked to Lucas, who had pulled down the covering from his mouth. I could see his full face. I nodded to him to let him know I was ready.

His eyes became fierce, and he nodded his head at me, "You've got this." The conviction in his voice made a sort of humming occur in my body, the Light was pulsing through me now with fervency.

By the time I had deflected his arrows and he was charging at me, I was glowing with the power of The Light, and had a shield formed over my entire body. In full faith that it would hold, I blocked his sword with my arm that took on the image of an actual shield. I felt no pain from the impact, but the force of it knocked Lucas's sword out of his hand. I used a light pulse to block him, and to my astonishment, it worked. He was repelled and thrown onto his back.

He rose and came at me again. At Pneuma's coaching, when he lost his sword again, I used three light pulses to block him and knock him back even farther from me. He rose again, and before his charge, she told me to hit him with as many light pulses as I could. At five, the last pulse fizzled before it reached him, but he was already on the ground.

"Well done, my love," Pneuma said, coming to embrace me. "You felt it?"

"Yes, Pneuma, it was flowing through me, and I no longer doubted it."

"And you were able to harness it."

I relished Pneuma's praise, but then quickly remembered Lucas lying on the ground. I turned quickly to check on him and saw he was already standing, back in his white clothes, and walking towards me. Pneuma had reassured me before we started that Lucas would only feel the effects of the pulses while we were training, but still, I was happy to see him up and walking.

"Well done, Sarah," he said, glowing with what looked like pride in me. "I knew you could do it!" He practically shouted as he wrapped me up in a huge hug.

"Thank you, Lucas!"

Once he sat me down, I exclaimed with the same exuberance, "I felt it that time. I felt The Light, and there was no doubt."

"Oh, I could tell," he said, rubbing his chest where more than one pulse had struck him.

"Did I hurt you?" I asked with concern.

"While we were training, yes, but I'm just teasing you now. I feel completely fine."

"Oh good," I said with relief.

"To the river?" Lucas asked, still wearing a huge smile.

"To the river," I seconded, turning back to say goodbye to Pneuma, but she was already gone. Lucas grabbed my hand, and off we went.

Lying on the riverbed and feeling completely relaxed, I asked Lucas, "Was that really what it will be like?"

I probably needed to be more specific, but Lucas knew me well enough to know what I was asking about. "Yes and no."

I laughed, "That's helpful."

"Oh, you need more details? What a surprise!" He chuckled, and I could hear the smile in his voice.

"Yes, please!" I said with a smile.

"The arrows and attacks are pretty standard. Unfortunately, though, you will rarely ever take on just one Terrobah at a time."

"Oh, I didn't think about that," I said, feeling some of my elation from earlier wane a little bit.

"No, no, remember what happens when you doubt."

"How did you know I was doubting?" I asked.

"Your poker face isn't as good as you think." I could tell he was looking over at me, so I turned my head to look at him. "You're doing incredibly well for just getting started. But you have to walk before you can run." He winked, which made me laugh.

"Sarah," his voice was serious, so I looked at him again. "You're stepping into who you were made to be. We all knew you were going to be capable, but not many of us knew how capable you really were. All Ganheela knows now."

I held my gaze to his and saw the truth in his eyes. I smiled and said, "But you might be a little biased where I'm concerned."

"Even compared to the others, you're still exceptional."

"Others?" I asked, confused by the thought. How had I not considered that there were others like me, others in need of training, others fighting on the side of The Light against the Terrobah? If there weren't, the Terrobah would have taken over the earth by now.

"Look at the time, we better be getting back," Lucas said as he rose.

"I thought there was no time here," I said with a smirk.

He smiled back at me as we walked out of the water.

"Lucas, will you please tell me about the others?" I tried asking sweetly.

He grabbed a fragi off the tree we went past and handed it to me. "Yes, I'll tell you while you eat."

"Others have trained here, then, obviously?" I asked.

"Yes, there are others here even now," he replied.

"Why can't I see them?" I asked, enjoying the fruit.

"Each Light Bearer has different needs, and as such, his or her Ganheela appears differently."

"How so?"

"Well, with you, this is the purest, most natural Ganheela I've ever seen. It's the closest to the other side that a soul has ever… projected, if you will."

I wasn't sure what to say, so I just kept quiet.

"You were already mature for your age on earth, and so I expected something like this. But you want for very little, and you are soothed by love and creation, completely at peace by it. Others take time to uncover the true nature of Ganheela. They have more stripping to be done. The darkness still has a hold on them to varying degrees."

"Will I get to meet others like me?"

"Yes, when we enter back into the time of your world. You will want others around you that are like-minded. The darkness has a strong pull, and you will need others that remind you of the power you each hold inside and to help you resist the temptation that comes with it."

"Temptation?" I asked. "What do you mean?" Lucas looked at me for a moment before continuing, choosing his words and the weight they held. "Power is a tricky thing. When you want power more than you want anything else, it starts to change you. The power of the Eklesi is supposed to be a gift that transforms you in beautiful ways. There are those who are turned by the power they possess. The world is steeped in shadow, and the shadow has a way of creeping back in. The greater their power, the greater the shadow they can potentially cast becomes. With very few who can match their power, it becomes easy to manipulate, control, even dominate. After a time, it is no longer the Light Bearer who wields the power, but their shadow; the darkness produced by their pride. It's here that even a Light Bearer can become a Terrobist, as they give into the darkness and become one with their shadow. They become creatures of fear, seeking to possess and rule others by their fear. They are both nightmare and shadow; death wrapped in darkness."

I felt the chill of that shadow come over me, even here in the warmth of Ganheela. I asked with hesitation, "Lucas, what does that have to do with me?"

"You had some in your lineage that chose to walk away from us, loving their power more than they loved The Light. And from what you've shown so far, you're even more powerful, and can carry more Light, than they ever could. We've seen nothing but Light in you, Sarah, but we also know how powerful the pull toward darkness can be."

I had somehow thought that, apart from battle, I could no longer be influenced by the Terrobah or be used for their purposes.

He held my face in his hands so that I had to look up at him, "Nothing will stop The Light that flows through you if you remain in The Light."

I had no idea what he was thinking now, but I could have stayed just like that forever. He leaned towards me and kissed my forehead, taking a breath while he did it. My heart was pounding at his nearness. I loved Lucas more than I had ever loved anyone else. When he pulled back, he was no longer smiling, and his eyes were glistening with tears as I'm sure mine were as well. Lucas had kissed me before on the forehead, but there was an intensity there I had not felt before.

I was right that Lucas's kiss was different, but I didn't realize why until a little while later in my final training with Pneuma. Lucas had been saying a sweet goodbye with his kiss. "Sarah Joy," Pneuma said, "You have defeated every scenario and completed your training. You are well equipped to return to your world. Your time has come."

With leaving lingering in my mind, I thought for sure I wouldn't sleep, but of course, I did. Pneuma came with me to tuck me in, as she had only done a handful of times since my stay in Ganheela began. Looking back, those had all been times when I was overly excited or anxious, and I imagined she knew her presence would bring about my sleep more easily. With Pneuma singing gently over me and the gentle breeze blowing across my room, it wasn't long before I fell into a wonderfully deep sleep.

✳ ✳ ✳

Instead of having fragi when I woke, there was a large banquet meal prepared in my honor to send me off. I had shared a few meals with Pneuma and Lucas before, and they were always filled with the most delicious foods and smells that were intoxicating. I felt a wave of sadness as I thought about leaving, but was immediately distracted by the berry I popped in my mouth. The best way I could describe it was like a strawberry fruit roll-up but in the best of ways. Not as sugary but bursting with a similar flavor. I laughed at my own description. I guess in some ways, I still felt sixteen.

I was delighted that Owen was able to join us for our last meal together in this place. Owen radiated joy, and he added more humor to our meals. And the joy of laughing in Ganheela never ceased to amaze me. As I looked around the table, I was so grateful for the three of them. I knew they would be a part of me always. I wanted to soak up every bit of their love and goodness as I could before I left. I would have friends around me that were a part of the Eklesi, but it wouldn't be like this.

I already knew where I would be headed and what I would be headed into—a battle against Uncle and the Terrobah in hopes of finding out where they were keeping Amelia. *Amelia.* My heart still ached every time I thought of her, which grew more frequent as I got closer to leaving.

That was my call now, to rescue those in need. I was there to fight the Terrobah and free anybody that I could. I would tell those who were freed and anyone else that I could about The Light, to bring about their Awakening. There were still so many captivated by the darkness, unaware of their chains and blind to The Light.

It wasn't just my looks that had matured in Ganheela; my physical strength had increased, as well as my wisdom and knowledge.

I no longer saw the world the way I had in the days before leaving for camp; and I no longer saw myself the same way either. I wasn't the fearful, small, unseen girl I'd been when I first met Lucas. I was a Light Bearer, fully convinced of the power that now dwelt in me. I was stronger than I ever believed possible and more loved than I had ever dared to dream. My mind rested on what I now faced.

"You've grown quiet, Sarah," Pneuma said.

"Yes," I replied, "Just thinking about what's to come." I didn't need to clarify what I was thinking for Pneuma, but I did it out of habit.

"My love, do not borrow trouble. Be in this moment, the next events will come soon enough."

"Worry always came naturally to me before; I worried a lot." I said, softly.

"And you will worry again, but you do not have power for the future, you only have power during the moment you are in. If you focus on what is to come, you will spend your energy and thoughts on the wrong thing. Stay in the moment."

"How do I not worry, just like that?"

"Every time a thought creeps in, give it a place. If it is a worry, let it go to the future it belongs in. If it is feelings from before, regrets, shame, and so on, release them behind you to the past where they belong. If a thought is about the moment, walk in it and bring it to The Light."

"It sounds a little too easy," I said with a smile at Pneuma.

"What you are going back to is anything but easy; to continue to choose The Light over the darkness is no small thing. Remember, my child, that I am with you now. You have my words from your time here to guide you. And when you need me most, call to me, and I will make myself known to you, even speaking to you."

"Really?" I asked, hopefully.

"Yes, I am everywhere at once, and will always be with you. You will not go alone, Sarah."

My leaving was inevitable. The time was drawing near. It helped to know that Pneuma would be with me in some form. I wasn't sure how the whole "calling her" thing worked on earth. Here, I just had to say her name, and she appeared. Would it be like that or like when Lucas had to try so hard to connect with The Light when we were on the run?

Though I had not asked the question aloud, Pneuma responded, "You will see." She said it with a smile and sparkling eyes, and somehow, I got the impression it would be more like Ganheela.

"I still feel like there is so much I don't know."

"That is true; there is a lot you do not know, but there is also much that you do. Your purpose is to complete the task that has been shown to you." She paused, "You will continue to learn from me even in your reality. Once you are back, things will be clearer than you assume they are."

"You are on a need to know basis," Owen chimed in, "so, in time, you'll know what you need."

I laughed, "That's not how that saying goes." Everyone else's laughter kept me laughing.

"It's not?" Owen said with a playful smirk.

Our meal ended, and without so much as a spoken word, the table was cleared, and I was standing in my room. I felt some of the unease return, so I began practicing what Pneuma told me about worry and the future. I didn't have power there, so I had to let it go. I walked onto the patio and stood there, just breathing in the beauty and life around me, releasing the future and what was to come. The worry had completely dissipated when I felt Lucas come up beside me.

"Is it time?" I asked, looking over at him.

"Almost," he said, staring out at the beauty before us. "I have something for you," he said, still not looking at me or making a move to give it to me.

"Do I get to have it?" I asked, teasing him.

"Yes," he said, turning his eyes to me. There was a gut-wrenching sadness in his eyes that I hadn't seen since we had been in Ganheela. I turned fully towards him and touched his cheek.

"I didn't think you could feel that here," I said.

He knew I meant his deep sadness. "Only if it's powerful. What I feel right now would cripple a mortal man on earth."

"It's not goodbye, yet," I said, stroking his cheek with my thumb.

"But this is goodbye to you being here, being completely safe and out of the reach of the Terrobah."

I couldn't speak. I knew I was only holding it together because we were in Ganheela. In my world, I would have been a wreck. As it was, a tiny tear still trailed down my cheek. He wiped it away with his thumb, then held his other hand out before me, closed tightly. As he opened his hand, a beautiful golden necklace with a circle pendant dropped down. In the pendant was a red jewel that sparkled brilliantly. I had dropped my hand from his face without realizing it and took the pendant in my hand, rubbing my thumb over the red ruby.

"It's from the river," he said softly. I felt another tear slip down my cheek.

"Here, let me." He took the necklace and unclasped the chain to put it around my neck. As he held it in front of me, I saw that there was an inscription on the back.

After he fastened it and the necklace dropped onto my chest, I turned it over to look, but I couldn't read what it said.

"What does it say?" I asked him as he stood before me again.

"It's the language used by the Eklesi. You'll learn pieces of it along the way, but just know it encompasses all I feel for you." His voice was steady and gentle, but there was agony in his eyes.

I dove into his arms as he hugged me fiercely. He pressed his lips to the top of my forehead, holding me there, each of us feeling the depth of this moment. Gently, he pulled back.

"Pneuma's calling us," he said with what seemed to be a forced smile.

I hadn't heard anything, but I was too wrapped up in the moment to listen to anything other than Lucas.

"Let's go," I said with more conviction than I felt, grabbing his hand for strength.

In the beautiful hall, at the front of the building, Pneuma and Owen were waiting for us.

Pneuma held out her arms, and I practically threw myself into them.

"Thank you, Pneuma, for everything." It seemed so little to offer her mere words, but she knew my heart.

"Go with The Light, Sarah Joy. You are ready."

I took one last deep breath, letting the truth of what she said inhabit me. I was ready. I knew they had prepared me well, and I didn't doubt that. All that remained was to face the unknown waiting for me back in the world I had left behind.

"I am ready," I said, and I truly felt it. Amelia needed me; she needed The Light. I was so very different from the girl that had come through the tunnel the other way.

Lucas and Owen joined me in the car, and before I knew it, we were out of the tunnel. No lights flashed; no warmth spread through my body. Colors grew dim and the light began to fade.

"No purification needed going this way, huh?" I said with a soft laugh as I looked at Lucas.

"No." He smiled at me.

My laugh no longer held the joyous quality it had in Ganheela, and Lucas and Owen didn't laugh along. All three of us were feeling differently already. I could tell how I felt, and the guys were fidgeting more and smiling less.

Even though I really wanted to, I knew there was no turning back.

CHAPTER 21

Everything about my former reality was worse than I remembered. The sun felt nothing like Ganheela; instead, here it was harsh and glaring. The sounds were disruptive, the smells foul, and the sights filled with darkness. From the rumble of the car to the storefronts, the trash and the dead plants, it was too much. What hurt worse was knowing that people here were blind to the pain in the world around them, walking in darkness while being so near to The Light.

We drove until it became dark, heading right back to the camp where we had come from. Since time had not moved here on earth, Uncle and the other Terrobah would just be arriving back from the police station. Uncle was still using the camp as his headquarters. He couldn't return to the Terrobah's actual headquarters until he had me, or he would face severe punishment. Just the thought of him made my stomach roll. How many lies had he told us? How much had he manipulated us? And how close had he come to pulling me to their side?

Lucas told me he didn't think I would have ever joined the Terrobah, even if he hadn't been assigned to save me. Even though I hadn't voiced it, I wasn't so sure. I had been very lonely, and I often gave into Uncle or Amelia just to avoid being left out. I was almost positive he could have swayed me after a time, especially because he would have told me anything but the truth.

"We're getting close," Owen said, seriously.

"How is that possible? We drove for a such a short time, and Lucas and I traveled for days." I asked, feeling panic rise up in me.

Owen and I made eye contact in the rearview mirror, so he answered me. "We came out in a different location."

"We did?" I looked at Lucas this time. I thought we had so much longer until we would get back to Camp Tuano. Now I was filled with questions and uncertainty and a frantic feeling that was no longer dispelled by being in Ganheela.

Lucas had been looking out the window, but he was now looking at me, I'm sure picking up on my panic. He placed his hand over mine.

I heard Pneuma's voice in my head, "While the destination is important, the journey to get there should never be overlooked." I smiled, hearing her voice and felt the calm that emanated from it.

"Pneuma?" Lucas asked. He had continued to watch me.

"Yes," I said, still smiling. "Could you hear it?" I asked.

"No, I just knew that only she could be responsible for that big of a change in your countenance." He reached out to me and pulled me close to him. "There aren't as many of them still here. Since the plans they had for you at the camp failed, some of them have fled. And some are making their way to the Terrobah headquarters."

He said this all very matter-of-factly, almost as if they were dinner guests that wouldn't be at the party. "And some of those who have stayed," he continued, "they don't feel loyal to Uncle. He has fallen from their high esteem and devotion. Most likely, they won't fight alongside him. He has maybe 12 still on his side."

I had fought 12 enemies in Ganheela and had defeated them, but in Ganheela, I was free from the doubt that followed me here. My mind told me over and over that here on earth, this task would be impossible. I could feel the fear rising.

"A few might return to his side once they see what you've become. To their core, they hate the Eklesi, and that might stir them enough to fight against us."

I tried not to think of the numbers again; Pneuma told me multiple times that the numbers didn't matter. If I focused on them too *much, then I relied on my own understanding of what would be true* about the outcome of the battle. I needed to believe that no matter the number, that with The Light, we would prevail.

"So, my first battle," I said to get out of my own head.

"No, it's not your first," Lucas said in all seriousness.

I looked at Lucas in confusion, so he continued, "You escaped the Terrobah at camp. You've already thwarted their plans once, and they were thrown into chaos."

"But I didn't do much, you did most of the ..." Lucas jumped in before I could finish.

"Oh, yes you did! The amount of courage it took for you to turn away from everything you had ever known to turn to The Light and come and find me? And you fully planned to take on the Terrobah to save my life. You never gave up. Your love for Amelia, and your love for me, compelled you forward. If The Light hadn't protected me, you would have even laid down your life for me. You are courageous, Sarah. Far more than you realize."

Even without The Light or my realization of the Eklesi, I had shown tremendous courage. Evidence that The Light was already with me, even though I was unaware, I had just known that something had to be done. Pneuma and I had talked of this, but I hadn't thought of that as a defeat to them. *The Terrobah.*

"Yes, I can agree it took courage, but I wasn't alone. I had you," I said.

"And today you won't be alone either. Owen and I will fight with you."

That made me smile. I hadn't trained with them very much on my side, but the two times I had, the targets had dissolved quickly. He must have thought I needed more reassurance because he continued.

"You also defeated many in Ganheela," he said.

"Yes, but that was Ganheela, and I'm sure you didn't come at me as the Terrobah will. You never wanted to kill me."

"That's true, but when I assumed the darkness, it wasn't my mind that came after you. I hated that training because I could in no way protect you. Pneuma had to remind me more than once that it was necessary for you to feel the full effect of the darkness attacking."

I didn't know how to take that in, thinking he had always been taking it a little easy on me. Knowing he hadn't been was a good surprise.

"You've already experienced victory over the Terrobah; remember that, Sarah." He kissed the top of my head. I sensed something in Lucas, so I pulled back to look at his face.

"What?" I asked. He didn't reply, so I asked again, "What's wrong?"

"The only thing you haven't faced is their true form."

"What does that mean?" He looked a little surprised at my question and then confused.

"Didn't Pneuma talk to you about how persuasive their voices are?" he asked, still looking confused.

I quickly recalled that Pneuma had taught me about how Uncle had had such a hold over me. I was feeling upset about how he'd deceived me over the years and how I was so weak against him. She explained how the Terrobah are persuasive not just with their voices but with implanting thoughts into your head, making it seem like they are your own thoughts.

I had trained against their invading thoughts. In my training, I pictured a helmet, and The Light then took the form of one, protecting me and my mind for however long I chose. But it wasn't until this moment that I realized I hadn't actually ever practiced using it against their voices.

"Why didn't I practice that, it seems like a very important piece?"

"While we can harness the darkness in Ganheela, their voices are never uttered there. They really can't be. The Light dispels them too fast for those training to even hear them."

"Well, what do I do about them now?" I was feeling anxious that they had an offensive weapon that I didn't feel ready for, so I leaned back into Lucas.

"The same helmet you utilized many times… you'll use that."

"Okay, so why did you seem worried about that?"

He took a breath before he answered, "Uncle will do anything in his power to try to get you to release the protection of the helmet. Your mind and your thoughts belong to you, and The Light won't remain there if you choose to let other things in. The Terrobah cannot win without getting into your head. They will try even harder once they realize you have been to Ganheela. They will see your physical appearance has changed, but more importantly, they will feel the change in you. Your presence and The Light within you will be painful to them."

Lucas continued, "Do you remember what Pneuma said will happen when they perceive the change in you?"

"They will change form?" I asked.

"Yes, they will return to their true form."

"I remember some of the glimpses."

Pneuma had prepared me well before she showed me, but the Terrobah were the stuff of nightmares, literally, as they were also the ones that caused nightmares. Pneuma had told me, "Outside of their human form, the Terrobah have no true physical body to inhabit, with only piercing red eyes to see through the dark. They are pure darkness and evil, living among the shadows yet mirroring what each person fears most. Powerless in their own right, they feed on fear giving them a foothold to step into reality. They whisper there, in the dark corners of people's minds, producing grotesque disfigurations of the things that terrify them most." After that, Pneuma gently grasped the sides of my head, and I saw a glimpse of the horror they were capable of producing, recoiling immediately in fear.

She assured me that no matter what form they took, I could defeat them. As we trained, she would put the picture there again before I had to defend myself. I stopped recoiling in fear but I still couldn't imagine taking on so many living images of the terrors that haunted me. While they couldn't read my mind, they knew my past, and they knew how much I feared losing Amelia. Pneuma had shown me a few forms they might take, and then she would show me the opposite pictures that revealed the lie behind each nightmare. That was how I was to resist being pulled into lowering my guard. I would fight the darkness with The Light and expose fear for what it was: a liar.

"You are prepared. If you were not ready, Pneuma would not have sent you," he said. His gaze affirmed the confidence he had in me.

"We're close enough that they will be able to sense us shortly." I jumped at Owen's voice. He completely startled me. I had forgotten he was even there because Lucas and I had been focused on each other.

They talked about where we should go. The plan was to be far from where the weapons were stored, and not near the lake because we didn't know what they would try to use out there. "It's dark," Owen said, "So the Terrobah will have a slight advantage." That gave me pause.

"Why don't we wait until morning?" I asked.

"They won't come out in the daylight, once they sense how much Light is coming," Owen responded, "They would just wait until dark to come back out anyway."

"Yes," Lucas continued, "It's best to face them at our full strength and not wait until night comes again."

The harsh reality of what we were facing quieted us all. I grabbed Lucas's hand as we passed a sign saying the camp was five miles away.

* * *

As the car rounded the last bend, I took stock of what we came with. The three of us were all dressed in hiking gear. Sturdy clothes and boots. Our protection came from The Light, not from armor made by man. We wouldn't carry packs or physical, earthly weapons.

We stepped out of the car with nothing in our hands. Lucas had taken my hand to help me out of the car and hadn't release it. I reached for Owen's hand after he shut his door.

We walked, united, to the open field where the campfire had been. Lucas and Owen had decided this was the best place to engage as the Terrobah couldn't hide as easily here in the open. With The Light coming from us, we would be able to see them. Lucas wouldn't be restricted by his human properties this time. He and Owen would wield the Light as immortals.

It sounded like a good plan until the trail from the parking lot led us to our destination. Seeing the chard ashes of the campfire, I was brought back to that terrible night and what had happened here. Amelia had been lured in easily by the Terrobah, and they had hurt her terribly. I felt the pain and the fear starting to come over me, but just as quickly, it was pushed back by the power that I felt walking between Lucas and Owen. The Light humming through us, and feeling their strength through their hands, dispelled any of my lingering doubts. We literally pulsed Light as we walked. And the fear and pain dissipated with every pulse.

We weren't in the clearing a minute before we saw movement in front of us. I felt both Lucas and Owen squeeze my hands, and we came to a stop. They had been waiting for us; Owen was right that they had sensed us coming, and Uncle had somehow known I would return here. He just had no idea what I had learned and what I had become. He probably thought I would come back in fear, ready for him to take me home. Instead, I came back to fight him.

As the Terrobah came slinking through the trees, they were still in their human form, but at the far side, a terrible screech came up that made me shudder. My eyes searched in vain for any sign of Amelia. Pneuma told me she wasn't there anymore, but I searched anyway. I was here to fight Uncle and his despicable gang, so I had to stay focused. My first mission was to fight the Terrobah that were here. They would continue to track me no matter where I went, so we had to stop them.

"One of the Terrobah was terrified at seeing us here," Owen answered my unasked question about the noise.

"Silence!" a voice roared from somewhere in the middle. I knew that voice well, and so did the Terrobah because they all quieted immediately.

Uncle came out of the trees and began walking towards us.

"Get ready," Lucas said in a whisper.

I quickly projected my helmet, and it appeared in my hands. When I was training, most of the time, it just appeared on my head. But this time I had to make a choice to put it on, and I did.

Owen squeezed my hand, causing me to look at him as he let go to turn his back to us. He began to send Light out behind us. I knew he was making a shield to our backs so that no one could sneak around undetected.

"My darling, Sarah," Uncle said with his hands outstretched in a peaceful gesture as if he expected me to run into his arms. "Sarah?" he asked again, a little more timidly and gently this time. The way he said my name was in stark contrast to the word he had just shouted at the Terrobah through the forest. I knew that he was trying to exert some power over me that he had used in the past, but I felt nothing.

"Who are your friends?" he asked kindly, still trying to make nice while walking towards us.

"I think you already know Lucas," I paused as Uncle looked at Lucas, trying to maintain his smile but failing just a bit as it fell into a sneer. "And this is Owen," I said as he returned to my side. It was too much for Uncle to try to smile at Owen, so he cut his eyes quickly back to me.

I could see the struggle as he tried to maintain his smile while looking at me. He had stopped about twenty feet away and looked at me differently now. It didn't occur to me before that maybe he thought The Light coming off of us was just from Lucas and Owen and that, up unto this point, he hadn't seen the changes in me. To him, it had only been a few hours since we fled the police station, but to me, it felt like a lifetime ago.

He was looking at me hard now, leaning his head towards me like he was trying to exert some influence over me. He glared at me with the intensity of whatever thought he was trying to force on me. He stopped for a moment, looking almost confused, but then his features contorted into anger, and his eyes began to glow a terrifying, evil red.

The red glow was there for just a second, making me wonder if I had imagined it, but I knew I hadn't. In their natural state, the Terrobah had horrifying red eyes. He took a breath, his now blue eyes shining as his features turned human again. He moved his hands down the front of his shirt, regaining his composure. Then, once again, he extended his hands to me and spoke.

"Sarah. Sweet Pea."

I focused on my helmet, which was still glowing mightily. I watched Uncle as he continued, "I see you may have been deceived by these gentlemen. You might see them as friends, but they have turned you on your own uncle. Think about that, Sarah. I have been with you, caring for you since the day your parents died. And if I'm as terrible as they have made you believe I am, why would they have allowed you to leave Amelia behind?" His voice was like honey and so gentle. I shifted my feet at the mention of Amelia's name.

Uncle continued, "They have filled your head with lies. They even made you see things at camp that weren't true. Even now, they have a hold on you that isn't good. They have made you grow up too fast, missing some of the best years of your life. With me, you can have a childhood filled with everything you desire."

I knew that without my helmet, I might have been tempted to believe him. But while I still heard his words, I could see them for the lies they were.

He looked frustrated for a moment when I didn't respond to his prodding, but changed back to his gentle side and continued, "I welcome you back with open arms, and we will help you in every way. Come home, beautiful angel, come back to your family."

I felt a slight jolt in my body at his use of my mom's term of endearment for me, but I was still unmoved by his words in any way. I lifted my chin slightly at the confidence I felt.

At that slight chin tilt, he became enraged. He knew he no longer had a hold on me. He screamed in rage, and his entire face turned red like fire. I thought for sure he would descend into his true form right then, and I braced myself for the transformation. But instead, he fired an arrow at me. I hadn't even seen a bow. It formed from him, as did the arrow. It was so unexpected that it took me off guard. Lucas reacted quickly, blocking the arrow before my shield was fully engaged. The arrow dissolved the moment it pierced The Light.

He screamed in rage again, but seeing what The Light did, I didn't feel a bit of fear as he uttered a string of expletives, all directed at me.

Pneuma told me I would be allowed to offer mercy, I figured now was the time.

"Uncle, The Terrobah and The Light have been at war since the beginning. The Light will prevail here today. If you give me Amelia, I am prepared to offer you mercy," I said, keeping my voice strong and controlled.

"This earth is the Terrobah's and all that dwells within it, you ungrateful brat. We are the ones who will prevail today. Your mercy means nothing to me." His voice was beginning to be mixed with something ancient and inexplicably evil. He spat and then let a torrent of hate-filled words flow forth, finishing as he screamed, "I will not stop until your wretched line is fully cleansed or destroyed! We destroyed your parents and will destroy you too."

He started walking backwards to the rest of the Terrobah, hissing out, "Today, you will meet all your nightmares. You will wish yourself dead, and I am so happy that I will be here to grant that wish."

If I hadn't had on my helmet, I was sure I would have been cowering in a ball on the ground in fear. I could feel the power of his words; they just had no effect on me.

"You have chosen your defeat today," I said in return to him.

By the screams I was hearing behind us, the Light shields to our backs were effective.

Uncle gave a command, and the Terrobah hoard began to shift into their true form, including Uncle. "He's transforming," Lucas said to me. He had told me in case I wanted to look away, but I would have to see him like this in another minute anyway, so I didn't flinch as his human characteristics began to change into the stuff of nightmares.

The red eyes he had hidden before now came fully into view, piercing and arresting from the horror they produced. His face and flesh faded away, and the shadows began pouring out of him. Terror gripped me as his face remained steady, but the shadows that formed beneath him began to produce images I can't repeat.

My shield was firmly in place. Lucas still held my hand and was radiating Light. He turned to look at me and said, "Ready?"

"Yes," I answered quietly, but confidently, looking him directly in his eyes.

"Yes. Yes, you are," he said. His reassurance made me smile and even laugh a little, which encouraged both Lucas and Owen to let out a laugh as well.

Our countenance caused another screech from the Terrobah, more than one this time. Apparently, they couldn't stand our joy even in their true form. I wasn't sure why we were laughing at such a serious time, but maybe this was why. The Light was joy, and all things pure, and the Terrobah couldn't stand it. The screech was quieted by the sound of a thump and slaps, followed by moans of pain. It reminded me of that boy I had seen being beaten. Maybe he had been a Terrobist and was still getting punished for any insubordination.

We looked back towards the trees as more Terrobah came out, and they quickly assumed different shapes. I cautiously searched for Amelia, knowing she wasn't there, but I couldn't help myself. I also couldn't help but count them. There were fifteen visible to us and probably more lurking in the trees. Lucas squeezed my hand, and I remembered that even if they outnumbered us, that numbers did not determine the outcome. The Light was more powerful than anything, and The Light was with us.

Lucas was reminding us of our strategy, "First?" Lucas quizzed me.

"Blast," I replied

"Yes, give it everything you've got. Next?"

"Ropes," I replied. This wasn't like the movies, the Terrobah wouldn't charge us one or two at a time, so we would blast them back altogether to confuse them, and then Lucas and Owen would tie up as many as they could with ropes made from the energy of The Light. The strength of each Terrobah would determine how long the rope held him. The stronger ones would escape faster. The weakest ones might lose consciousness before they were even tied up.

"Third?" he continued.

"Fight."

"Formation?"

"Triangle," I said, as each answer reminded me that I was, indeed, ready for this fight.

We had moved so that Lucas was in between Owen and me. We stood with our backs to one another, shoulders touching, or in my case, arms touching, given our height difference. I had my forcefield up and glowing strong and could already see my fist-shaped blasts forming on my hands. Uncle's shriek filled the air, the arrows started flying, and his army poured towards us.

I thought again about my forcefield around me and my helmet; they were firmly in place. I even gave myself permission not to notice the form of the Terrobah. Some were in their human forms, specifically to torment me, while others were pure Terrobah. Arrow after arrow sparked and disintegrated in the light of the forcefield in front of me. There was no fear in me, only a strong humming pulse of The Light. I'm sure it helped that I felt Lucas's presence.

The power was surging so strong within me that I was almost overwhelmed by it. I had to get this pulse out, I was so ready. I was ready to release the biggest pulse I'd ever done and almost did. The power surged even stronger within me, but Lucas cautioned, "Wait." He said it slowly, so I knew he just meant to let them get a bit closer. It was all I could do to continue to contain it.

"3, 2, 1," he whispered. "Now!"

The blast pushed forth from my hands in giant fists as they joined with the blinding light coming from Lucas and Owen. Every single Terrobah was blown back and writhed in pain as we kept the blast going. I didn't look away from my targets but could sense the entire forest surrounding us was lit up, The Light shooting to the sky as well. Anyone around us would have seen that beam of light, so it was a good thing we were in the middle of nowhere. I'm sure Sergeant Tanner wouldn't know what to tell the boys down at the station.

"Keep going!" Lucas shouted. I pushed harder but could feel the blast surge was waning in me.

"Forward!" he said. We began to walk forward towards the Terrobah who were mostly on the ground. They were shrieking as they writhed around in agony, but my helmet protected me from the worst of that as well. Their shrieks would have caused me great pain without it. Others weren't even moving as they had been completely incapacitated.

"Get ready," Lucas shouted, which I knew meant he and Owen would begin to tie up the Terrobah who were down from the blast, while I would continue smaller blasts and defend them from any Terrobah that overcame our initial blast more quickly than others.

"Now!" he shouted as we released our blast. He and Owen moved faster than I had ever seen them move. Their hands moved back and forth, quickly creating a vibration that pulled energy from The Light. From there, they stretched their hands apart, as though they were pulling a rope out of thin air, then quickly bound any Terrobah who seemed to be overcoming the effects faster. It all happened so fast it looked like they were simply wrapping pretend ropes around their would-be assassins.

One of the human Terrobah, who was still unbound, started getting to his feet, and I blasted him back down, sending Owen to him next. Two more stood to their feet, so I fired one hand at each of them, knocking them down but not as forcefully, given the blast was divided. Lucas moved to secure the first one as I moved to blast the other one again.

It was all moving very fast; eight Terrobah were harnessed, but all the others had now returned to their feet, with six moving straight toward me. Lucas and Owen had to join me because I no longer had enough energy to incapacitate the Terrobah long enough for them to be tethered.

We were in our triangle formation now, the remaining Terrobah surrounding us. We had our backs to each other, Lucas and Owen sending out blasts while I regained some strength. It seemed the Terrobah had their sights set on me, probably at Uncle's orders, but somehow Lucas lured them more towards him or managed to rotate our triangle at just the right moment for me to avoid the attack. As Lucas and Owen sent out debilitating blasts, I could feel the strength of The Light increasing within me, and I returned to the fight sending out renewed blasts of my own.

Each vile creature looked different from the next, sometimes changing form right in front of me in an attempt to frighten or distract me. The only one that had any real effect on me was one that looked and spoke like Amelia. Her face was wretched and emaciated, hair missing from her head, bones protruding from her ribs, and her skin clinging to her paper-thin frame. She ran towards me, screaming, "Sarah! You left me! You left me!" I stood spellbound by her accusations as my living nightmare came closer and closer with each step. I screamed in pain and horror, and for a moment, The Light faded from my hands. Owen heard the voice of the Terrobah and turned to see what was happening. His aim was swift, as he blasted it back, returning it to its shadow form.

The thought that they would use the image of my sister made the power within me surge. I recovered from my fear, and with a force I had yet to obtain, blasted the next one to come at me into the ground, brushing my hands back and forth as if to say I'd made short order of him. We were winning, and I looked over at Lucas to affirm my hopes.

Yet, when I saw him, somehow, Lucas had broken formation without me noticing and was beaten and bloody on the ground. Another Terrobah sat on top of him, thrashing at his chest and making him scream out in pain. But something wasn't right about the picture before me; Lucas had never screamed out in pain when he was being tortured. I used my shield to hold them back but waited to blast until I was sure. I couldn't take my eyes off my targets to look around for Lucas, and I couldn't feel him next to me. I yelled, "Lucas!" causing another Terrobah to rush at me. With one hand, I held the shield against the two, and with my other hand, I pulsed with Light and knocked him back a bit. He seemed weaker than some others, so I punched hard again as I heard, "That's not me, Sarah!" Lucas's real voice was strong and healthy behind me.

The Terrobah that received the pulse from my right hand felt the force of their deception with another pulse. The more they used the image of people I loved, the more I felt The Light pulse with my anger. With the creature now fully incapacitated, I could fully focus on the two that were imitating Lucas and his torturer. It still pained me to hear his voice cry out in pain. As I blasted a pulse at the fake Lucas and his torturing Terrobah, it hit me that I didn't actually know if Lucas and Owen could be harmed.

Lucas was sure harmed while he was at camp, so didn't that also mean that he could be hurt today?

The questions churned so much in my head that worry began to drown out all other thoughts. I hadn't realized how much until I heard, "You're going to get them killed, Sarah." My blasting slowed as that thought hit me right in the heart. The anxiety overtook me, and my helmet stopped projecting. I desperately tried to picture it and get it back when the same putrid voice whispered, "You are worthless. You couldn't save your own sister, and you won't be able to save your friends."

That one made my shield falter as well because I had always felt worthless. *I was worthless, wasn't I?*

I dropped to my knees with my head in my hands, screaming for the voice to leave. Surrounded by shadow, I heard the voice repeat itself, growing louder and louder.

No, Pneuma told me I was . . . wait, what had she said.

The thoughts were coming harder and faster, each feeling like a shot to my ribcage, and I knew Uncle was somewhere tormenting me. I needed help, but I couldn't even call to Lucas or Owen. My forcefield was starting to fade and shimmer; I was losing it, but again I remembered Pneuma. Right before my forcefield disappeared I whispered weakly, "Pneuma."

Immediately, the shadows fled, and a brilliant Light struck down from above. My weapons returned to me, and I heard her voice thunder, "Sarah Joy, you are worthy, you are chosen, and you are a Light Bearer."

"I am a Light Bearer!" I screamed in agreement. I believed Pneuma, and at once the darkness that drew near fled back to its source in Uncle. The two Terrobah were almost upon me. The fake Lucas again begged me to help him while the torturer gave him another lashing.

I stared into the red eyes of his Terrobah, and for a wavering moment, I felt fear. But once again, Pneuma's voice came to me, "Do not be afraid, Sarah. I am with you wherever you go."

I felt such a strong surge of power. The Light was so much more powerful than any of their weak attempts to stop it. I felt the surge of power grow as I thought about Pneuma and Owen and Lucas. They were imitating Lucas, my Lucas, recreating the torture he'd endured at the camp. I blasted both Terrobah with such power and strength they were knocked flat, unconscious, and smoking. I knew that if I continued while they were in this state, I could eventually erase them from existence. They could not hold up forever against The Light. I felt anger surge in me, and more power came forth from me. I wanted to eliminate them, I wanted to *kill*. But then I heard Pneuma speak, "That's enough, my child." Her voice was enough to stop me in my rage.

Her words from training came back to me. "At some point, you will have to erase another being from existence. It will change something in you when you do." Her eyes had pierced right through me as she finished by saying, "Do not let your anger darken your heart."

As I looked down at the two forms on the ground at my feet, they no longer looked frightening; they looked pitiful. My anger was gone. My heart pitied their wretched forms, and I turned away to find my next opponent.

I glanced back to see that Lucas's and Owen's backs faced me as they were both finishing off a Terrobah.

Suddenly, Owen was struck so hard his body flew backwards, straight into me. I bore the full brunt of his weight, and the air was knocked out of me as I was pinned to the ground. As I gasped for breath, I lifted my head to see that a forcefield of Light was forming over both of us. Lucas was shielding us as he continued fighting with his other hand. But I knew Lucas couldn't hold them off alone forever.

"Owen," I whispered. I wasn't trying to be quiet; it was just all I could manage with him on top of me.

I could feel him trying to get up, but I didn't have the strength to help him. I pleaded for strength to come from The Light, and somehow, as the power of The Light surged through me, I managed to get us both upright. That's when I saw what was sticking out of his right side towards his back. Somehow in the fight, he had been pierced with an arrow that was still blazing red with heat. Owen was gasping for breath, and I could tell he couldn't breathe because that thing had gone into his lungs. He slumped back down to the ground.

"Owen!" I screamed.

I knelt down next to him and whispered, "What can I do?"

"I...can...already... feel..." he tried to say to me.

"What?!" I shouted, thinking he was going to say he could feel himself dying. Could he die? I didn't think so; he was immortal, right?

"The Light..." he breathed in sharply, "it's pushing...it out."

And then I saw what he was talking about. The arrow was slowly moving out, and the shaft of the arrow had started to dissolve in The Light as well.

Owen's breathing was starting to get better, but he was still taking shallow, gasping breaths.

"Can I help?" I asked as I noticed that Lucas's forcefield had started to shimmer, meaning we had very little time.

"Yes...wrap your arms... around," he didn't even have time to finish before I wrapped my arms around him and let him breathe deeply like Lucas had done for me so many times. It was a much shorter recovery for him than it had always been for me. A few quick seconds, a few breaths, and the arrow was out, and then he was breathing deeply on his own.

"Okay," he said, "Thank you, Sarah."

I watched him rise, still stunned that I had helped a Mythreal recover. "Forcefield!" he shouted and then turned away from me to face the Terrobah. Lucas's forcefield was weakening, and for some reason, I thought that was what he meant. I had been distracted by being a part of his healing, and my forcefield was not up. I didn't realize the mistake until I felt the pain of an arrow piercing my back. Lucas's forcefield had fallen the moment before I was shot. I screamed in agony as another found its target in my back, and I fell face-first to the ground.

CHAPTER 22

I was floating in the river in Ganheela. It was peaceful and calm, then agitated. But, that couldn't be right, the waters were never agitated. Suddenly, I could feel the warmth of the water, whereas before the water was neither cold nor warm, it was just…perfect. Now I felt warmth on my back. All at once, the warmth became searing heat. I was burning alive in the river. I woke up screaming in pain as someone lifted me.

"Sarah!" I heard an agonized scream. And then a blood-curdling scream erupted. My eyes were closed, but they still almost felt blinded by light that accompanied it.

"Sarah, Sarah, I'm so sorry," Owen said. He was the one holding me, and I realized Lucas was the one screaming.

"Oh, Sarah, I'm sorry you're in pain, it's all my fault." I forced my eyes open a little, but it was difficult to keep them that way.

Owen had me wrapped in his arms. I knew he was trying to heal me, but the pain only grew worse.

The blinding light began to dim, and I realized the screaming had stopped.

"Sarah, Sarah, are you okay?" I heard Lucas say as he came close. I tried so hard to open my eyes for him, but with the searing pain, I just wanted to be pulled under into whatever awaited me. Maybe it was the river in Ganheela.

Yes, I'm okay, I'm slipping away to Ganheela.

I started to feel the water again.

"Sarah, don't you dare." Lucas's voice was firm. "Open your eyes, Sarah," he said, more gently this time, almost pleading.

I slowly managed to open my eyes and was rewarded with his glorious face. "You have to focus, Sarah. We have to get these arrows out; their poison is seeping into you."

He looked at Owen, "We have to pull them out," Lucas said.

"I have already been trying, but they won't budge." Owen's voice sounded strange, a mixture of frustration and agony, a sound I'd never heard from him before. I couldn't be sure because now that my gaze was on Lucas, I had to stay fixed there or I knew I would surrender fully to the river.

"We have gotten them out before," Lucas said, a trace of anger returning to his voice.

"I know, but these have different tips on them. They hook themselves into their target. If we pull them out, it might rip through her lungs and heart. Lucas, if we do this, she might die."

I tried to push aside my pain to summon The Light from within, hoping maybe I could help them in some way. I screamed in agony as they tried again to remove the Terrobah's arrows from me. My attempt to use The Light, coupled with the intense pain I felt, drained any energy I had remaining. Lucas and Owen were still talking, and I felt tugging on my back, but my new focus was on breathing. I could barely breathe; each breath became more labored than the last.

"Pneuma, help!" Lucas screamed out in despair.

I had closed my eyes to focus on breathing. I couldn't see Lucas, but I could imagine what his face looked like. I wanted to comfort him, to remove the anguish from his face. I tried to lift my hand, but it wasn't responding, not even a little bit. I couldn't open my eyes now either. It must be the poison. I lay unable to move on the remaining ashes of the bonfire where Amelia had been... I felt myself drifting further away.

"The ropes!" Lucas exclaimed as his communication with Pneuma ceased. "The ropes!"

"Ropes?" Owen asked.

"We can use our Light ropes. The energy from The Light should weaken the hold the arrows have, and we can get them out," Lucas answered.

I was barely breathing, and their voices seemed distant. I tried to hang on; to keep breathing.

"That much Light in that concentration will be very painful for her because of the poison, but if it's what Pneuma told you to do, then it's the only way," Owen said.

"Owen, hold her against you so that you can heal her the moment the arrows are removed."

Lucas's voice was distant, but I heard him say, "Sarah, I'm sorry."

I tried to pull in one more gasp of air as I felt the pain intensify even more, but then I heard and felt nothing.

"Sarah, Sarah Joy." I heard my name so sweetly. I knew this voice. This voice knew my name. It was my mother's voice, and I wanted so desperately to see her. I wanted to see her, but I couldn't.

"Not yet, beautiful one. I will see you again someday, but now you need to stay and hold up The Light." Her voice was so near, I was sure I could touch her. Yet, my eyes couldn't open, and my arms couldn't move. Was I dreaming? Was I living in a distant memory? Was I going to wake up as a 9-year-old child, to my mother stroking my hair and wiping the tears from my face? Had this all been a bad dream?

"Sarah," I heard another voice. It was a man, but it wasn't my dad. Why couldn't I open my eyes? I heard his voice again, but he sounded hurt or in pain. I also knew this voice. And this voice also knew my name. Who was it?

I was so weak, I couldn't open my eyes, and yet my desire to comfort that voice was strong. I could feel the voice pulling me away from my mother, away from the comfort I felt there.

"Sarah Joy, my beloved child," another female voice called to me. "You have done so well, showing mercy, fighting, bringing The Light, and healing." As the voice continued, I started to remember: Pneuma, Ganheela, the Terrobah, Uncle, Lucas.

Lucas! His was the voice calling to me. I had to get back to him; he was in such pain. And just as I thought it, my eyes flew open, and he was there before me. "Lucas," I said softly.

"Sarah!" he exclaimed, smiling through his tears. He lifted me in his arms and stood. We clung to each other, both overwhelmed at the joy of being together.

"You can put me down now," I laughed. "I've been healed."

As soon as my feet hit the ground, I looked briefly around. The forcefield was gone, and the rain of arrows from the Terrobah had stopped. But before I could make sense of what I saw, I felt arms from behind me come around, embracing us both in a big bear hug.

"Sarah, I can't believe you're back," I heard Owen whisper.

"Owen." He looked at me like he couldn't believe I was alive.

I turned back to Lucas, and he was looking at me in much the same way as Owen. "We thought we had failed you. We thought we had failed The Light. But you are unbelievable."

"I don't know what you are talking about, Lucas; you saved me. I was dying, took my last breath, and the next thing I knew, I was in your arms."

"Sarah, you were gone. We thought we hadn't gotten the arrows out quickly enough."

I thought about that for a moment. "Well, I feel great, so whatever happened, I'm thankful. I wouldn't be here if it weren't for you both." I reached out to grab both of their hands, giving them a squeeze. It was then that I saw the Terrobah lying on the ground and remembered exactly why we were there in the first place.

"Did we win?" I asked, still feeling a little fuzzy on all of the details.

Lucas was silent.

I looked around me to see remnants of Terrobah either laid out on the ground or tied up in ropes.

"It looks like we won," I said, trying to figure out why the guys weren't celebrating.

"Lucas, please tell me what's going on," I said, not liking the confusion I felt.

Lucas's voice quivered and shook. "I… I did something I've never done before. I let anger and pain overtake me. When you were dying, I was consumed by the pain and burning Light came out of me."

I had been looking at him, but I moved my gaze to the Terrobah, their forms shredded and smoking. It was clear. These weren't coming back again.

I looked back at Lucas, still confused. We had won, so why was he upset? "Lucas, what is it? What aren't you saying?"

"None of our kind has ever been able to do something like this before." He paused. "I thought it would consume me. I thought I was being pulled into the darkness."

Owen responded softly, "Lucas, it was The Light that came through you that saved us. It was Light and not darkness. If it hadn't happened like it did, we wouldn't have been able to save Sarah."

I reached for his hand again, but for the first time ever, he pulled away from me.

"Lucas."

"I don't want to hurt you, Sarah," he looked down at his hands, fearful of the power he wielded.

"You would never hurt me." His head was bent and his eyes closed, so I moved to stand in front of him. I reached for his face, but he jerked his head back slightly at my touch. I reached for his face again, holding it in my hands.

"Lucas." His eyes opened and shimmered with tears, "You would never hurt me, you saved all of us." He didn't respond. "Do you hear me?"

It took him a moment, but then he responded with a soft, "Yes."

"I love you," I said it in a way as if I were expecting an answer from him.

His face cleared a bit, and he returned, "And I love you, Sarah Joy."

"That's better," I said. For all the times his gaze comforted me, I knew this one time I returned the favor. The fear left his face.

I released his face but quickly grabbed his hand. I reached out to Owen with my other hand and said, "Okay, boys, what's next?"

"Well, Lucas took care of the Terrobah," Owen said with a quip, like that was just one small thing on our to-do list. The way he said it made a smile spread across my face. He was back to his joking self.

"Yes, a little too well," Lucas said softly.

"What do you mean?" I asked not really believing he was upset that a few Terrobah had expired. I looked at him, then allowed my gaze to follow where he was looking. I saw ashes rising in the air. A Terrobah had been finished off and blew away as if it was only dust.

Lucas hadn't replied, so I continued with, "What were we supposed to do with them instead?"

Owen jumped in. "It would have been nice to have a few conscious for questioning, but it's no biggie, smoldering Terrobah are good too," he said, once again trying to lighten the mood.

"What was I thinking?" Lucas muttered.

"You weren't, old friend," replied Owen. "What came out of you wasn't something anyone could control. It was only something The Light could produce, and it saved us all."

"No, no, now we can't ask them about Amelia! We don't know what they're planning next for Sarah. We won't know who their next target is."

I let him continue to berate himself for just a moment longer, but then I'd had enough. "Lucas," I said firmly. He turned his eyes to me. "This isn't like you. You don't doubt yourself. You do what has to be done, even when it's hard. So, what's so different about this time?"

As he looked at me, tears filled his eyes. "I could have killed you," he whispered. His face was filled with so much pain.

"But, you didn't."

"It doesn't matter," he said fiercely.

"Yes, it does. There is a big difference between life and death. Lucas, I remember that pulse, and besides seeing a blinding white light behind my eyelids and hearing you scream, I felt nothing but the pain of my wounds and Owen's arms."

He was looking at me with confusion.

"You're seeing this Light fire as something similar to what the Terrobah do, but all I saw was Light. It may have come from a place of anger, but not all anger comes from fear. This anger came from love; it came from The Light."

He looked at Owen, who was smiling at me like I had just given him the best news ever. Owen looked to Lucas and said, "She's right, Lucas. The anger you were overcome with was righteous and pure. If there had been any darkness, she would most likely have died because of the poison already in her."

As we watched Lucas process this, his face changed to one of understanding.

"You're still one of us," Owen said, "You can still come home any time."

Lucas's countenance immediately changed and he embraced Owen, pounding him on the back, as the relief became more evident on his face.

"See!" I said, matching his smile.

He turned to embrace me, lifted me up in his arms, and spun me around, laughing at the fate he had escaped.

I giggled at his enthusiasm. "Lucas, put me down!" I said, not really wanting him to. I loved to see him this way. He sat me down, and while he was still beaming, I said, "You are pure light and goodness. Nothing will ever change that."

"Now to clean up," Lucas said with his smile firmly in place.

There were a few Terrobah in ropes that weren't too far gone from Lucas's blast to be revived. I walked around with my forcefield firmly in place and my helmet on, just in case. Since Lucas came to terms with what happened, he was glowing, more than both Owen and me. It was almost like when he had come out of the furnace. That moment felt like years ago. I laughed to myself, thinking that for me, it really was like years had passed.

I walked by each one of the Terrobah, but I didn't see the one that I was looking for. I would know Uncle when I saw him, even if he was smoldering in his true form.

"Lucas?" I asked.

He turned and looked at me. "I don't see Uncle."

He seemed taken aback by that, like he couldn't believe he had forgotten to look for Uncle himself. He started marching around the field, looking at the Terrobah.

Lucas was all the way to the other side of the field when I felt a chill go down my spine. "Uncle," I whispered, and turned just in time to see him. He had returned to his human form and charged at me from the woods. I gasped in shock as he fired arrow after arrow as he ran at me. My forcefield was dissolving the arrows, but I would still need to defend myself against the physical attack if he got close enough.

Of course, he was the last one remaining. I could feel anger rise in me at the thought of him cowering in the woods. He'd waited for his chance to catch me alone and off guard, and like the coward he was, he attacked.

I blasted him back, but it barely slowed him. I blasted again with the same result. But then I felt Lucas and Owen on either side of me, touching me.

Uncle never stood a chance. Lucas, Owen, and I stood shoulder to shoulder, and with our collected strength channeling the power of The Light, we sent a pulse so strong that it cratered the earth, leaving Uncle smoking at the center. We didn't stop firing until he stopped twitching. We kept blasting until we were on top of his smoking, still form, which had transformed back to the Terrobah.

"That's not him," Lucas said. His words were laced with the confusion I was feeling.

"What do you mean?" I asked in almost a shout.

"It's not him… it was a decoy," he said slowly.

We had taken care of all of the Terrobah but hadn't managed to get Uncle. That last Terrobah had been told to pose as Uncle, to make the coward's escape more failproof.

We heard a hellish moan behind us and turned quickly together. The Terrobah that Lucas had been working on was now moving and returned to its charred human form. It was Tommy. Lucas and Owen moved to stand over him, ready to blast.

"Where is Uncle?" Lucas demanded.

Tommy just sneered at Lucas in between his grimaces of pain. His ugly red eyes remained, and his blackened flesh just made it that much worse.

"I'm going to ask you one more time," Lucas said slowly, but with a command to his voice that I had never heard before. He had his hand out, and energy was flickering around, almost as if it were lightning. Tommy stared at Lucas with fear flashing in his red eyes.

"Where is Uncle?" Lucas asked again.

"I don't know," the creature gasped out.

Lucas made the lightning in his other hand and tilted his head to the side to challenge Tommy's statement.

"I really don't know!" He cowered in fear before Lucas.

"Tommy!" I said, feeling angry enough to blast him as well. "Tell us!"

He looked at me as if I had gone crazy, but answered, "I don't know, ok! He was supposed to leave with you. But now… the Boss will be coming for him." Tommy's red eyes squinted in morbid delight as the thought of Uncle's torture ran across his mind.

"Where would he go?" I demanded next.

Tommy turned his gaze to me, tilting his head and producing a cruel smile. "He's probably heading to where he sent Amelia, but he didn't tell a single one of us where that is."

"Amelia!" I shuddered to think where they might have gone.

"And Ben is her guard." At Tommy's words, I felt like I was going to pass out. Amelia was still in the hands of two of the worst Terrobah, and who knows what lies they were poisoning her with. The world started to spin.

Owen grabbed my shoulders to steady me. I had too much Light pulsing through me to pass out, but I began to feel the emotional effects of what my sister was now facing.

"Where did he send Amelia?" Lucas demanded with lightning glowing in his palms.

Tommy cringed away from him, "I swear I don't know, he didn't tell anyone but Ben."

"Ugh," I moaned thinking of her with those two who were pure evil. What lies were they telling her now, about me even?

"She is much easier to sway; our truths are sinking in with her." Tommy's red eyes glowed, and I turned away, trying to think of anything other than the fact that I had left my sister with these monsters.

Amelia had been in no condition to be moved when we had left, but I thought I still had time to rescue her. Pneuma had told me the Terrobah had taken Amelia, but I had hoped the other Terrobah knew where she was.

"You have a beautiful target on your back now, Sarah," Tommy hissed as his human voice gave way to the Terrobah within. I whirled around to glare at him. "We can see The Light perfectly wherever our weapons pierce. You were marked by us, and some-day, eventually, you will be one of us."

Before the last word finished crossing his lips, Lucas blasted him unconscious.

"Is that true?" I asked Lucas, trying to twist myself so that I could see my back.

"The Light is brighter in those areas. So maybe he was telling the truth about it being easier to see," Lucas paused. "But I don't think it's their mark." He trailed off.

"What do you mean?" I asked, still trying hopelessly to see my back.

Lucas was behind me, touching my back over those areas. "Lucas?" I questioned, even though I couldn't see him standing behind me.

"Those areas have become stronger than ever before and the thickness of The Light seems to have spread to your entire back. It's almost like you've gained a permanent shield on your back."

"What?!" I asked in astonishment, again trying to see what he was describing.

"Even if they can see this, you're not an easy target. What they think is a target is actually a shield. Their weapons will bounce off you."

"My wounds are now actually a defense?" I asked calmly, no longer needing to see what was back there.

"It appears so. What they meant for evil has become your good," Lucas said in awe.

"Does this not normally happen when Light Bearers are wounded?" I asked. Neither of them answered, so I turned to fully face them with the question still on my face. Lucas was looking a bit stunned, so I focused my attention on Owen.

"Owen?" I entreated.

He cleared his throat, as if trying to get past some emotion. "There aren't many Light Bearers that survive a physical attack of the Terrobah," he said, "and never one of this magnitude."

That's why he was having trouble speaking, I shouldn't have survived this, but I did, and I was better than before.

"You're a warrior, Sarah, just as we knew you would be."

I let his words wash over me, feeling the same confidence that he exuded as he spoke. I was a warrior, I wasn't weak. I was worthy of The Light that worked to save me and make me stronger than I had ever been before. I wasn't easily persuaded by darkness, even when they took their best shot at me. I was strong and capable in The Light. The Light secured my destiny and placed me in my family, but Amelia came from the same line, and had been persuaded by the darkness. I had always seen myself as the weaker of the two, but I was actually stronger in The Light than she ever would be in the darkness. But if she could fall, couldn't I too? Tommy's words haunted me. *Eventually, you will become one of us.*

"Are you okay, Sarah?" Lucas asked.

"Yes," I said. Even with all of the questions swirling around me, I knew for now, I was okay.

CHAPTER 23

The sun started to rise across the field, and the sight and stench of the Terrobah overwhelmed my senses. By the time everything was finished, there were only six Terrobah remaining, and they were all incapacitated on the ground, secured in ropes. The rest had been obliterated to ash or they had fled.

"What happens to them now?" I asked Owen. Lucas had gone to look around the camp to see if there were any clues about Amelia or any stragglers.

"They stay here," Owen replied matter-of-factly, intent upon his work of securing their ropes.

"What?"

"They stay here," he said again as if I hadn't heard him the first time.

"No, I mean why would we let them stay here, won't they just eventually get free and come after me again?" I said, feeling a bit angry that we had done all this work for nothing.

"No, these ropes will erase their memory of their current target, and they won't escape these bonds on their own. Other Terrobah will come and take them back."

"They won't remember me?"

"No, they were sent here for a purpose, and all of that has been erased. None of these Terrobah will have the ability to track you anymore." I liked the sound of that, but I was still confused.

"You said take them back, back where?"

"To their, uh, headquarters," he said, focusing on a knot that seemed particularly tricky, but I wouldn't be distracted.

"To their headquarters? So, we just let them go free, and they don't answer for what they have done?"

"They will answer for what they have done, from both The Light and the darkness." He trailed off.

"How? I don't understand, Owen. Why can't we just take them to Light jail or something?" I asked, feeling frustrated.

Owen smiled and shook his head at my use of the words "Light jail."

"There is no such thing. They aren't allowed in places of The Light." He stood as he finished tying up the last of the Terrobah and turned to look at me.

"So how will they be accountable to The Light?"

"They just were; you dealt out some serious accountability for what they've done," Owen said with a smile.

"Owen," I said with a laugh, but a slight trace of frustration. I couldn't believe that's all the punishment they would receive. Was that all we came back for?

I said as much to Owen, who lost his smile. "Obviously, we were hoping to capture Uncle and get more information on Amelia. And then some are just no more." He said, trailing off.

"Well then, shouldn't we make them all 'no more' so that they can't hurt or deceive anyone else?" I asked, feeling angry that he seemed so reluctant to hurt the Terrobah.

"That isn't our purpose." The sound of his voice jerked my eyes to him. He said it so firmly that I felt it in my bones.

He continued, "We are the Eklesi of The Light. We belong to life itself. We do not take life if it can be helped. Any life, no matter how undeserving."

I felt ashamed at how quickly I wanted to deliver the death blow, but also slightly confused.

"But there's no hope for them, it's not the same as with humans."

"Only the One who gives life decides when life should be taken back."

"But they are also darkness, and humans aren't even aware of how they're being manipulated by the darkness. Surely keeping them alive is the worse option here," I said.

"Again, Sarah, that is not our purpose." I felt his words in my bones, and this time, I agreed, feeling the full conviction of their meaning.

We were quiet for a few moments. "Wait," I said, "You also said something about the darkness punishing them."

His face looked pained as he replied. "What we did to them here was just a taste of what they will feel when they are taken back to their headquarters and are punished for their failures."

I could tell Owen truly felt bad to offer these Terrobah up to their masters or whatever they were called, to be punished. It hurt him to think about it.

"How can you feel so deeply for them?"

"They were once just like us," he said as he looked towards where the sun was coming up over the forest. With his gaze fixed on the sun's light, he took a deep breath, and his smile returned.

"I feel like you don't want me to ask, but I kind of can't let it go. The Terrobah were like you and Lucas?" I asked in disbelief.

"Yes, and that's all I can say." His smile had fallen again in sorrow, and it looked like regret. He continued, "Sarah, have you ever felt pity for someone, even though they made choices and kind of deserved what was coming to them? Doesn't part of you still wish you could change their past?"

I knew what he was getting at. I had always felt for people like that. Amelia, most of all, but there was also the boy Ben beat in the woods. I had even offered Uncle and the rest of the Terrobah mercy before we fought them. My thoughts returned to Amelia. She had run towards the darkness so long that choosing Ben over me must have seemed like the right choice. If only she hadn't chosen Ben, she could have left the camp with Lucas and me. Despite all of that, I would still do anything I could to save her.

I simply said, "Yes," in reply. It was all I could manage to get out. I still wanted more for Amelia.

Lucas returned a short time later. He had found nothing indicating Amelia's whereabouts, but he did pack up our belongings so

I would have clothes and toiletries—things I still needed here in this world. He put them in the car, along with Amelia's things. He didn't think I would want to look through her stuff here. He knew me so well.

"So, what's next?" I asked. I pushed down the sadness, and anxious excitement coursed through me as we all walked back toward the car.

"Our time together is done," Lucas replied gently.

"What?!" I asked sharply, completely taken aback. I stopped dead in my tracks.

"Sarah, it's time." His voice broke a bit, and he cleared his throat. "I have to leave you."

"What about Amelia? Aren't we going after her?" I asked, feeling somewhat deflated and confused.

"No, Pneuma hasn't revealed anything further about her location. After this loss, Amelia will be heavily protected. Owen and I were only given permission to help in this one battle, and you are not yet ready to go and fight alone."

"So, that's it? I just have to give up on her?" I felt tears come to my eyes.

"No, Sarah, never give up on her. You will free her someday." He said it with such assurance that I held on tight to his words, hoping I would save her someday.

"But our time together is done?" I reached for both of their hands.

"Owen will drive you to your new home," Lucas said, clearing his throat against his unsteady voice.

"Where are you going?" I whispered, looking at him through tears.

"I can't tell you that, Sarah. Our mission is different from yours." He spoke softly, gently. There was no rebuke in his voice, just the truth as it was.

"What if they come after me?" I wasn't feeling any fear in that moment, I was just grasping at straws to get Lucas to stay.

"They will." He stared at me with the same look of confidence as before. "And you will always have help."

"But how will you know I need help?" I asked.

"You call for help, and the help you need will come."

"But," I stalled, getting a little frustrated that I couldn't sway him even a little.

"Sarah," Lucas said kindly and calmly. "You are ready. You are the most accomplished Light Bearer I've ever seen. A few Terrobah are no match for you, Sarah." He said my name in a way that I had to look up at him. "But even with that, you are never alone." He said each word slow and measured.

I knew that was true, I had just seen evidence that I was part of a force that could not be defeated. The Eklesi had dealt a mighty blow to the darkness today.

"You can do this, Sarah Joy, warrior princess." Lucas winked and smiled at me.

"Warrior Princess?" I asked, coming a little out of my funk at the name he had just called me.

"Oh," he said, acting a little silly, "As you know, your name means princess."

"I think I remember Pneuma saying something about that."

"Well, you are a princess of The Light, and Owen and I both bear witness that you are a fierce warrior. So…" he paused in a dramatic way. "You are a warrior princess." He bowed with great flair to show his reverence for such royalty, flashing his brilliant smile as he did so.

"I AM a warrior princess," I said, receiving the honor he was bestowing on me with a smile to match his in return.

I turned to look back at the field, but I could no longer see it through the trees. I couldn't believe all that had happened and that we had accomplished together. It was amazing, the things my eyes had seen, and the forces my mind and body had been able to exert. I was in awe of the power of The Light inside of me.

Owen said something to Lucas, and the two of them embraced. When they were done, Owen looked at me and said, "I'll be in the car," as he turned to finish walking the path that way.

My eyes watched him. I was reluctant to turn my attention to Lucas because I didn't want to say goodbye. He gently took my left hand into both of his, pulling them up to his chest. My eyes had no choice but to follow my hand up and continue on to look him in the eyes.

"You have done so wonderfully, Sarah, but it's still hard for me to see you go, for me to let you be on your own."

"I won't be on my own, right?" I said with a small smile.

He returned the smile. "Of course not. You are never alone; The Light is always with you. And Pneuma will pop in from time to time."

We both laughed a little at that. She had been with us this whole time in the battle, even if we weren't aware of her presence. "But I'll still be without you," I said, bringing us back full circle.

"Yes," he said, dropping his eyes. He reached to touch the necklace he had given me as it still hung around my neck. I had forgotten it was there and felt some happiness that I would have a part of him with me, all while I still had a deep, painful ache at having to say goodbye.

"I wish you could stay with me," I said softly, as a tear rolled down my cheek.

"I know," he said, gently touching my face with one of his hands. "But, a new mission has been chosen for me, and I must go." The quiet of the morning forest fell around us.

"Lucas, I uh…" How would I ever begin to put into words how I felt about him and everything that he had done for me? The worldly love I had known before was inadequate for how I felt about Lucas. I wasn't teenage, flighty, in-love with him, but I had a deep, deep, forever-ingrained, unconditional love for him. I couldn't even look at him. "My words are failing me, so all I can say is thank you and…" my voice broke off with emotion, "and… I love you."

"And I love you, Sarah Joy." He wrapped me in his arms, and we stayed like that for a long while. I think he was letting me breathe in whatever else I might need from him. Love, strength, courage. I breathed deeply while I listened to his heartbeat.

When I felt contentment flood my soul, I knew it was time to say goodbye. I took one more deep breath and squeezed him around his waist one more time. Then, I pulled back, and so did he. We looked into each other's eyes for another long moment, then he nodded his head at me as he had done in training to tell me, "You've got this."

I nodded back as our fingers slipped apart. Lucas moved backward and then turned to walk through the trees until I could no longer see or hear him. He was gone from my life and gone from this world for a time. My heart ached for him, and the separation was already making it hard to breathe as the tears ran down my cheeks.

I knew deep down that he would be back and that I would see him again. I had to force myself to take a steadying breath as I stared into the trees after him. I turned my head to look down the path where Owen waited. I knew that I had a new life before me. I allowed myself one last glance towards the spot where Lucas had disappeared, but my new life was calling to me.

With that thought, I turned back to walk down the path toward my life as a Light Bearer.

ACKNOWLEDGEMENTS:

Light Bearers: The Awakening came to me through a divine dream. There was no story outline, no idea of where I would end up in the end. Each time I sat down to write, I would pray, and I would begin to type. I am so thankful for the friends and family that came around me during this process, understanding my need to get this dream onto paper so that others could read it and gain hope from it. Thank you, readers, for taking a chance on this first-time author. I know your time is precious, and I'm thankful you decided to spend it here.

Thank you, to my husband. Without you, there would be no book. You never wavered in your belief that this book was important, and you have gone to great lengths to help me get it published. *I would have given up long ago if I hadn't had your encouragement* and understanding. You sat beside me for each edit, I said it was just to start, but you remained by my side as you do in every aspect of our life together. Our first sixteen years have certainly been a wild ride, and I'm very much looking forward to the next sixteen together.

Thank you, Allison, for being my very first reader. You volunteered and read the book in its rough, rough beginnings without formatting and without an ending. Your read-through and encouragement spurred me on to the finish line.

Thank you, Rachel Magee, for giving an author's perspective on the book, for your encouragement of the project, and for your encouragement before the book even began.

Thank you, Carol Jones, my editor, for taking on this project. As a freelance editor and collaborative writer, you have your pick of projects, but from the first pages, you saw something special in mine. Being a first-time author, you took me under your wing explaining the book world, editing, and so much more to me as we tackled this very special project together. I can't thank you enough as you went above and beyond to help me edit, format, and get it to publication. You added polish to a dream and made it a novel.

Thank you, Sharon, Joy, Irma, Cindy, Katie, and Allison, for being my rearguard. Whenever I think of you, my team, I see an army of angels. You have prayed for me, for my family, and for this book and I am eternally grateful.

Thank you, Shauna, for mentoring me, crying with me, rejoicing with me, and praying with me. You are my angel.

Thank you, Beth, for grabbing my hand and making me take the first steps, literally, to being a writer.

Thank you, Eric, for lending me a police officer's perspective to put our law enforcement in the best and most accurate light.

Thank you to my friends. I am beyond blessed to have so many friends that love and support me, that I cannot list them all here, but I had to say thank you. Thank you for your prayers and your support of me and *Light Bearers: The Awakening*. I am thinking of your many faces as I type this and saying a prayer for each of you.

Thank you, to Candi, for loving me and for loving this book. You have enjoyed it, proofread it, and believed in me. You bless me.

Thank you to my mom, for passing on the gift of creativity and imagination. For instilling in me a great love of reading and for supporting me in this endeavor.

Thank you to my dad, for always seeing me as a winner, even when I was covered in mud or recovering from surgery. You always see light in me no matter what.

Thank you to my entire family for not acting like I was completely crazy to write a novel. Knowing I am a physical therapist, you could have really questioned my sanity. But instead, you have encouraged me and all promised to buy copies as soon as the book is out, and that means the world to me.

Thank you, to my precious sons. You have given up hours of your time with Momma to make this book a reality. Thank you for your sweet prayers for me and for all of my readers. If any of you asks what is next, my reply is, "I'm taking my sons to Disney World!"

Finally, and most importantly, thank You, my Heavenly Father, for the dream in May 2018 and for all of the words that followed. Thank You for the opportunity to glorify Your Name and serve Your people in writing this book.

FROM THE AUTHOR:

Thank you for reading *Light Bearers: The Awakening*. It was my pleasure to write, and I hope it was a pleasure for you to read. Stay tuned for the sequel, *Light Bearers: The Deliverance*, as we move a few years in the future to see what Sarah, Amelia, Owen, Lucas, and even Uncle are doing, as well as many new characters whom you are sure to enjoy.

While reading this book, if you were stirred to hope and want to learn more about The Light, please visit this page: www.mindyhite.com/thelight.

I love you, dear readers, and hope to be with you in the pages of my next book again really soon.

Mindy